D0906288

THE INNER CIRCLE

JONATHAN FAST

DELACORTE PRESS / NEW YORK

Published by
Delacorte Press
1 Dag Hammarskjold Plaza
New York, N.Y. 10017

ACKNOWLEDGMENTS

Lyrics from "Hey Jude" by John Lennon and Paul McCartney:
Copyright © 1968 Maclen Music, Inc. *c/o ATV Music Corp.,
6255 Sunset Boulevard, Los Angeles, California 90028.
*For the U.S.A., Canada, Mexico, and the Philippines:
Northern Songs, Ltd. for the rest of the world.
Used by permission. All rights reserved.

Lyrics from "Bye Bye Blackbird" by Ray Henderson and
Mort Dixon: © 1926 WARNER BROS. INC.
Copyright Renewed. All Rights Reserved. Used by permission.

From DEATH OF A SALESMAN by Arthur Miller:
Copyright 1949, Copyright © renewed 1977 by Arthur Miller.
Reprinted by permission of Viking Penguin Inc.

Lyrics from "Feel Like I'm Fixin' to Die Rag"
courtesy of Joe McDonald.

Manufactured in the United States of America
First Printing

Designed by Jo Anne Bonnell

Library of Congress Cataloging in Publication Data

Fast, Jonathan.
The inner circle.

I. Title.
PZ4.F257In   [PS3556.A779]   813'.5'4   78-24579
ISBN 0-440-04031-0

*All characters depicted in this novel
are fictional, and any resemblance to persons
either living or deceased is purely coincidental.*

For Scott Waugh,
and in memory of his brother, Stuart,
and the San Francisco days.

TONY VALENTI

One summer night Tony Valenti came banging on the door of my West Hollywood apartment, panting for breath and raving about murder.

"You've got to help me, Lou—let me stay here, just tonight. You're the only one I can trust. Everybody else is out to kill me. There was a goon with half an ear who tried to run me off the freeway . . ."

He glanced furtively over his shoulder at the front door; then he crossed to the Chinese-style windows, all the time keeping close to the wall, out of view of anyone who might be standing on the street, and tugged on the pulley system that closed the drapes. After that he seemed to relax a little.

He was twenty-eight but that night he looked older, his face pale, his eyes sunken and fearful. He had a Roman nose, high cheekbones and thin lips which he was constantly wetting with his tongue (I had to remind myself that every Saturday night this desperate man made fifty million people laugh until their sides ached). He was wearing a calfskin jacket, tailored jeans, boots with pointy toes and a silk shirt open to the solar plexus. Around his neck hung four chains of heavy gold, his trademark.

"I see," I said sleepily. "Everybody's trying to kill you." I hitched the sash on my plaid bathrobe and looked at the clock on the mantel. One A.M. Then I wandered over to the window, parted the curtains a few inches and peered out. From where I stood I had a clear view of the intersection of Fountain and La Cienega; there were no pedestrians in sight and the few cars parked along the street had been there all evening. Beyond Fountain the whole south side of Los Angeles spread out below me, row after row of house lights twinkling in the smog, a full moon floating over the flatlands like a big slice of lemon.

There was some truth to the stories of full moons turning men into wolves, or so claimed a friend of mine who used to work in the mental ward at Bellevue. The full moon signaled peak business hours; the bum trippers and suicides, psychos and schizos, crowded in the doors until it looked like Bullock's a week before Christmas. Now I don't believe in astrology or any of the other "religions" that Los Angeles breeds like maggots in a rotting orange, but I do know that the moon can raise the tides twenty or thirty feet and that the human body is ninety percent salt water.

And a full moon in conjunction with a little too much booze and cocaine, for a guy who's already a trifle paranoid . . .

"Let's call your wife," I said gently, "and see if she'll come over and pick you up."

"She left me. She hates my guts."

"There must be someone . . . ?"

"You don't have anybody when you get where I am. Your old friends turn on you. They envy your talent, your success, your money. And the ones who take their place, the lawyers and agents and managers, they're jackals; they *eat* your talent and they tie up your money so you're a slave to them for the rest of your life."

His fingers moved to the golden chains, and he pulled at them as though they were choking him, as though they were holding him to a life he had stumbled into by accident, a life from which he could find no escape.

"That's why I came here," he continued. "I knew I could count on you. You're different from the others, Lou; you're from back East. You've got—*substance*. Remember the good times in New York? Remember the night we got drunk and slashed the tires of Malcolm's Lincoln Continental, and all the time he was watching us . . ."

"Right," I interrupted, before the nostalgia got too thick, "and I'll tell you what else I remember. I remember when you got your own TV series and you were coming out to Hollywood. You were going to introduce me to all the agents and producers, send them my screenplays, help me get a foot in the door. And I remember when I moved out here and you wouldn't answer my calls."

"I was really busy," he pleaded. He came so close I could see my face reflected in the round black mirrors of his pupils. "You wouldn't believe how busy I was. But if you let me stay here tonight, I'll introduce you to every goddamned producer in this town. I know an agent who will have you working every day of the year."

In his excitement he had seized me by the shoulders; I could feel the tension of his fingers through the rough wool of my bathrobe, as though he were trying to drag me along with him down into the mire of fear and suspicion.

"Nobody's trying to kill you!" I grabbed his wrists, pulled his hands away. "It's a fantasy, it's all in your head. It's the fame and the cocaine and having your ego blown up like the Goodyear blimp. You're turning into a raving paranoid and you'd better get a grip on yourself before they have to tie you in a strait-jacket and pack you off to Scripps."

We stared at each other in silence. After a while he said, "You're not going to help me?"

His voice was a whisper. He looked white in the moonlight, like a ghost rattling his golden chains, searching the drafty corridors of West Hollywood for salvation.

The creak of a hinge jolted him like an electric shock. He spun around. Carol was standing at the bedroom door, all six feet of her wrapped in the bed quilt, like an Indian squaw. Her corn-silk hair fell straight to her shoulders, and her big green eyes were sleepy and puzzled.

"What's the ruckus?" she said. Then she noticed my visitor and her eyes opened wider.

"Carol Goodkind," I said, "Tony Valenti."

"Wow," Carol whispered, and, "pleased to meet you."

She stuck out her hand, but Tony just stared at her wistfully. After a while he said, "You've got a good thing going, don't you? Bini and me, we used to have a good thing too— before I got so fucking famous. We had a big old apartment in New York, on the Upper West Side, thrift-shop furniture but we were so happy we didn't even know we were broke. We'd go to a double feature at the Thalia and then we'd get Szechuan food at one of those restaurants on Broadway. The whole thing never cost more than twenty bucks but I felt like a king. Now I go out and drop a hundred and it don't mean shit. I was a goddamned idiot. I gave it all up for them and now they're going to kill me."

"Who?" Carol said gently.

"Everybody. The Inner Circle. Do me a favor? I know Lou's after the big bread. Don't let him make the same mistake I did." He took a deep breath. "Well, I don't want to spoil the party. Guess I'll be on my way." He added as an afterthought, "You wouldn't have a cigarette, honey?"

Carol went back to the bedroom and returned with a pack of Dorals. "They may be a little stale," she apologized. "Somebody left them here months ago."

Tony's hands were shaking so, he could hardly line up the end of the cigarette with the flame from his gold lighter. Finally he succeeded, puffing gratefully.

"So at least the visit wasn't a total waste. Good night, Lou."

"If you really want to stay . . ." I began.

He shrugged. "What's the difference?" He was

bitter, defeated. "They're all in my head. Too much fame, too much cocaine, right, buddy? Take care."

He patted my cheek with his fingertips—they were icy cold—and smiled.

"Was that really him?" Carol said after he had left. "Tony Valenti? I didn't know he was a friend of yours. Oh, I love him!"

"You and everybody else," I said. "That's why he thinks they're all trying to kill him."

The roar of him gunning his Porsche reached us from the basement parking lot, swelled as he came out of the driveway and diminished again as he drove out along La Cienega, out into a night that held for him terrors beyond my imagining.

"Want some tea?" Carol said. Now that we were alone she dropped the quilt and padded naked into the kitchen. The ring-shaped neon fixture blinked a few times before it caught, then it buzzed like a mosquito. I sat down at the Formica-topped table and rested my head in my hands while Carol put the water on.

"It would have been easier to get me into bed," she said, "if you'd told me you had friends who were movie stars."

"I don't know how it could have been any easier than it was."

"How do you know him?"

"We went to NYU together; we were in the same freshman English section. I helped him with his papers. Sophomore year he left to go to the Actors' Studio. He did some off Broadway and we stayed in touch. Then he auditioned for the lead in *Dino's Pizzeria*, and he got the part. I remember when he had to tell Strasberg he was going to Hollywood to star in a situation comedy about a dumb wop who runs a pizza parlor. That was some scene. And the rest, as they say, is history."

"What was he like?"

"Insecure. He wanted desperately to be your friend. He'd give you little presents—silly things—and do schtick to make you laugh. I remember he used to imitate John Cameron Swayze in the Timex commercials. *This wristwatch was strapped to the tail fin of a hydrogen bomb . . . yes, folks, it's still ticking!* But deep down he was serious, hardworking. I liked him very much. Too bad fame turned him into an asshole."

"Chamomile or Red Zinger?"

"Coffee."

"You know, stimulants take years off your life," she said, reaching for the jar of Nescafe instant. "You won't be able to go back to sleep."

"I don't want to go back to sleep. I feel rotten. I should have let him stay here. What the hell kind of person am I anyway, to turn away an old friend who comes to me pleading for help?"

"But you said it was all his imagination."

"Yeah, but what difference does that make? Imaginary problems are every bit as bad as real ones. Worse. Real ones you can deal with, you can call the police. Imaginary problems you're stuck with. Jesus. Ten years ago I wouldn't have treated him like that. Maybe Hollywood's making me into a bastard too. Maybe failure can louse you up just as badly as success."

"Oh Louis, stop. You're not a failure. You're the best magazine writer in California. In the country."

"Journalist, dear. And even if it's true, I still have to work my ass off to clear twenty grand a year. Carol, there's money out there, more money than simple folks like us ever dream of. I drive down Doheny and I see the Mercedes parked bumper to bumper . . ."

"You told me they were leased."

"They are leased. But even leasing a Mercedes costs a bundle. That's the real reason I was rude to Tony. I'm eaten up with envy. Ten years ago we were both bums. Today he's worth a couple of million and I'm still a bum."

"You are not. Stop talking like that. You're kind and funny and brilliant."

"More! More!"

"Oh Louis."

She brought the two steaming mugs to the table, and a plate of cookies she had baked from soy flour and sunflower seeds and a dozen other ingredients I wouldn't feed to my dog, if I had one.

"You don't suppose," she said, "somebody really *is* trying to kill him?"

"Why?"

"I don't know. Maybe he owed money to the mob. Or is that just on television?"

She sat down across from me. The steel frame of the director's chair must have been chilly on her back, but she didn't seem to mind.

"He's making so much money I don't know how he could go into debt."

"Gambling? Drugs?"

"Well, I've read in the gossip columns that he's partial to cocaine—but cocaine is cheap if you've got a hit TV series. As for gambling, he never used to when I knew him. But if he did run up a big debt in Vegas let's say, he'd be more valuable to his creditors alive. He'd be in a unique position to help them with certain kinds of favors—promoting other entertainers, influencing film studios and networks. Know what I mean?"

She nodded. "You don't like my cookies, do you?"

"I love your cookies."

I took one from the plate and bit into it.

"I better get home," she said. "Unlike some people, I have to work tomorrow."

"That's right, I'm sorry. Seeing Tony—I lost track of the time."

"I forgive you," she said, leaning over to kiss my naked dome.

We dressed and I drove her home in my silver Honda Civic, crossing the Hollywood Hills at Laurel Canyon. The drive was fast at two in the morning and the view of the valley, the endless grids of light, the distant silhouette of the mountains, was a pleasure.

Carol lived in Toluca Lake, in a two-story apartment house, a boxy concrete bunker inhabited entirely by young divorced women with screaming children. She had moved there from the suburbs of Chicago six year ago, leaving behind a job as a secretary at a big insurance company, a computer-programming husband whose circuits had calcified at the age of thirty-two, a circle of women friends who talked about nothing but the care and feeding of their new babies, a life like a tunnel with no light at the end; and she had come West with Betsy, her delicious five-year-old daughter, to find a style of existence which was, while not necessarily less rigid, certainly less conventional, with its health foods and Yoga and courses in self-perfection.

The apartment house circled a court with an azure-blue swimming pool and a cherry-red Coke machine. Every apartment opened onto a long terrace overlooking the pool, and as we walked along we could look into other windows—nobody seemed to think much of blinds—at half-furnished lives: a chair, a sofa, a coffee table, a framed print of big-eyed children standing beneath a street lamp. There are so many divorced women in Los Angeles, sometimes I can't help but wonder where they all come from. And what becomes of their ex-husbands? Somewhere in the United States there must be a city filled with divorced men.

We stood outside her door, kissing good night beside Betsy's tricycle. Betsy was spending the summer back in Chicago with her grandmother and we were both torn between missing the little demon and celebrating Carol's liberation. When I finally took my lips away, Carol said, "Not so good."

"Thank you."

"Don't get angry. You're the best kisser in the world when your heart's in it. Trouble is, you're thinking about Tony Valenti, not me."

I admitted I was.

"And telling yourself you're a rat for not letting him stay in your apartment."

"If you can't turn to your old friends, then you really don't have anybody."

"Well, it doesn't sound like he was much of a friend."

"Let's forget it," I said. "It's late."

By the time I got back to West Hollywood my

eyes were crossing; that's what happens when I'm very tired. I half undressed and lay down on the bed and fell asleep with the television just starting up an old Ronald Reagan movie.

The next thing I knew it was noon and the sun was shining in my eyes. I rolled out of bed, switched off the TV and stumbled into the bathroom. Washing woke me up a little more. I put on a pair of beige polyester slacks and a Hawaiian shirt, a pair of loafers and a tennis hat to shade my poor naked dome. The California sun may be great for oranges, but it's rotten for bald scalps. Then I left my apartment and tripped downstairs, stopping to say hello to the fags below me, who were trying to squeeze a huge antique armoire into the door of their apartment.

As the valley is populated by young divorcées, so is West Hollywood filled with fags. (Maybe that's what happens to the ex-husbands—they turn gay?) This is probably because West Hollywood has some of the oldest and most stylish apartment buildings in Los Angeles, many dating back to the misty dawn of history—that is to say, the 1920s—many of them built by set designers moonlighting from their studio jobs. In the morning they erected Egyptian temples for D. W. Griffith, in the afternoon they built Egyptian-style bungalows for Goldsmith Construction and Realty.

The house I lived in was a vintage example of the period: The Pagoda Towers, a humble stucco structure gussied up with Chinese-style gingerbread, and red and black enameled beams, pagoda-shaped gables, fierce gargoyle dragons on the rooftops and a bronze gate to the street. Of course it was aging like a silent-film star, wood cracked, enamel peeling, bronze fittings green and moldy—but that only added to the charm.

I stopped in the lobby for the mail, mostly advertisements and a letter from the bank threatening to repossess my Honda if I didn't send them a payment soon. Then I continued down the stairs to the basement garage.

I drove over to the Schwab's at Sunset and Fairfax and bought the afternoon *Herald Examiner*. As always, a gang of bit players and character actors were sitting at the counter, sipping coffee and socializing. Whenever actors get together they horse around and tell jokes—regardless of how long they've been unemployed—and the feeling of good humor was one of the things that made Schwab's so appealing. Today, however, I was struck by how miserable they all looked. One woman whom I've seen on TV admiring the shine on her daughter's plates, was weeping.

I dropped into a booth and ordered some sweet rolls and coffee. I opened the paper and saw a three-column photo of Tony Valenti with his Porsche wrapped around him like a ball of crumpled tin foil.

Tony Valenti Killed in Car Crash
Young Actor Was Star of Popular Television Series
Friends Say He Was Depressed After Wife Left Him

The article went on to describe how Tony had driven into a concrete piling on the Hollywood Freeway at around 2:30 A.M. last night. Earlier that evening, it said, he had quarreled with his wife, Bini Valenti, on the telephone. She had been living in New York since their separation in December. Then Tony had gone to visit his lawyer and personal manager, Martin Rubin, complaining of suicidal depression. Mr. Rubin phoned Dr. Abraham Kellerman, Tony's analyst, who agreed to come over immediately. Mr. Rubin tried to detain Mr. Valenti, but the young actor refused to stay, insisting that he had an urgent appointment. Millions mourn his passing. Services will be held at Forest Meadows, Sunday noon.

Below the article was a picture of Tony Valenti in his prime, twinkling eyes and a sassy smile, and next to him a pretty pixie of a girl with short black hair parted on the side. They might have been brother and sister, but the caption said they were husband and wife. The second article ("Early Stardom—but a Tragic Personal Life") covered his childhood, his career as an actor in New York, his sudden rise to superstardom on television, his unhappy marriage and bouts of depression, his rumored reliance on alcohol and drugs.

I tore out both articles and folded them into my wallet. Then I leaned back, my pants squeaking against the vinyl upholstery of the booth. Depression. Alcohol and drugs. As if that explained everything. He wanted to be a star, and he got to be a star, but it didn't bring him happiness; so he went and wrapped himself around a concrete piling. And all you folks who loved to watch him every Saturday night, you can all rest easy knowing that the famous and rich are miserable too. When they stop by your house in the middle of the night, complaining that people are trying to kill them, you can laugh at them and slam the door in their face. What's the difference? They're *stars*; they've got everything; they're invulnerable. If they act a little strange, well, that's just to be expected; it's the booze and the cocaine.

But whatever you do, don't stop to think that their problems might be real; that a goon with half an ear might be trying to run them off the freeway; that some weird thing called the Inner Circle might be conspiring for their demise. Don't dare believe that for an instant because then you'll see that the blood is on your own hands.

And you're an accomplice to murder.

Suicide, I mean.

BINI VALENTI

Before writing for *BonHomme* magazine, I had imagined naively that the offices would be oak-paneled, shag-carpeted pleasure pits with bosomy secretaries bounding half naked through the halls. Alas, the building was austere, the atmosphere amiable but business-like, and the women, with the exception of one black beauty in a skimpy T-shirt who sat at the reception desk, extremely clothed. There was not even an example of the famous centerfold art, which certainly would have been preferable to the dull abstracts hanging in the lobby.

I told the black girl that I had an appointment with Flora McReese and waited while she tapped the buttons on her switchboard. She had vampire fingernails and on the T-shirt, "Bitch" lettered in sequins. I'd take her word for it.

"Miss McReese will see you," she said after a moment. Her office is just past the . . ."

"Thanks, I know how to find it."

In fact, I'd been writing regularly for *BonHomme* since I came to California five years ago. They paid the highest rates, almost enough to elevate me to the middle class. And Flora liked my work and bought nearly every story I proposed. In the last two years I'd only had one story killed.

Flora was the senior articles editor, although she looked more like a librarian from Omaha. She had mousy hair, a severe nose, a dumpy figure which her dresses, usually striped or polka-dotted, only accentuated. The crowning touch was her harlequin glasses. Contrary to appearance, she was quick and witty, always searching for the pun, the double entendre, the means of introducing the topic of sex, no matter how inappropriate, into any conversation.

I pecked her on the cheek as I came in; then I sat down opposite her desk and said, "Tony Valenti was murdered."

"Oh?"

She folded her hands on the desk and regarded me with a birdlike stare, raising and lowering her eyebrows as if to shake away a bug lodged on her forehead. This odd tic, I had learned, was a sign of interest.

"What," she said, "makes you think so?"

I recounted the details of our meeting the previous night.

When I had finished she said, "I remember ten years ago when Rosalee Romain died. Practically everybody who's ever written for *BonHomme* came up with a murder story. One story was that her shrink accidentally gave her an overdose of barbiturates and set up the suicide to cover his own incompetence. Another account said she was having an affair with a prominent senator; she threatened to talk to the press and he had her bumped off for fear she'd ruin his chances at the presidency. There were all sorts of theories. But there weren't any facts. All you had at the end was a lot of speculation.

"That was in the sixties when the public was just beginning to get wise to the covert activities of the CIA. Everyone was fascinated by the idea of plots and conspiracies. Today, I don't know. The climate of the country is different. People want to trust, they want to believe. That's why they're turning to religion. Do you think Jimmy Carter could have been elected ten years ago?"

I shook my head.

"But today people want to trust his Southern charm," she continued, "they want to believe in his concern for human rights. Personally, I think he must be a great lay." She grinned at me. "They're so slow down in Georgia."

"In other words," I said, starting to get up, "you're not interested." I was a little irritated by the length of the lecture when a simple no would have sufficed.

"Au contraire, my dear, I'm fascinated. What I'm saying is, give me hard facts. No hypothesis, no speculation, no rumors."

"It's a deal," I said, sitting back down. "I'll need expenses."

"As long as it's reasonable."

"About three thousand dollars."

"That's not reasonable."

"Look Flora, I don't know how long this will take. I want to work on it exclusively, and frankly, I'm just about broke. I spent the last five months on that screenplay and nobody will even look at it."

"Still having trouble with the movie people?" she asked, concerned.

"I can't get a foot in the door. Everywhere I go it's *Who have you worked for? What have you written?* They're not interested unless you're already a proven commodity."

"Three thousand dollars is a lot of money, Louis." She jotted some figures on her desk pad and continued, "Let me see what I can do. I'll speak to Fletcher"—he was editor in chief—"this afternoon. Will you be home later?"

"Either home or at the office. I really appreciate it, Flora."

"It's just because I find bald men irresistibly sexy. Don't forget to have Annie validate your parking ticket . . ."

She tossed me a kiss as I strode out the door.

The article in the *Herald* said that Tony had been to see Marty Rubin the night of his death. Chances were that was the same Marty Rubin I had tried to contact a couple of years ago while researching an article on theatrical lawyers, a partner in a law firm called Weston, Rubin, Weiss & Penny. He had refused to speak to me at the time, but that didn't mean anything: Lawyers never like to talk unless they've got their meters running. Anyway, he seemed like a good place to start, so when I got back to The Pagoda

Towers I lay down on the bed, rested the phone on my belly and dialed information for his number.

Recently lawyers have been replacing agents as artists' representatives for some very good reasons: Most artists get their work for themselves. The agent merely negotiates the terms and structures the deal. Now, since this is legal, contractual work, it makes more sense to have a lawyer do it. Furthermore, a good lawyer will be able to advise his clients on investing their money so it doesn't disappear too quickly. And he will also be equipped to handle the numerous law suits that come in the wake of every deal. Marty Rubin acted in all these capacities for Tony; in addition, I imagine, he held his hand during marital difficulties, cheered him up when his ratings fell, maybe even helped him procure that expensive white powder called cocaine.

I dialed the number and told the girl that I wanted to speak to Marty Rubin.

"I'm sorry," she said, "Mr. Rubin is out."

Her voice was nasal and tinged with Brooklyn despite all her efforts.

"When can I reach him?"

"Not till next week."

"It's urgent," I said. "It concerns Tony Valenti's death."

"I'm sorry but he cannot be reached."

"Somebody like Marty Rubin doesn't disappear without leaving an emergency number with his secretary."

"He's down on the Baja peninsula and there aren't any phones—oh, I wasn't supposed to tell. Don't say I told you, please. He'll fire me and this is the first steady job I've had in two years."

"What's he doing in Baja the day after his number one client dies?"

"I can't say anymore so don't ask."

"You tell me or I'll tell him you blabbed about Mexico."

"Oh, I'm such a fuck-up. All right. Everybody was calling him and nagging him about Tony's death. Mr. Rubin was the last person to see Tony alive."

"Not quite the last," I said.

"What?"

"Nothing. Go on."

"Anyway, everybody was calling him and he said he couldn't think straight anymore and he had to get away and have some time to himself. He and Tony were really close friends. They were like brothers. He was really broken up about Tony's death."

"So he flew down to Mexico?"

"Mr. Rubin's got a twin-engine Cessna. He flies whenever he has the chance. He flies to Catalina for lunch, even."

"Where exactly in Baja did he go?"

"I don't know."

"If you're holding back on me . . ."

"No, I swear I don't know."

"I assume he'll be back Sunday in time for the funeral?"

"I guess so. You promise you won't tell?"

"It's our little secret," I said and hung up.

Next I decided to get in touch with Bini Valenti. She had been living in New York since the separation, but I was certain she would fly out as soon as she heard the tragic news. If she managed to get the 9 A.M. flight on American, she would have checked into her hotel an hour ago. I called the Beverly Wilshire Hotel and the Bel-Air. Then I called the Beverly Hills. Yes, Mrs. Valenti had checked in around noon. No, her room was not answering.

Well, if she wasn't there, I had a pretty good hunch where she would be. I changed into my brown suit and drove out to Glendale, got lost, and finally found the big iron gates to Forest Meadows. I told the man in the kiosk that I was part of the Valenti party; I wished to view the body. He told me to go straight along Heavenly Rest Drive, make a right at the Shrine of the Resurrection and I'd find the Mortuary Building just past the Inspiration Duck Pond. He sketched the way on a light-green map with an orange border. I had the uncanny feeling that I was at Disneyland.

The Mortuary Building was a sprawling Tudor mansion complete with mullioned windows and old oak doors, and sculptured box hedge all around. Los Angeles, what a place: apartment houses disguised as pagodas, mortuaries pretending to be English mansions —even the buildings are putting on airs. But it's all so innocent, like kids dressing up at play, that it's hard to be angry.

A tall erect woman in a dark-gray suit greeted me in the foyer. She whispered that the Valenti party was having "visitation" in the Hunt Room upstairs, and I whispered thank you and set off in the indicated direction.

The hall was carpeted in green and soundproofed so that I could hear the creaking of my brown oxfords, which I hadn't worn since the *BonHomme* awards dinner last year (nominated, but didn't win).

There were several visitation rooms, each with a

different motif. The Music Room, the Library. The Hunt Room had crossed flintlocks on the walls, braces of pistols and powder horns, and a huge oil painting over the fireplace of geese flying south—or maybe they were starting in the south and flying north. The furniture was oak, purple velvet, overstuffed; and the coffin was raised on a platform, open like a massive chest.

A tall old man with a white mustache sat in a wing chair and wept soundlessly, while two plump women on a love seat were more vocal in their grief. One of them was puffy-faced and pink with a black beret and a veil; the other, gray-complexioned with a trace of mustache on her upper lip. A young man who looked remarkably like Tony was holding their hands and comforting them. Three middle-aged men in dark glasses stood in a corner whispering. And a beautiful young woman knelt to comb the hair of a little boy, no more than five, itchy and squirming in his first suit, while a girl perhaps a year younger watched with enormous brown eyes. There was no sign of Bini Valenti.

I took off my hat, a dark fedora, and entered the room. The two plump women raised their eyes, the young woman with the children looked up, the three men turned; then, seeing I was neither friend nor relation, they returned to the business at hand. I stepped on the platform and walked to the edge of the coffin.

Tony wore a dark suit of conservative cut, the sort of thing he himself would not have put on in a million years. His hair had been trimmed and his eyes closed; his flesh had a waxy sheen and too much color. I was happy to see they had left him his gold chains in addi-

tion to another ornament: A brown clay fetish perhaps
two inches tall, hung around his neck on a leather
thong. It was a stumpy little figure with a skull's head
and cat's paws in place of hands, probably Indian or
pre-Columbian.

"Tony," I whispered, "I'm sorry."

Suddenly I felt a tension pass through the room;
the air became heavy like the air before a thunder-
storm. At first I thought it was something I had done,
I felt so guilty anyway being there under false pre-
tenses. But when I turned around, I saw they were all
looking in the other direction, toward the door where
a small woman had just appeared. She was in her
twenties, with short black hair parted on the side, held
back with a barrette, and enormous sunglasses which
nearly covered her pixie face. She wore a loose black
dress belted at the waist and her figure was slim, boyish.
Bini Valenti; I recognized her from the picture in
the paper.

She avoided looking at anyone as she crossed the
room; she kept her eyes focused on the coffin as if it
were a hypnotist's gold watch. With every step the
tension grew. When she reached the love seat where
the two fat women were seated, one of them—the one
with the veil—jumped up and blocked her path. Bini
Valenti tried to ignore her; she tried to walk around
her, but the fat woman wouldn't let her pass.

"Go away!" the fat woman shrieked. "Get out!
You have no business here."

One of the men in dark glasses rushed to the fat
woman and took her arm.

"Mama, please," he said softly, "don't get excited."

"Why shouldn't I get excited? She's a murderer.

She murdered him. Murderer!" She searched for something stronger. "Whore!"

The two other men joined them now, trying to quiet her, while the first apologized to Bini: "She's hysterical, she doesn't know what she's saying . . ."

"I know what I'm saying. I'm saying she's a murderer and a whore! If she didn't go to bed with every man she met, Tony would still be . . ."

"Sofia!" The name was like the sting of a birch rod. It was the old man with the mustache who had spoken. His face was red with rage and his hands were trembling.

"Sit down," he said, "and shut up."

"Don't tell me what to do, Mario Valenti!" She hesitated. Then she straightened her dress and sat back down. She was still glaring at Bini. I heard her whisper, "Whore."

Meanwhile Bini Valenti stood rooted to the ground, biting her lower lip, staring at the floor. Tears were welling in the corners of her eyes.

I walked over to her and said, "Can I help you?"

"I just wanted a last look at him." Her voice was high and thin and threatening to crack.

I took her arm and led her up to the platform and let her lean against me while she looked at Tony.

She made a funny twisted smile. "He looks so— *healthy*."

I nodded. We stood there a minute longer and then she said, "Help me leave, please."

So I walked her off the platform and across the floor, past the flintlock rifles and the flying geese and the hostile eyes of the Valenti clan. As we left the darkness of the Mortuary Building, the sweeping lawns appeared sun-bleached, like an overexposed photograph. I wondered how many hundreds of thousands of gallons of water it took to keep them lush and green in this desert climate.

"Where's your car?" I asked.

"I came by cab."

"I'll drive you home then."

She didn't object.

I steered her toward the Honda which, fortunately, I'd parked by the Inspiration Duck Pond, only thirty or forty feet away. Nobody's graceful crawling into a Honda—it's like squeezing into Cinderella's glass slipper—but she was so small and supple she made it look easy.

"Where are you staying?" I asked, wedging myself into the driver's seat.

"The Beverly Hills," she sniffed and burst into tears.

"Hey, don't cry."

I touched her arm, and she took it as an invitation and buried her head in my shoulder. A woman who was passing by stared at us sympathetically.

"I didn't murder him," she sobbed.

"Of course you didn't."

"He killed himself, the stupid son of a bitch."

"Think so?"

Gently I slipped my arm from behind her neck and started up the motor. We drove out of the cemetery, through the crazy quilt of taco stands and gas stations that constitutes downtown Glendale, and onto the freeway.

"He always drove too fast," she said. "It was a test

for the passenger. If you could ride in the Porsche without flinching or screaming, that meant you trusted him."

"But wasn't he a really good driver? I mean, didn't he drive in races sometimes?"

She nodded. She looked better.

"He used to go up to Bakersfield and race. A couple of times he won and they gave him a big gold cup. The two Emmys he got for *Dino's Pizzeria* are in the closet, but the racing trophies always went on the mantel."

"Then don't you think it's unlikely he'd drive into one of those concrete pilings? Unless maybe he was drunk—or stoned."

"Tony didn't drink much. And he *didn't take drugs!* Joyce Haber printed that cocaine story to get back at him—he snubbed her at a party or something." Suddenly she turned around and stared at me. "Who are you, anyway?"

I knew that tone of voice. What she meant was, *You're a reporter, aren't you?*

"I'm an old friend of Tony's from back East. Louis Pinkle's the name."

"*You're* Louis Pinkle?" She stared harder.

I laughed. "I didn't think I was famous."

"Tony talked about you all the time! You went to NYU together. And there was some girl, who lived on St. Mark's Place, whom you were both in love with, only she was in love with a black guy who owned an enormous Lincoln Continental, and one night . . ."

"And one night we both got drunk and went out and slashed the tires. Custom white sidewalls. Seventy bucks apiece."

"And then the black guy . . ."

"Malcolm was his name."

"Right!" She was enjoying this. "The black guy cornered you in the hallway of her building and stuck a razor to your throat and said he'd kill you both if you didn't buy him a new set."

"That's right. We found out he was watching from a window the whole time we were doing it. It's one of those stories that's ghastly while it's happening but quite funny five years later."

"It's a pleasure to meet you after all these years, Louis."

She stuck out a tiny hand and I shook it.

"The pleasure's mine. Tony really talked about me?"

"He told that story. Hundreds of times."

"It's funny. I thought he'd forgotten I existed."

"He changed after we came to California. He was running all the time. All day at the studio, then he'd come home and study his scripts all night. He liked to give the impression that he didn't care about anything, but he worked his ass off. On the weekends he'd go racing; that was the only pleasure he had in life. No booze, no drugs, no Hollywood orgies. No women."

"Then why did you leave him?"

"Cause I got *bored*! I had a cook and a maid and a cleaning lady. There was nothing to do around the house and he wouldn't let me get a job. So all I did all day was shop. I'd have the chauffeur drive me along Wilshire, up Canon, down Rodeo. *Bonwit's, Magnin's, Saks, Giorgio, Hermès, Gucci.* I'd come home with the trunk full, but I'd be all empty inside. I was going out of my mind. So finally I told him that

I loved him very much and I was going back to New York and he could come if he liked."

"And he didn't?"

"Of course not. And give up what he'd dreamed of all his life? Oh no. So I left him, but that's not why he killed himself no matter what his stupid Aunt Sofia thinks."

"That was the plump lady who was shouting at you?"

Bini nodded. "She always hated me. They wanted Tony to marry an Italian. Fuck them all."

After that she was silent. She withdrew into herself and I tried to attend to my driving, which was not quite so good as Tony Valenti's.

I steered the Honda into the file of Mercedes and Rolls-Royces that were lined up on the circular drive of the Beverly Hills Hotel. The building was a pink spun-sugar fortress, mock-Moorish in design, where the room service came on silver trays and the hundred-dollar hookers traveled in teams—as if one alone were just too boring. The car park who opened the door for Bini was a handsome boy with a blond mustache.

"You're Mrs. Valenti, aren't you?" he asked.

Before Bini could reply, he was off and running: "Listen, I've just finished a screenplay about what it's like to work at the Beverly Hills Hotel. I've got a meeting at Warner's next week—they've already given me the go-ahead, but we've got to finalize some of the details. I mean, I won't even be working here after Friday. Like I was saying, instead of having *walk-on* parts like they do in most movies, we're going to have *drive-on* parts, know what I mean? And I was wondering if you'd be willing to do one?"

He delivered the entire speech in seconds, without pausing for breath.

"Talk to her agent," I said, taking over for Bini, who was speechless. "It's Mr. Lazar. And I'm warning you, she takes a percentage of the gross from the first dollar."

"I've got to get back to New York," Bini said as we entered the hotel. "From the moment I arrived here they've been hustling me. Some man met me at the airport—he wants to ghostwrite Tony's story using my name. Why won't they leave me alone?"

"Let's go to the Polo Lounge. You need a drink."

"Come to my room and we'll call room service."

But when we got to her room, instead of calling room service, she locked the door. She stood right in front of me and said, "You're very kind."

She rose up on her toes—that brought her level to my chin—tilted her head back, closed her eyes and half opened her lips. Her teeth were small and sharp, and she was wearing a perfume that smelled like clover.

"Close to death," she whispered after we were through kissing, "makes me want to be close to life. Make love to me."

"Let's have that drink first," I said, stalling for time. In a few minutes, I was reasonably sure, her mood would pass and I'd be off the hook. Those passions cool as quickly as they flare up.

By five the Polo Lounge was filled with film types and pop stars. They sat at pink tables with braided wire legs, making deals in the shadows of tropical foliage, green plastic foliage, a jungle of it. As a matter of fact, that's not a bad symbol for the place—

a plastic jungle. We hid at a corner table and within seconds we were surrounded by industry people heaping condolences on Bini. A big man with a little mustache, a quality producer named Pinkerton who was an old friend of Tony's, joined us for a drink. I took the opportunity to tell him the story of my new screenplay, *The Climber*, hoping he might want to make a deal on it. Sitting in the Polo Lounge without making a deal is like walking through Vegas without playing a slot machine—virtually impossible. And when again would I be likely to have a few minutes alone with a big-time producer? He said no thanks, but someday he'd be interested in hearing some of my other ideas; then he gave Bini his condolences and excused himself. I bought her another martini and when she seemed to be slightly anesthetized, I spoke my mind.

"Do you think Tony could have been murdered?"

Her head snapped up, her eyes were fearful. "Why?"

I described her husband's late-night visit.

"Did he ever mention a club called the Inner Circle?"

She looked at the light fixtures and said to herself, "The Inner Circle. The Inner Circle. Yes, he did—a long time ago. I remember because I thought it was the name of a play. He said he'd been invited to be part of the Inner Circle, and I said, 'Yes, the play by Brecht,' and he said, 'No, that's the *Caucasian Chalk Circle*. Wrong circle.' "

She laughed, recalling it.

"What kind of organization was it?"

She thought hard. "He wouldn't tell me. He said it was a secret."

"He must have told you something. Why else would he bring it up?"

"Just to make me curious. Tony was like that."

"And he never mentioned it again?"

She bit her lip and shook her head.

"How long ago was that?"

"We were still in New York . . . Tony wasn't working . . . I remember now! It was the night before he auditioned for *Dino's Pizzeria*. We kept toasting his success."

She raised her glass. "To health and wealth and Hollywood. . . ."

"Isn't it 'health and wealth and happiness'?"

"No." She shook her head and started crying again.

I passed her my napkin. I felt like everyone in the Polo Lounge was watching us—and they were.

At five to six I told Bini I had to be at an appointment. I said I would see her at the funeral and she was to call me if she had any night panics. She was so skittish and high-strung that I was afraid she might do something crazy. Having somebody to phone, somebody to open your heart to—even if he is a stranger—can mean the difference between life and death.

I drove across the hills on Coldwater and down Ventura Boulevard until I came to the big wood sign that said SpaMaster Showrooms.

This was where I had first met Carol two years ago. I was going through a dry spell at the time, six or seven months without a woman. Celibacy in the East isn't so bad, but out here in the West where the sun superheats your skin and the women walk around half or three-quarters naked, and every billboard displays vast vistas of flawless flesh, it's worse. *BonHomme* wanted a short piece on "The Hot Tub Phenomenon." (They love anything with "Phenomenon" in the title. They also love anything with "New," such as "The New Vegetarianism" or "The New Asexuality.") So I was going around to the different showrooms and when I got to SpaMaster I saw Carol, all six feet of her, and lost my heart. I lost most of my mind, too, except for a tiny red-hot center that kept frantically thinking, *How can I get her undressed as quickly as possible?*

Now, by coincidence a photographer I had been working with, a guy named Bill Shiner, had left his camera in the trunk of my car. It was one of those sophisticated box-shaped German jobs that costs a thousand bucks. I got out the camera and told Carol I was a photographer for *BonHomme*; if she let me photograph her nude in one of the tubs, we'd give her free publicity. I know it sounds underhanded, but I was a desperate man. Anyway, I was half joking; I thought she'd laugh at me and that would be the end of it. But no, the idea must have turned her on because a minute later she had the shades drawn and in another minute I was witnessing one of the greatest natural wonders this side of Canyonlands National Park. She turned on the spa and jumped in. I started fooling with the camera, turning knobs and pushing buttons with the utmost professional aplomb, telling her how to pose (a childhood dream come true), snapping pictures and having a truly wonderful time. Occasionally I'd look up, murmuring something photographic like, "Hmmm, have to stop down the ASA . . ."

While I was helping her out of the water some fifteen minutes later, I asked if she'd like to have dinner with me and to my delight she agreed, assuming she could find a baby-sitter. As I was leaving she took the camera and held it in front of my face. "By the way," she said, pointing to a little window on one side of the box, "this is the viewfinder, and this"—she indicated a cylinder on the other side—"is the lens. You were holding it backward."

I was lucky to find a space on the street; while parking I could watch Carol locking up. She was wearing a skimpy halter top, tight jeans and a fancy squash-blossom belt that my friend Alex, "The Bead Brujo," had given her. She noticed me when I got out, smiled her toothy smile and unlocked the door.

"Can I help you, sir?" she said.

"Yes, I'm looking for something special in the way of a tall blonde."

"Perhaps if you'll come into the back room with me I can show you something you'll like."

"I'll bet you can," I said, grinning.

She relocked the door and flipped the OPEN sign to CLOSED. Outside on Ventura the neon was going on, restaurants and giant all-night supermarkets, car dealers (big cash rebates) and more restaurants. Kids were cruising in surfer vans, boxes with big balloon tires and little windows in back, like fish eyes. The dusk was crimson; the sun, a steel plate fresh from the furnace.

Inside, Carol went around turning off the spas: the Imperial, a ten-foot Fiberglas tub backed by a photo of a Bel-Air mansion to help the buyer "conceptualize the setting"; the Executive, an oversized bathtub for the office—assuming your office is forty feet long; the Back to Nature, which looked suspiciously like an old wine barrel; and the Mighty Midget, the big-selling economy model.

I remember back East, whirlpool baths were for Uncle Murray when he broke a blood vessel in his leg. Here you had the caldrons installed on your redwood deck so you could invite the neighbors for a nude soak on Saturday night.

"Do you know," Carol said, her voice suddenly grave, "that your friend Tony Valenti died last night? He crashed into one of those concrete things on the freeway. The paper says it's suicide, but after that scene at your apartment I've got to wonder."

"You and me both," I said, and I told her about the day's events. When I mentioned visiting *BonHomme*, Carol interrupted to report that Flora McReese had called (I leave the SpaMaster Showrooms phone as my office number, which often causes some confusion) and Fletcher had accepted my article unenthusiastically. Half the advance I had requested was on its way. This news alleviated some of my anxiety; I could make another payment on the Honda and take care of the rent for—what month was it? I counted backward on my fingers. Last March? Could I really be that far behind?

While I talked, Carol took some towels out of a cupboard and led me to the back room where a Mighty Midget was bubbling happily away.

This was the demonstrator model—no fooling! If a couple couldn't make up their minds about buying a spa, Carol brought them back here, gave them towels and left them alone for a half hour. Or however long they wanted to stay. The record was two hours and twelve minutes; the couple came out grinning, walking as though their legs were rubber, and bought an Imperial.

I undressed, folding my clothes neatly over the back of a chair, and slipped into the delicious water. One hundred degrees, five hundred little jets of air massaging the knots out of my muscles. Carol joined me a minute later, shedding her jeans the way a snake slithers out of its skin, piling her hair into a plastic shower cap.

"Bliss," I said. "Heaven." I leaned back and folded my hands behind my head. In fifteen minutes I felt as though my entire body had been turned to mush. "Let's go back to my apartment," I suggested, "and try and think of new sexual perversions."

"Can't," she said.

"Why not?"

"I have other plans."

She climbed out of the tub and started to towel off her long, long legs.

"What other plans?"

By the time she had formulated her reply, we were both dried and dressed and she was staring into an oval mirror on the wall, brushing her hair.

"Fritz Uhler," she began, "the Dutch spiritualist? He's giving a lecture at the Hotel Miramar in Santa Monica. He's going to answer questions from the audience and make spirits appear, and . . . well, you might as well say it and get it over with."

"Say what?"

"That you think it's a lot of horse shit."

"I don't think it's a lot of horse shit," I said. "I just

don't understand why you waste your time with that crap."

"Because I believe in it! Because it makes life richer and more mysterious and beautiful. And because a life after death gives everything a deeper level of meaning."

I shook my head with disgust.

"What I want to know," she continued, peeved, "is why it makes *you* so angry. Going to a lecture doesn't hurt anybody; it doesn't cause pain or waste the environment or take money out of people's pockets."

"I'm not angry," I said, supercalm. "I simply think that you're deluding yourself. If you saw somebody walking around in a dream, you'd want to wake them up, wouldn't you?"

"Well I don't think I am walking around in a dream. I think *you* are. Look: For the past five thousand years people have believed in the spirit world."

"What's that supposed to prove? For five thousand years people believed the earth was flat and the universe revolved around it. A consensus of opinion does not make a truth."

We walked out through the showroom. She unlocked the front door and we stepped into the street.

"For your information, many ancient people believed the earth was round. The scientists of Atlantis . . ."

"Spare me the scientists of Atlantis."

"Oh, you're so sarcastic and superior!" She slammed the door behind her and locked it, jabbing with the key.

And we stood there on the street corner shouting at each other.

"Not superior," I said, "rational. I believe in verifiable facts. If I can see it with my own eyes, if I can touch it and hear it, or if I can have it on the authority of two reliable sources—note the inclusion of the adjective *reliable*—then I believe in it. Some nut who claims he's in psychic contact with Queen Victoria does not constitute a reliable source."

"Louis Pinkle," she said, shaking her fists at me, "sometimes I want to kill you!" Then she calmed herself down. "We're having one of those fights again. Now, I think we should try and figure out what we're *really* fighting about, 'cause I don't think we'd get this angry if we were just arguing about the existence of a spirit world."

"True," I said, "and very perceptive. Obviously something more is at stake."

"I think I'm angry about your attitude toward me. When it's anything concerning sex or cooking or taking care of you—any of the things women are supposed to do—you can't get over how great I am. But whenever I try to use my brain, you put me down. Thinking's for men. Louis Pinkle, big New York intellectual; Carol Goodkind, dumb California sun bunny."

"I never feel that way about you."

"You do and you don't even know it. That's the other thing that drives me crazy about our relationship. You're so involved in your articles that half the time you don't even know I exist. You start a project and I don't hear from you for days. Then you pop up for a meal and a fuck and then you're gone again. I mean, really! What kind of relationship is that? I could move back to Chicago and you probably wouldn't even notice as long as I left a few meals in the fridge."

"If it's so awful, why do we keep seeing each other?"

"Because it's not *so awful*. And because I love you."

"Yeah, I guess that's the bottom line. I love you too. And I'm sorry if I put down your brain—which, incidentally, I think is terrific—or ignore you. Let's kiss and make up."

"Okay."

We did, right there on the street corner in front of two fascinated twelve-year-olds, who chewed gum and gaped until their mother showed up and hustled them along.

"Come back to my apartment," I said when we were done. "We'll make a long night of it."

"Nope. I've got to go to the Miramar and hear Fritz Uhler."

It pissed me off that she didn't want to come home with me, even after I had admitted that I was wrong. I picked a phrase that I thought would hurt her most: "All you California girls are the same; you always prefer a séance to an orgy."

It worked; her temper flared like a barbecue when you squirt lighter fluid on the coals. "Fuck you, Louis," she hissed, opening the door of her powder-blue Mustang, sliding into the driver's seat.

"Carol . . ." I said.

I ran over to the window, but she rolled it up before I could say anything. I tried to pantomime that I was sorry, that I hadn't meant to make her quite that mad; but she gunned the engine and I barely had time to leap out of the way. I stood there watching the taillights recede down Ventura Boulevard, wondering whether

I should follow her to the Hotel Miramar to apologize, or give her a day or two to cool off. The latter seemed the sensible alternative, so I got in my Honda and drove home.

3

MARTY RUBIN

The Memorial Mausoleum had been conceived in the same spirit as the Great Pyramid of Cheops or the tomb in which our Russian friends display Lenin. It was a series of low Gothic buildings formed from huge blocks of stone, with narrow windows and arches five feet thick, as though built to withstand a direct nuclear strike. And no wonder. Here were laid to rest our greatest cultural heros, Jean Harlow, W. C. Fields, Irving Thalberg, to name a few. An enclosed bridge spanned the drive, connecting the mausoleum with a half-scale Cathédrale de Notre-Dame, which housed, weirdly enough, a full-sized reproduction of the Sistine Chapel ceiling.

I parked the Honda at the end of a quarter-mile file of limousines and walked the rest of the way. The day was obscenely sunny, and the chauffeurs were sitting on the grass, smoking and talking. Having arrived an hour late, thanks to oversleeping and taking the wrong freeway exit, I was worried about getting inside before the services had ended. As it turned out, the mausoleum was so crowded I couldn't have gotten inside anyway; people were packed in solid. They crowded the marble steps at the entrance, standing on tiptoe to catch a glimpse of the celebrities, and a couple of photographers I knew were using their cameras like periscopes. I smiled to think that Tony's last appearance was SRO.

Ten minutes later the crowd at the door parted and the parade began. Nicholson and DeNiro, Polanski and Faye Dunaway. It was unusual for TV stars to socialize with screen stars in the rigidly stratified Coast community, but many of them knew Tony from New York days, from the Actors' Studio, and many respected him as a performer. Flashbulbs burst as photographers raced along, trying to get as many famous faces as they could in the same frame, while the evening news people concentrated on not tripping over their camera cables. The parade continued: aging producers chewing on cigars and young agents hiding their claws in the pockets of their Saint Laurent suits. The immediate family came next: Aunt Sofia in a black veil, supported by a priest; tall, proud Uncle Mario; and all the others I had seen at the wake. And finally Bini, clutching the arm of a slim, sharply tailored man in sunglasses. The press bore down on them until he actually had to push them away, like mayflies. They walked faster and faster, seeking the refuge of the limousine. I ran and shoved until I was alongside her.

"Mrs. Valenti . . ." I called.

Her escort grabbed me by the lapel, half ripping it from the jacket. My only good suit.

"Leave her alone!" he barked. "Don't you bastards have any respect . . ."

Then Bini recognized me. "It's Louis! Oh Louis, I'm so glad you came." She let go of his arm and took mine instead.

"Sorry," he said. "I thought you were another reporter."

"Forget it," I said. I asked Bini how she was holding up and she made a brave smile.

"I'm so angry at the reporters, there's no room for hurt. Ride back in the limousine with us—please?"

I agreed; I'd pick up my Honda later.

The chauffeur saw us coming. He must have been used to this sort of thing; he had the door open and the motor idling, and the moment we were safe inside he raced around to the driver's seat. In the intervening seconds at least thirty photographers had clustered around the limousine, aiming their single glass eyes in through the tinted windows. Suddenly I knew how it felt to be a goldfish. And then they were all behind us, and we were gliding down Heavenly Rest Drive in hermetic, air-conditioned silence.

Bini sighed and lay back in the plush upholstery. Her escort took off his sunglasses—aviator glasses tinted brown on top—and massaged the bridge of his nose. His eyes were surprisingly small and pale, like underground animals dragged into the light. He lit up a cigarette, an exotic fragrance, pungent and earthy.

"They're jackals," he said dramatically.

He was forty-two or forty-three, tan and in fine physical shape—probably tennis twice a week and a swim in the pool every evening after work. He had brown curly hair and a nice straight nose, but a receding chin spoiled his face. Furthermore, I thought there was something nasty about those lips. Perhaps they sneered too often.

"Sorry about your jacket," he went on. "You know Carrol's in Beverly Hills?"

I nodded. It was one of the more expensive men's shops.

"Stop by there tomorrow. I'll arrange for them to fit you for a new one."

"Don't be silly," I said, "it's just a little tear."

"No, I insist."

"I couldn't."

"I don't want to hear any more about it," he said. "I'm going to have my secretary call and they'll be expecting you. Tell them Marty Rubin sent you."

"It's too bad," I said, "we couldn't have met under pleasanter circumstances. I'm Louis Pinkle."

"Tony's oldest and dearest friend from back East," Bini explained.

"It's beautiful to meet any friend of Tony's," Marty said. "This is a terrible tragedy, him dying so young."

"How was Mexico?" I said.

"Mexico?" He repeated it as though it were the name of a man he'd never met. "Oh yeah, Mexico. Great. I played some tennis, swam in the ocean—it's a beautiful beach down there. At sunset these young girls ride horses bareback down the beach. It's like a United Airlines commercial." He laughed.

"I didn't know you were in Mexico," Bini said.

"I just got back this morning."

"You didn't tell me." Her voice was accusative.

"The strain of Tony's death was too much for me," he admitted. "I had to get away by myself. But I was embarrassed to be off playing tennis at a tragic time like this."

"It's nothing to be ashamed of," Bini said, putting her hand on top of his. "Death means different things to everybody and we each have to deal with it in our own personal way."

She looked at me significantly and I remembered her request at the Beverly Hills Hotel.

We rode for a time in silence. Then Marty said, "I'm just curious—how did you know I was in Mexico?"

"You're smoking a Delicado. There's no smell quite like it."

He frowned at me. He rolled the cigarette in his fingers until he could see the brand name on the tip. Then he smiled and nodded.

"Very good. You're very observant, Lou."

"Of course you could have bought them in Los Angeles," I pointed out. "It was just a lucky guess."

"Where can we drop you?" Marty Rubin asked as the limousine glided down the broad, mansion-lined boulevards of Beverly Hills, past rows of coconut palms so tall they tickled the clouds.

"To tell you the truth, Marty, I'd like to talk to you alone. If we could drop off Mrs. Valenti first . . ."

"It's fine with me," Bini said. "I'm going to have a dry martini and a bath and curl up in bed."

We left Bini Valenti at the Beverly Hills Hotel, and Marty ordered the chauffeur to cruise up Sunset in the direction of the strip.

"Now, Lou, what's on your mind?" he said.

"What can you tell me about the Inner Circle?"

"The inner circle of what?"

"Frankly, I don't know. Some kind of organization Tony got involved with just before his career took off. He mentioned it once to Bini years ago, but wouldn't say what it was. I thought he might have told you. A manager can be closer than a wife."

"Particularly when the wife puts the make on every guy she meets."

"Bini's a little promiscuous?"

Marty whistled and grinned. "I'm not putting her down. She's a terrific little girl. But she told me to pick her up early for the funeral so we could talk, you know? And when I got there she put the make on me!"

"What did you do?"

"Gave her my usual advice: Never commit to a project you'll regret later on."

I laughed.

"Tony was like my brother," he went on. "It would have been incest. Or adultery, or something."

"What about the Inner Circle?" I reminded him.

"You got me. I could make some calls."

"I'd appreciate it."

"What's your interest?" he asked.

I shrugged. "Curiosity. And . . ." I hesitated. "Well, Tony once mentioned that he felt this Inner Circle might be after him."

"The poor kid." Marty shook his head sadly. Suddenly he had a thought. He pushed a little switch on the armrest, which lowered the glass partition a crack, told the chauffeur to go to 9200 Sunset, and slid it back in place. "You don't mind if I stop at the office to pick up some papers? Good. Jesus, I knew Tony was getting a little paranoid, but I never dreamed it was so bad. Inner Circle." He shook his head. "When you're a kid and you've got a hit TV series, you know everything there is to know and nobody's going to argue with you. You've got *yes*-men everywhere. They tell you what you want to hear and pretty soon you start to believe them. Every day it's harder to tell the difference between fantasy and reality."

A few minutes later the limousine pulled to the curb in front of 9200 Sunset, a monolith of black glass and chrome that housed half the top theatrical lawyers, agents and producers on the Coast. The chauffeur ran around to open the doors for us.

Nobody walks in LA, and they walk even less on Sundays. I miss that about New York—walking down Madison Avenue and window-shopping, running into old friends, and before you know it, clocking ten miles. Good for the heart and the soul—and the waistline. As far as I could see on Sunset, there was not a person in sight, and the only man in the lobby was a black guard in a blue uniform, who grinned and tipped his hat.

"Hi, Henry," Marty said. "We'll just be a few minutes."

The elevator was playing a lush arrangement of "Hey Jude."

"Tragic thing," Marty said, pushing a button marked "4." He took off his glasses. They didn't fit right; they left footprints on the bridge of his nose. "He could have been another Brando. *Take a sad song and make it be-eh-eh-ter. Remember to let her under your skin* . . . This is our floor."

The door was mahogany, with the names Weston,

Rubin, Weiss, and Penny set in raised brass letters. Marty picked a key from a leather case and fitted it in the lock.

The reception area was all old-English-looking—chairs with lions' paws for feet, a dark leather couch, a coffee table neatly stacked with *Variety*, *New West*, *Esquire*, and *Time*—obviously contrived to give an atmosphere of respectability and age in a land where the oldest legal firms dated back no more than fifty years. Corridors went off to the left and right, opening into conference rooms, a legal library, more offices.

Marty Rubin's office was the largest. The tinted windows gave a sweeping view of West Hollywood's stubby stucco apartment buildings; the taller, sparkling-windowed office buildings on Sunset; and above them all the hills, brown and humpbacked, covered with crazy rows of private residences like gaily colored matchboxes.

"See that?" Marty said, pointing to a picture on the wall, a big oil painting of a couple of sheep. "That's a Constable. An original. I bought it last week."

"He has a way with sheep," I agreed.

Rubin laughed. "A way with sheep? That's priceless. What a sense of humor!"

"Could I use your phone?"

"Sure, follow me."

He led me into a small conference room and left me alone. I leaned back in what was no doubt a Chippendale, put my feet up on the distressed table top and dialed Carol's number. It rang nine times before she answered.

"Oh, it's you. I ran all the way from the pool. What do you want?"

"Is that any way to talk to the man you love?"

"If you're calling me to apologize . . ."

"Nothing of the kind. I'm stuck at Ninety-two hundred Sunset and I need a ride to Glendale, to pick up my car."

"Take back what you said about séances and sex and California girls."

"I will not be coerced."

"Then take a cab."

"At the moment my wallet contains six dollars and two canceled credit cards. Furthermore, the lapel has been half torn off my only good suit."

"Poor boy. How are your hands?"

"My hands? My hands are fine."

"Can you make a fist and hold up your thumb?"

"I suppose so."

"Then go do it!"

I returned to Marty's office and found him sorting through papers.

"I'll be through in a minute," he said, signaling me to a chair. "This is the damnedest thing. A lawyer I know is representing a college professor named Irvin Becker in a suit against World International. Becker wrote a book called *An Inquiry into the Psychology of a Gambler*. He sold it to World for ten thousand bucks and they made it into a movie called *High Rollers*, their biggest grosser in twenty years. Becker thinks he deserves some of the money. He says World International implied they were going to do it as a television show—otherwise he never would have agreed to sell so cheaply.

"Think of the poor schmuck. He spends his life

teaching smart-ass college students, living in some dirt-water town in Idaho, taking home fifteen thousand a year if he's lucky. By some fluke he writes a book that gets turned into the biggest movie in years. It's his one chance to get a little piece of the American Dream and he blows it. So he decides to sue.

"The friend of mine who's representing him calls me this morning—Sunday morning—at eight. They've got to go to court on Monday with an *expert witness*. That's somebody who knows the film business inside out and can testify as to what constitutes *standard practice*. He's got four guys lined up, all respected, experienced members of the film community. Over the weekend all four· call up, canceling. They've all got crazy excuses. Obviously World International put the screws on them. So he asked me if I'd do the job."

"And what did you say?"

"I told him I'd do it."

"Aren't you scared about getting blacklisted?"

"Sure I am. But sometimes you've got to do crazy things. I mean, you've got to live with yourself. You've got to look in the mirror every morning when you shave. I couldn't stand the idea of the poor schmuck getting such a screwing."

Marty grinned at me—a really likeable grin—and dialed the phone.

"Billy?" he said. "I'm glad you're there. A friend of mine needs a ride home. Can you send a cab over?"

"No," I objected, "it's all right. I'll walk."

He waved for me to be quiet and continued: "He'll be waiting at the garage entrance on the alleyway. He's wearing a brown suit with a torn lapel." Marty winked. "A young guy, kind of nice-looking, and, uh . . ."

"Bald," I said.

Marty laughed. "Bald. Yeah, that's right. Beautiful." He hung up and said to me, "The cab will be here in ten minutes. They bill us, so don't give the driver anything."

"Listen, I don't want to . . ."

He stopped me. "Anything I can do for a friend of Tony's makes me feel better. Now let's not hear any more about it."

We shook hands. Marty stayed to make more calls, and I took the elevator to the garage level and walked to the entrance.

It looked out on a narrow alley below Sunset, deserted except for a lizard waiting to get run over. I sat down on the curb and watched the lizard do push-ups. A few minutes later a battered old red Cadillac, squat and tail-finned, pulled up across the street. Two kids got out and walked toward me.

One of them was an Oriental type, possibly Hawaiian, six two and built like a bull, with a pageboy of straight black hair and a girlish face, long eyelashes, smooth cheeks, an indolent smile.

The other was a drugstore cowboy: plaid shirt with pearl buttons, Levi's, high-heeled boots. He had blond hair and blue eyes and a chin like a clenched fist.

They stood in front of me.

"Hi," I said.

"Come on, Baldy," the Oriental said, "you coming with us."

"First of all," I said, rising to my feet and edging

away, "being bald is nothing to be ashamed of. It's a result of an excess of testosterone, the male hormone. So, in a sense, it indicates virility. And secondly, I have no intention of going anywhere with you. You're not my type. I like . . ."

But at this point the Cowboy twisted my arms behind my back and began pulling me to the car, while the Oriental ran ahead to start the engine. Halfway across the alley I recovered my wits enough to smash my heel down into his instep. He let go, shrieking with pain, and I dashed back into the garage.

The elevator, with typical Pinkle luck, was on the lobby floor. I pressed the DOWN button so hard my fist hurt, and muttered, "Come on you motherfucker, come on damn you!" I could hear them running after me, their footsteps echoing through the cavernous garage.

The instant the elevator arrived, I leaped inside, pressing 4 and CLOSE. The doors started to slide shut. Then a hand came into the space between them, smacking against the rubber bumpers, and they popped open again.

They joined me in the elevator, the Oriental grabbing me from behind, his hand under my chin, and jerking back my head so that my neck was shot through with pain. Meanwhile the Cowboy put his knee into my groin, knocking away my breath. My knees buckled and my body doubled up trying to protect the family jewels.

"Easy, Baldy," the Oriental said.

"It's the excess of virility," the Cowboy said and laughed. "We're taking you for a little ride," he whispered as they dragged me across the garage like a piece of heavy luggage.

One thing about crime in Los Angeles—it always sounds like a bad television show because that's where the idiots learn their dialogue. In some distant part of my brain it occurred to me that they were going to kill me and that they were going to do it while voicing cliché lines they had heard on *Kojak*.

They stiffened at the sound of another car.

"Come on," the Oriental said to his buddy, and they tried to drag me faster. I scraped the floor like a sack of potatoes.

The car passed the garage entrance, a blue Mustang convertible with a tall blonde in the driver's seat.

"*Carol*," I called, but my voice was a whisper; I couldn't catch my breath. It was like a dream where you pump your lungs and nothing comes out. I guess she didn't hear me because then the Mustang disappeared around a corner.

"Come on, you cocksucker," the Cowboy hissed.

"Carol," I called, and this time my voice was a little louder.

Then, like an answered prayer, the Mustang drove into the garage, spotlighting us in its headlights.

"Let's get out of here," the Cowboy said.

He hesitated long enough to kick me in the head, then they ran.

A second later I heard a car door opening, high heels on the concrete.

"Oh my God," she whispered, bending down next to me. "Can you hear me?"

I seemed to be under water. My vision was blurred,

double images, blue dots swimming in front of my eyes. In what seemed like another universe, somebody named Louis Pinkle was wondering if he'd suffered brain damage and if he'd ever be able to write again and if not, would he have to get a job as a janitor and mop floors in public washrooms.

"His right ear," I murmured. I had to tell her.

"Shh, darling, save your strength. I'm going to call an ambulance."

"His right ear . . . only half an ear . . . he's the one who killed Tony . . ."

"Whatever you say, darling. Now lie still."

While she was calling the ambulance, somebody turned off the lights.

I woke up in a private room with pale-green walls, a color TV set, and a view of Westwood rooftops, which led me to believe that I was a resident of UCLA Medical Center. Soon a nurse came in and helped me climb onto a rolling table. My entire body was one large, dull ache, and when I moved my neck it felt as if a dentist were probing the vertebrae with a sharp metal tool.

The rest of the day they wheeled me around as though I were a Danish cart in an advertising agency.

First a urologist, hand in latex glove, gave me a rectal examination to determine if I could still have a sex life. Prostate, testicles; results negative. Thank you, God. Then he did a kidney series, an IVP and a cystoscopy. Kidneys, negative. Thanks again.

A technician X-rayed my head and my neck from every angle, and an orthopedist fitted me with one of those plastic and foam rubber neck braces my Aunt

Pearl always used to wear. Whiplash—otherwise, negative.

And finally neurology, the tests I had been dreading. Understand that when I woke up in that hospital room, I couldn't remember my phone number and I wasn't too sure about my street address. Life is difficult enough with all systems operating; at half power I would probably be filling tacos at Jack in the Box. A pretty girl who claimed to be a neurologist examined my X rays and recorded my EEG and something else called an EMG, and pronounced my brain in full working order. I told her I loved her and would be her slave for life, and she laughed; if the offer still held by next week, she'd take me up on it.

They kept me in the hospital three more days; in the morning I'd urinate into a jar to see if my kidney was bleeding; in the afternoons I'd stroll through the corridors making suggestive remarks to the nurses; and in the evenings I'd watch people get the shit kicked out of them on television, get up and brush off their suits and walk away whistling.

The first day a Mr. Perez came to visit. He was a big bear of a man with coffee skin, a stirrup-shaped mustache, longish hair and sideburns, dark stubble where he shaved. His eyes were brown and liquid. He wore a blue polyester leisure suit and a lot of fake Navajo jewelry.

He introduced himself, letting me admire his Beverly Hills Police Department badge. He must have been pretty smart to become a detective so young—I doubted if he was thirty—or else he was Jerry Brown's nephew.

"I know you've been through a very rough experience, Mr. Pinkle," he said, "and I'll make this as brief as possible."

He asked me my age, my place of birth, and my profession, jotting down my answers on a little pad. When I said that I was a free-lance writer, his eyes lit up. He put down his pad and said, "What do you think of Bellow?"

"Bellow?"

"Saul Bellow. What's your opinion of his work?"

"I . . . I like it."

"But don't you think the Nobel Prize should have gone to Graham Greene?"

"Maybe."

His voice became animated and he began to gesture with his hands, enormous hands with black hairs on the back.

"What I mean is, Bellow is basically a photographer, like Roth and many of the other modern Jewish writers. His prose is marvelously descriptive, but does he have anything to say?"

"I don't know. Does he?"

Perez's brow wrinkled in concentration. "I think not. Greene, on the other hand, is a philosophical novelist. He deals with the dilemma of man's place in the universe as symbolized by his own struggle with Christianity. Don't you agree?"

"Well . . . to tell you the truth, I haven't read any Graham Greene in a long time."

"Who is your favorite novelist, Mr. Pinkle?"

"Kurt Vonnegut?" I hazarded.

Perez nodded solemnly. "His *Cat's Cradle* was a miracle of compression. But don't you think his recent works are becoming overly mannered?"

He looked to me for approval, like a cocker spaniel; when I nodded, he beamed.

"This is such a privilege for me. I never get to discuss literature with a real writer."

"I never get to discuss literature with a real cop," I said. "But could we get on with it? I'm very tired."

He apologized and got back to the business at hand: "Tell me, as clearly as you can recall it, what happened."

Ever since awakening in the hospital I had held the firm conviction that the goons had been summoned by Rubin while he was "calling a cab"; but now that I was speaking to the Law Himself, I had second thoughts. Before I put Rubin through a lot of trouble I should be damn sure he was the guilty one, and frankly, it didn't make much sense. He wouldn't have wanted to silence me unless he was a member of this Inner Circle that had put away Tony. But how could a man with thirty or forty percent of Tony Valenti benefit from his demise? Talk about killing the goose that laid the golden egg. My brain still felt like somebody had slipped chewing gum between the gears and I worried that I might be missing some obvious fact and drawing illogical conclusions. So rather than implicate Marty Rubin, I threw together some half-assed story about how I had been searching for a travel agent in 9200 Sunset—a travel agent who was open Sunday—when the goons had accosted me.

"Probably junkies," I said of my assailants.

"Perhaps."

Perez reached in his lapel pocket and brought out my wallet, a worn black-leather Buxton.

"The nurse gave me this," he said. "How much money were you carrying?"

"Six dollars."

He removed a five-dollar bill and a single. "Could they possibly have been waiting for you in particular? Do you have any enemies, anybody who might want to do you harm?"

I shook my head, puzzled.

As he was leaving, Detective Perez confessed that he had written several short stories and would give all for my opinion of them. I told him I was a journalist and I doubted my advice would be worth anything. But at his urging I agreed to look them over after my recuperation. He had such enthusiasm, I couldn't disappoint him. Hopefully he'd forget by then.

Carol came in soon after Perez left. She had been out in the corridor all afternoon, waiting to hear about my condition, and she looked a mess. Her hair was all over the place and her white T-shirt and shorts were streaked with blood—my own, I realized with a start. I think she had been crying.

"Are you all right?" she asked in a tiny voice.

"Fine—except for one thing," I replied in my highest, squeakiest voice.

"Oh my God," she whispered. She pressed her fist to her mouth.

"No, no," I said in my normal register. "I'm just kidding. Everything's great except for a little soreness in the kishkas."

For an instant she was angry; then she smiled.

"You fink! How could you worry me like that?"

"It's my irrepressible good humor. Now listen.

Where are my clothes? You've got to get me out of here. I don't have any health insurance and between the X rays and the EEGs and the three doctors, this fiasco has got to cost me a couple of thousand bucks."

Carol sat down at the edge of the bed and took my hand.

"Don't worry, Mr. Rubin is paying for it."

"What?"

"I said, 'Mr. Rubin is paying for it.' I think it's very generous of him."

"It sure is," I agreed. "Especially since he was the one who put them up to it."

"Louis, what are you talking about?"

"Who else knew I was down there? And the police detective said they didn't take any money. They wanted to kill me. They wanted to kill me because I know about the Inner Circle."

"What's the Inner Circle?"

"I don't know," I admitted.

"But you just said you knew . . ."

"Carol, I'm a sick man. Don't argue with a sick man."

She sat there for a minute, watching me with concern. Then she said, "Louis, if Marty Rubin wanted to kill you, why did he take you to the hospital?"

"He took me to the hospital?"

"He came down to the garage while I was calling an ambulance. When he saw you lying there unconscious, he practically went into shock. The cab arrived a couple of seconds later and . . ."

"Wait a minute! There really was a cab?"

". . . and he and the driver stretched you out on the

back seat. When we got to the hospital he insisted on a private room. He was really worried."

"They must have followed the limousine back from the funeral. Maybe they've been following me ever since the night Tony stopped at my apartment— following me and waiting for the moment when I'd be alone."

"Louis, that sounds awfully paranoid."

"By the way, did I thank you for saving my life?"

"I just couldn't see you hitching all the way out to Glendale."

"And next time I'll even go to see Fritz Uhler with you."

A curious look came into Carol's eyes, distant and troubled.

"A sacrifice . . ." she murmured.

"No sacrifice at all. I'll be delighted."

"No, that's what Fritz Uhler said. He was taking questions from the audience and I asked him about Tony's death. He said it was a sacrifice. A sacrifice to the spirit world."

"That explains everything," I said and started to laugh. But at that moment a storm cloud crossed the sun, plunging the rooftops of Westwood into darkness and bringing a sudden drop in temperature that raised gooseflesh on my skin.

My second day in the hospital I called Flora Mc-Reese. When I told her what had happened, she came over immediately, stopping just long enough to pick up a box of candied fruit and an obscene get-well card. Greeting cards are a passion with Flora; she sends them at every opportunity.

"Solid, concrete evidence," I said, showing her my medical report.

"It certainly seems to be."

"Furthermore, I have a quote from Detective Lester Perez of the BHPD. Me: 'Is it possible that I was a random victim of junkies?' Perez: 'I don't think so. It seems to me they were waiting for you in particular. Somebody wants to do you harm.'"

Her eyebrows were oscillating at a high interest level.

"Remarkable. And it's usually so difficult to get any sort of statement from the police."

"So I'm on the right track?"

"I'd certainly say you are."

"Great. I need another thousand dollars."

"This is going to be very difficult, Louis. At least give me something to tell Fletcher."

"I'm going into analysis."

"Do you really think *BonHomme* should pay for that?"

"I'm going into analysis," I explained, "with Tony Valenti's shrink. The only way I'll get to talk to him is by posing as a patient. You know how they are about doctor-patient confidence. His name is Abraham Kellerman and . . ."

"Kellerman?" Flora's eyebrows went up and stopped. "Now that is odd." She walked over to the window and then she walked back.

"What?" I said.

"And nobody's made the connection—"

"What connection?"

"—although it must be coincidence. It must be."

"What coincidence? What are you talking about?"

"Abraham Kellerman," Flora said slowly, "was Rosalee Romain's psychiatrist, the one who was rumored to have killed her with an overdose of barbiturates."

4

ABRAHAM KELLERMAN

I was still weak when I checked out of the hospital. Carol took me to her apartment in Toluca Lake and stayed home from work for two days nursing me. She pumped me full of vitamins and wheat germ and brewer's yeast. I was too weak to protest. The weird thing was, I think the stuff worked—my constitution improved—although I'd never admit it to her and give her the satisfaction of saying I told you so.

Bini Valenti had sent flowers to my hospital room—Rubin must have told her I was there—and a note apologizing for her absence. At this moment in her life, the note said, she couldn't bear going near a hospital. Would I call her when I was released? So, while I was convalescing at Carol's, I rang her up and told her I was all right. She said that my injury had been her salvation; her concern for me had drawn her away from her own tragedy. Instead of worrying about her own life, she was worrying about mine.

There's a malady I call Doctor Chauvinism that everybody suffers from: My dentist is The Best Dentist in New York City; the surgeon who did my Uncle Murray's hemorrhoids is The Best Surgeon on the East Coast; the doctor who delivered you is still practicing in Brooklyn and he is probably The Best Obstetrician in the Entire World, communist countries included.

Naturally when I told Bini about the terrible psychological stress I'd been under, and mentioned that I'd been thinking of seeing an analyst, she told me she knew of The Best Psychiatrist in Beverly Hills. As it happened, he had been Tony's psychiatrist too. He didn't take many new patients but she would call him and ask if he'd see me as a special favor. She mustn't go to the trouble, I said, but she insisted. And before I knew it I had entered into that great American institution, psychoanalysis.

Abraham Kellerman was in his seventies, an energetic yet grim little man. Shaking hands with him, I could look down on his stooped pink head with its continents of liver spots, its cloud cover of wispy white hair. His nose was round, but the rest of his face was drawn and severe, with deep lines on either side of his mouth. Wire-rimmed bifocals made the bottom half of his eyes bigger than the top. He wore baggy tweed pants—the jacket of the suit was spread across the back of a chair—and a short-sleeved beige shirt, which made his arms look like sticks.

"As you know," he said, "I have a busy schedule;

I turn down three or four patients a week. But I have agreed to see you for a very special reason: As Tony's analyst, I feel responsible for his suicide. Frankly, I have been so filled with guilt the last week that I find it almost impossible to carry out my usual work. Since you are the same age, and a close friend of Tony's, I am hoping some transference will be possible. I will deal with my own guilt while I help you with yours. It is a trifle unorthodox, but why not? The Chinese sage Confucius said, 'How do you expect to heal others when you cannot heal yourself?' We will heal each other, yes?" He smiled, and his whole face was transformed, suddenly warm and kind and sympathetic.

His office—one room of a big apartment in Century City—was furnished with contemporary pieces: chairs of chrome tubing with leather slung across them, an arc lamp, a shag carpet with a red and blue free-form design, Miró prints on the walls, and an enormous desk.

"No couch?"

"It is better," he said, gesturing for me to take one of the chrome chairs, "if we can see each other. Freud was a Victorian and the Victorians were fond of chaises. Today we are more chair-sitters, I believe. Tell me, what is the problem?"

He had sat down opposite me, only a few feet away, and was staring at me across the top of a church steeple he had formed with his fingers.

"The problem. Well, there are lots of problems. For one thing, I don't have enough money."

"How much money is enough?"

"Enough to marry Carol—she's a girl I've been seeing for a couple of years. She has a kid to support, and if we got married her ex would cut off her alimony. Enough money to go to a restaurant once in a while and to buy myself some new clothes. I don't even have a suit anymore. Enough money so I wouldn't have to spend all my time worrying about the payments on the car and the rent and my goddamn bank loans. If I could just sell one screenplay I'd be out of the hole, I could settle my debts and then I'd be free to concentrate on my writing. But that first sale, that's the killer. Nobody will buy from you unless you have a track record and you can't get a track record because nobody will buy from you. It's Kafkaesque. Well, I guess I'm meant to be broke," I said lightly and laughed.

Kellerman's right eyebrow went up.

"What do you mean by that?"

"Nothing." I shrugged. "Just being philosophical. I guess a lot of my troubles stem from my relationship with . . ."

"Louis, if you please. Let us return to that statement you made: *I guess I'm meant to be broke.*"

"It was just a joke."

"A joke is only a way of saying something serious. Who meant for you to be broke?"

"Nobody. It's just a fact of life. I'm broke and Walter's loaded."

"Who is Walter?"

"My brother. He draws a hundred grand and he's only a year older than me."

"And who said that you should be broke and Walter should be wealthy?"

"Nobody. Look, Dr. Kellerman, I really think we're

barking up the wrong tree. As I see it, my important problems come from my relationship with Carol and the way she's always trying to . . ."

Kellerman's voice was suddenly harsh, commanding. "Louis is poor and Walter is rich. Answer me: Why?"

"Because Louis is the artist and Walter is the businessman"—I burted it out before I could stop myself.

Kellerman smiled.

"Jesus," I said thoughtfully. "That's what my father always used to say. Louis is the artist, leave the business to Walter. You see, when I got home from school, I'd sit in the kitchen, drawing pictures, and Walter would go do deliveries for Goldin's Pharmacy. And I'd feel guilty because Walter was working, but Pop would say, 'Forget it. You're the artist, leave the business to Walter.' And you know what he'd say to Walter? He'd say, 'You help Louis out one day when he's a starving artist in Greenwich Village.' It's so obvious—why didn't I ever see it before? I'm being poor to please my father."

"That's very good, Louis, very good. We'll talk more about this tomorrow."

I thanked him profusely, shaking his thin old hand in both of mine, beside myself with gratitude. I was halfway home before I realized that I had completely lost track of my reason for going to see him.

"I've been having a recurring dream," I said the next time I found myself seated opposite Kellerman. "I dreamed that Tony Valenti was murdered."

I waited for him to say something, but he just sat there watching me. I went on: "I know what the papers say about suicide, but I think it was murder."

He still wasn't talking. Those piercing eyes—I felt that he could see through me and that all my secrets were printed along the inside of my spine. My heart began to pound and the room swam before my eyes. I couldn't keep up this masquerade another minute; I had to bring it to a head.

"The night of his death," I rushed on, "he came to my apartment. He told me that a group called the Inner Circle wanted to get rid of him."

Kellerman's eyes had closed. He sat in the easy chair facing me, limp and relaxed, breathing easily; he might have been asleep. Minutes passed. I felt awkward. I didn't know what to do, so I just sat there.

Then he opened his eyes and said, "Tony Valenti was a very troubled young man. He used drugs. At times he evolved vivid paranoid fantasies. The Inner Circle was one of his fantasies. He suspected everyone who tried to help him—his wife, his manager, even myself—of being a member of this conspiracy. For Tony it was a defense, a system for safeguarding his neuroses. I have the impression that you are the heir to Tony's fantasy, that he left it to you before he killed himself and now you feel that you must nurture and protect it. Would I be correct in assuming that you intend to expose this Inner Circle and bring its members to justice in order to avenge Tony's death?"

"I guess so," I said weakly.

"I think we had better explore more of your feelings about Tony Valenti. Our time is almost up but tomorrow we'll try to reexperience what you felt when Tony came to visit you."

I wandered out to the street, my mind in a daze. From a crusading journalist I had been reduced, in fifty short minutes, to a self-doubting neurotic. Was the Inner Circle no more than a paranoid's masterpiece? The evidence seemed to support that conclusion, and yet I could not accept it. I knew that Tony had been murdered, I knew it! And I also knew that if I spent one more hour with Dr. Kellerman, I would be certain of nothing.

I drove into Hollywood, down to Sunset and Vine, where the boulevard starts turning rinky-tink and every third shop caters to the tourists with glossies of old-time stars and novelty items and tacky souvenirs.

I found a parking space on a side street and walked back to a gaudy shop in the middle of the block called The Great Spectacle. The window was filled with the most outrageous glasses: harlequin frames like giant butterflies, pink rimless "Lolita" glasses shaped like hearts, glasses with designs inlaid in colored rhinestones right on the lenses. Then there were posters of various celebrities wearing Great Spectacle spectacles, including Kansas Richie who, according to the copy, had all his 371 pairs of glasses custom made there.

When I went inside, Chester McCann spotted me immediately. He grinned and signaled that he would be with me in a minute; then he went back to fitting a pair of rhinestone-monogrammed, fuchsia-tinted, pearl-rimmed rhomboid-shaped glasses on a tall black man in a purple velvet suit. Meanwhile I examined some of the frames on display, trying on the silliest and making faces at myself in the mirror.

Chester McCann was a real, honest-to-goodness dispensing optician licensed by the state of California;

he was also a flack and a talent manager and the com-
poser of such notable songs as "Pasadena Sunset." He
had come to Hollywood after the war to make a career
in the movie business. He had done time at all the
major studios and most of the smaller ones, and he had
known, with varying degrees of intimacy, nearly
everyone who had worked in or near a movie until
the early sixties; that was when his career fell apart.

Chester was barely five feet tall; he wore loud sports
jackets and Brylcreem and bow ties, and he loved
ethnic jokes. His wife had died of cancer in 1952, leaving him to care for their only child, a ten-year-old girl.
In 1961, while a sophomore at Bennington, she committed suicide. Chester started to drink and didn't stop
until 1967 when he woke up in the hospital with
cirrhosis of the liver and malnutrition. A compassionate
doctor, who was himself an alcoholic, talked him into
joining AA, and Chester began to put his life together. He studied to be an optician because he felt
that the insecurity of show business was one of the
factors that had made him drink; and yet, as with
alcohol, he found he could never get it entirely out of
his system.

When he finished fitting the black man, he hurried
over and pumped my hand enthusiastically. Chester
was all energy and enthusiasm.

"Are you ready to hear," he asked me, "the next
great singing sensation of the century? Barbra
Streisand, Liza Minelli and Dionne Warwick all rolled
into one?"

"Uh—sure," I said.

A little girl was standing behind the cash register,

processing the black man's Master Charge card. She couldn't have been more than eighteen, fragile and skinny with straight blond hair and a sweet face.

Chester called to her: "Sweetheart, this is Lou Pinkle, a very dear friend of mine. He wants to hear you sing. Feel like doing a song?"

Smiling shyly, she nodded.

"Terrific," Chester said. He led me to a seat. "Try to imagine you're in Vegas," he continued. "The stand-up comic's just finished. Now the dancing girls come on, nothing but a couple of feathers. The orchestra plays an intro—"

He dashed behind the counter in the back of the store and returned, slipping the straps of an accordion over his shoulders. He ran his fingers over the keys and buttons, playing a few quick scales and arpeggios; then he began to squeeze out thick harmonies, introductory chords.

The little girl came out from behind the cash register in a sultry walk, flashing her teeth.

"Now remember," Chester said, "she's wearing a black lamé evening gown, low cut. The spotlight follows her. The audience is whistling and stomping."

I was surprised to hear such a big voice come from such a little girl:

Pack up all my cares and woes,
Here I go, singing low,
Bye-bye blackbirrrrrrrrrd . . .

"Very nice," I said. "Chester, can I talk to you for a minute?"

Where somebody waits for me,
Sugar's sweet, so is he,
Bye-bye blackbirrrrrrd . . .

"Chester," I said, trying to be heard above the accordion. "Did you know Rosalee Romain?"

"Oh yes, a sweet sad girl. We were at Fox together —Now listen to the way she does the chorus . . ."

No one here can love or un-der-stand me . . .

"But were you close personal friends? Did she ever discuss her analysis with you?"

"That close we weren't. I said hi, she said hi. Once we had coffee together. She was very shy and uncomfortable with people. She never knew what to say."

Oh what hard-luck stories they all hand me . . .

"But I'll tell you who would know about her analysis. Mashenka Andreevna. Remember her? She was the acting coach at Fox in the fifties."

"Right," I said, "she was the one who had to be on the set whenever Rosalee shot a scene. And if Mashenka didn't like it, Rosalee would insist they shoot the scene over. Drove the directors nuts."

"Exactly."

Make my bed and light the light,
I'll be home late tonight,
Blackbird, bye-bye . . .

"Shenky came in here for glasses last week," Chester continued, pumping great bellows of sound from the accordion. "I've got her address. She's running an acting school a couple of blocks from here. She knew Rosalee better than anybody— Now watch how we do the end."

I said, Blackbird, bye-bye . . .
Blackbiiiiiiiiiiiiiiiird! Bye-byyyyyyyyyyyyyyyyyye!

She opened her arms and emptied her lungs, and all the people who had gathered at the window to watch burst into applause. The little girl bowed and Chester smiled.

"What did I tell you? A star is born. I got her a meeting at William Morris for next week. Now if you could write a little something in *BonHomme* magazine . . ."

"I'll see what I can do."

"Great. I'll get you Mashenka Andreevna's address."

MASHENKA
OSPENSKAYA
ANDREEVNA

The Andreevna School of Dramatic Arts was located in an industrial area on Melrose, across the street from a barbed-wire-fenced film processing plant, in a two-story cinder-block office building of thirties' vintage. In the lobby, on a black felt board with white plastic letters, Ms. Andreevna's name appeared between Sofi Aladabra, Polar Energy Massage, and Herbert Beel, Private Detective.

I climbed the stairs to the second story. The floor was flecked linoleum and the walls shimmered in eerie flickering neon. I read the numbers on the milk-glass windows and when I came to 214, I stopped at the door and listened:

"*Where were you all day? You look terrible.*"

"*I got as far as a little above Yonkers. I stopped for a cup of coffee. Maybe it was the coffee.*"

"What?"

"I suddenly couldn't drive anymore. The car kept going off the shoulder, y'know?"

I turned the knob and pushed back the door, trying to make as little noise as possible. The room was dark except for a bright area on a platform where a boy in blue jeans and a girl in a cotton print dress were sitting on straight-back chairs, playing their scene. I also had the impression of rows of benches, of young people in rapt concentration. While I was standing there, waiting for my eyes to adjust, somebody hissed, "Shut the door."

I did; then, when I could see a little better, I tiptoed to the last bench and sat down next to an intense young woman.

The boy on stage was saying, "It's so beautiful up there, Linda, the trees are so thick and the sun is so warm. I opened the windshield and just let the air bathe over me. And then all of a sudden I'm going off the road."

I noticed a woman of sixty or so sitting next to the platform, regarding the actors with a critical eye. She had waist-length black hair, coarse and streaked with silver, angular features and absolutely smoldering eyes. She was lean and wiry and she wore a black leotard, a long green skirt, sandals and, around her firm neck, a modernistic choker that seemed to have been stretched from a lump of silver toffee. Her body was extraordinarily youthful, but what struck me even more was her remarkable poise, the way she held her chin and shoulders, the way she arched an eyebrow when the boy faltered on his lines. She had the bearing of a queen.

She said nothing until the scene was finished; then she had the lights turned up and gave the other students first crack at the actors. When arguments developed, Mashenka Andreevna—"Shenky," they called her—would intervene at the moment those arguments threatened to lose bearing on the scene and become arguments for their own sake. Finally she herself delivered three or four terse sentences of criticism. Her English was near perfect, her Russian accent still strong. I had the impression that she was respected—even venerated—by the students, but also feared.

She assigned new scenes to some of the students, told others to work on old scenes, and dismissed them. They filed out of class, talking passionately about acting, playwrights, the theater. They were the handsome kids I see waiting on tables and parking cars, the ones who are still young and naive enough to think they have a chance in an industry that uses actors like toilet paper.

A few students lingered around Mashenka Andreevna, asking her advice on various matters. I waited at a distance, and when they were through I approached her. She smiled at me and nodded, and I could see those blazing eyes scrutinizing every detail of my dress, my bearing, my face.

"And what can I do for you?" she said.

"Ms. Andreevna . . ."

"Call me Shenky, everyone does. The old names are difficult to say, yes? Mashenka Ospenskaya Andreevna. Too long! Nowadays it is all streamlined and freeze-dried, and I have my freeze-dried name. *Shenky*. Hah!"

"Shenky"—I found it almost impossible to call her that—"my name is Louis Pinkle. I'm a journalist and I'm writing a piece on . . ."

"Yes, yes, you're writing a piece on Rosalee and you want to know is it true that she never wore underwear." Her voice was weary, disgusted. "What I want to know, Mr. Pinkey, is why you people keep digging? This girl suffered so when she was alive, she lived in such pain and anguish, why not let her rest in peace?"

"Because," I said, "I think she was murdered."

"You're absolutely correct."

"Excuse me?"

"You're absolutely correct. She was murdered. First we said, 'We will love you, Rosalee, if you show us your tits.' And then we said, 'How immoral! I wouldn't take my family to a movie where a woman shows her tits!' We said, 'She can't act, she's a piece of meat'; and when she studied acting we said, 'Why the nerve of her, the pretension.' When she was alive we held her under a microscope and tried to pull her wings off, and when we killed her, we all stood in a circle and said, 'I'm sorry, I'm sorry, I'm sorry.' "

"That's not exactly what I meant."

"I know what you meant. You've uncovered a conspiracy involving high government officials, yes, I've seen it all before. Scraps of gossip, newly disclosed 'facts.' Innuendo. You people make me sick."

"If you'd shut up for a minute," I said, "I'll tell you what I found out."

"How dare you talk to Mashenka that way!" she flared. She turned her back on me and began collecting

yellow legal pads scribbled with notes and the mimeo-
graphed scripts strewn around the platform.

"I don't mean to be rude," I said, bending down to
help her, "but when you say 'you people' it makes me
feel like a leper. It so happens I'm not that kind of
journalist; I never wrote a piece on Rosalee Romain
and I'm not going to start now. Actually, I want to
know about Kellerman . . ."

"Ach, Kellerman," she grunted.

". . . and how Rosalee felt about him. I came to you
because I've heard that you knew Rosalee better than
anybody."

"That is true," she said, still not bothering to look
at me.

"I wish you'd talk to me," I said standing up, facing
her. "I don't know who else to go to."

She stood up, too, and stuffed the scripts into a big
leather briefcase. She handed the briefcase to me,
saying, "Come. Buy Mashenka a drink. We will talk."

We drove in separate cars to an Italian restaurant
a couple of blocks away, an old-fashioned place with
sawdust floors and ceiling fans, where the manager
greeted Mashenka with an embrace and practically
wept to learn we wouldn't be staying for dinner. At
his insistence we had our drinks at a table, and over an
excellent antipasto I told her Flora's story about Kellerman accidentally giving Rosalee an overdose.

"Yes," she sighed, "I have heard this too. So many
stories! But I do not believe it. Kellerman is a very
careful little man."

I mentioned that Tony and Rosalee had both been

his patients and now both were dead, a certain amount of mystery surrounding both their deaths—at least as far as I was concerned.

"It is interesting," she said, "but only coincidence. You would probably learn that Rosalee Romain and Tony Valenti also used the same dentist. Certain doctors get reputations in show business, and all the actors flock to them. I remember in the thirties a plastic surgeon named Weiss. He fixed Jean Heart's nose and suddenly they were breaking down his door for nose jobs! Then you know what happened? Her nose collapsed! With God as my witness, it fell in during a day's shooting. All his patients were hysterical that theirs would go next." She chuckled into her vodka. "So it's not such a remarkable coincidence. I knew others who were psychoanalyzed by Kellerman, all of them big stars."

"Did Rosalee ever tell you about him?"

"Oh yes, Rosalee told me about everything—until the break. She raved about what a marvelous man he was, but I had an impression of a cold-blooded manipulator. He took control of Rosalee's life; he became her Svengali. That is not my idea of a good analyst. A good analyst teaches you to stand on your own feet and make your own decisions. I will tell you something, Mr. Pinkey, Rosalee might not have killed herself if Kellerman had taught her to find her own strength. That is what I try to do always; help them find their own strength."

"Pardon me for saying this, but you sound a little bitter."

"And why shouldn't I? I taught her everything! The

famous Rosalee walk—it was my creation. The way she smiled, the low voice, even her makeup. All my work. I was the head dramatic coach at Fox for years before she ever came there. When they brought her to me, she was another contract player. I made her special! I was the first to see the qualities: the sexuality, the warmth, the sensitivity. I mined those qualities, I purified them and polished them until they glittered like gems. Mashenka made her a star! And then she went to see your fine Dr. Kellerman and learned she was too dependent on me. Well, she could have simply told me, 'Mashenka, we cannot be friends anymore,' but that was not Rosalee's way. You see, she was a coward. She could not confront me, so instead she had me fired. After seventeen years! Of course I asked why, but nobody would speak to me. I tried to get in touch with Rosalee but she wouldn't accept my calls."

"Could you get work at another studio?"

"Not in nineteen sixty-two. Producers were making films independently and the studios were like graveyards. The last thing they wanted was an acting coach. But Mashenka survives. Through a revolution and two world wars, Mashenka survives. I borrowed a little money and I opened my own school, and look at me today; I turn away students, my classes are so crowded. One of my—alumni, do you say?—yes, alumni, one of my alumni is starring in a play at the Ahmanson, another has his own TV series." Her voice dropped to a whisper. "One of my girls makes porno movies but I'll soon have her working legitimately."

"You're great," I said, and I meant it.

She lowered her eyes shyly to her drink; a surprising gesture from such a proud, strong woman.

"It is only survival," she murmured. "We must survive."

"Shenky, there's something I've always wondered about. I remember seeing a picture of Rosalee when she started modeling and her hair was sort of mousy brown. Was it your idea, dyeing it platinum?"

"No, the credit for that went to a young man in the legal department at Fox. His name was . . . Bowden? Rudin?"

"Marty Rubin?" I asked, my heart starting to pound.

"Yes, Rudin. He saw her on the lot one day—pretty young contract players spent more time being decorous than acting—and convinced her to dye her hair blond. They never mention him in Rosalee's biographies, but that young man, Rudin, was terribly influential in her career. He brought Rosalee to my attention as well as to Zanuck's, yet he never claimed any credit. And this in a town where every man who's ever met a star claims to have created him. It's curious, yes?"

"I'll agree," Flora McReese said, sitting behind her desk, "that it's an unusual coincidence."

"It's more than a coincidence," I insisted, pacing back and forth in her office. "Rosalee Romain and Tony Valenti, both discovered by Marty Rubin, both in analysis with Abe Kellerman . . ."

"Now wait a moment, Louis. You still have nothing to substantiate the claim of murder, nothing to suggest it except what Tony said at your apartment that night, and it sounded to me like he was in the midst of a psychotic episode."

"What about the goons who beat me up? And didn't

you tell me that somebody called you after Rosalee's death with a story about Kellerman murdering her? What about that? Whoever suggested it must have some evidence; I'll go talk to him . . ."

"You can't."

"Why not?"

"It was Arthur White."

I stared at her dumbly. Arthur White was one of the writers I most admired, a muckraker, but a muckraker with compassion and respect for life. He had won a Pulitzer Prize for his exposé of the Teamsters. Furthermore, he was scrupulously honest and he shied away from sensationalism. If he had proposed the article, then he must have known something, but I'd never find out now. He died in 1968, knifed and beaten to death in a side street in Silver Lake. The murderers were never found.

"Don't you see?" I whispered. "They knew he was onto it, so they murdered him—just like they tried to murder me."

"Louis, thousands of people are murdered in Los Angeles every year. You can't assume they were all involved with this Inner Circle."

"They murdered him," I said louder, banging my fist into my open palm, "they murdered Arthur White!"

"Why don't you sit down and I'll have my secretary bring you some tea. It's not good to get so excited so soon after leaving the hospital . . ."

"I'm not excited, goddamn it! Now what did Arthur have to go on? He must have mentioned something when he called you about the story."

"Louis, that was ten years ago. Do you know how many articles have been proposed to me in the last ten years?"

"You must remember something, you've got a mind like a steel trap."

"Flattery will get you everywhere, darling. Now let me think. It was something about—something about an interview with Rosalee's maid. I'm sorry, my mind's a blank. But you might try talking to Arthur's widow— I believe she still lives at the same address in Tarzana."

6

ARTHUR WHITE

Tarzana is an upper-middle-class neighborhood in the San Fernando valley, about twenty-five minutes from Beverly Hills. In the early days, when Los Angeles was a big orange grove, the entire township belonged to Edgar Rice Burroughs, purchased for him by his friends, John Carter of Mars, the Moon Maid, and naturally the notorious vine-swinger after whom the property was named. Now Burroughs' picture can still be seen in the local post office and his grave site is rumored to be under a huge oak near the Ventura Freeway, although, sadly, no marker exists.

The Whites' home was a modest ranch house not too far from the freeway, a building of mortared stone with green wood frame and picture windows overlooking a broad expanse of lawn, where the swirling streamers of lawn sprinklers sparkled in the sun. The front door featured a brass knocker the size of a pie plate and Scotch-taped next to it, a note in pencil: "Come around back, I'm working in the garden."

I walked to the driveway and around the house, fighting my way between a Ford Granada and some kind of exotic philodendron that was planning on taking over the neighborhood. Los Angeles is filled with strange tropical plants that flourish in the hot, sunny, arid air, growing so fast you can almost see them creep along; and if one of these days the gardeners go on strike, we'll all be done for.

Behind the house I saw a white garage, flaking paint, with a basketball hoop over the door, a big swimming pool surrounded by a wooden fence, and a patio of brick and flagstone where a woman of fifty, dressed in a soiled man's shirt and jeans and gardening gloves, was kneeling in front of a brick barbecue. The barbecue had been filled with dirt and planted with fifty or so strange and beautiful cactuses, most of them types I'd never seen before. When I appeared, a large black dog that had been lying in the shade beside her, barked and lunged and tore a two-inch circle out of my left pants leg before Mrs. White yelled, "Down, Cupcake, down!"

Obediently, the dog lowered her head and trotted back to her master. Mrs. White came forward, pulling off her gardening gloves.

"I'm so sorry, Mr. Pinkle—you are Mr. Pinkle, the man who called this morning? Yes, I'm so sorry but you know how it is; now that Arthur's dead and the children are gone I'm all alone, and I'm afraid Cupcake is a little overprotective."

She was a small, energetic woman with close-cropped silver hair, a face pleasantly tanned and wrinkled, and clear blue eyes. Everything about her was efficient and self-sufficient, and I could easily imagine her knitting afghans, throwing pottery, and writing a cookbook in between picketing for Chavez and the farm workers.

She glanced at my knee and said, "Oh dear, she's torn your pants. Cupcake, you awful thing!" She slapped the dog on the nose and Cupcake lay down and whimpered. "Please let me pay for it."

"Out of the question. They're just an old pair. Nice doggy, nice doggy."

"I don't know what got into her."

"She probably senses fear," I suggested.

"Maybe that's it. Would you like some lemonade?"

"No, please. Go on with whatever you were doing. Like I said on the phone, I have a few questions about some of Mr. White's work."

"You must understand," she said, kneeling by the barbecue, "Arthur didn't discuss his work with me. I rarely saw him when he was involved in a project. He'd be running everywhere and talking on the phone six hours a day. And when we were together he seemed to be listening to a radio station my ears couldn't perceive. I don't mean to give the impression that he neglected me, no; but when he died I tried to remember him, and all I could remember was a ghost of a man rushing to meet a deadline.

"Once he said to me, 'Kitty, are you scared of dying?' And I said, 'Yes, I suppose I am. I've never thought about it much.' And he said, 'Kitty, that's why I write so much. I think if I leave enough paper with my name on it, people will have to remember me after I'm dead.' And then he got up to make a phone call. But dear me, I'm rattling on. What did you want to know about Arthur?"

She picked up a small cactus, a mass of wiry stems with bladderlike leaves of gray velvet shaped like clam shells, and began to tap it free from the rusty coffee tin in which it had been potted.

Cupcake lay on the ground beside her, front paws together, regarding my every move with suspicion. I stayed rather still.

"I was curious about an article he was working on right before his death, an article on Rosalee Romain."

She held the coffee tin upside down and the cactus slid into her open hand, all the dirt intact, a black plug veined with thousands of ivory roots.

"Root-bound," she murmured, holding it for me to see. "We've rescued the little darling just in time. Now let me see, Rosalee Romain; no, I can't recall anything."

"It was about her being murdered."

"Like I said, Arthur rarely spoke to me about his work."

Leaning over the barbecue, she made a hole with a trowel and began gently fitting the cactus in a space between two others.

"But I do have his files," she continued, "and you can look through them if you like."

"I'd like it very much."

"If you'll just wait till I have this little darling tucked into bed."

"That's a fascinating cactus. I've never seen one like it."

"Actually, it's a succulent. Cacti are a subspecies of

succulents; they have thick fleshy bodies instead of stems." She pointed to a plant like a green tumor studded with fine white needles. "That pincushion, for example. *Mammillaria.* That's a cactus."

"What's this succulent called?" I asked about the plant she was putting in the soil.

"Heaven knows. Some hybrid. There now."

She firmed the edges of the soil with her fingertips and watered it with a big red plastic can. Then she got to her feet, brushing the dirt off her knees, tugging her shirttails, which she had left untucked.

"After Arthur died I gave most of his things to his brother's family—I didn't want to make the house into a museum to his memory, if you see what I mean. I was going to give his files to USC—that's where Arthur went to school—but they never came to pick them up. So I had a boy who lived down the block help me move them to the loft on top of the garage. I don't think I've been up there since."

As she spoke she led me toward that building, Cupcake padding along at her side.

"Los Angeles is a funny place," I said. "They build houses without attics and basements. I don't know where people are supposed to store their pasts."

"People in Los Angeles don't have pasts," she said without a trace of bitterness. "I don't believe anyone remembers Arthur, despite all the pages he signed his name to. Life out here is like a cactus flower, gaudy and brilliant—but brief. Sometimes I think about moving back to New England—we're from Boston, you know—but now my life is out here, for better or worse."

Inside the garage was an aging Volkswagen and a

variety of things stacked against the walls: a rusty Schwinn bike with training wheels, two surfboards, a lawn mower and a baseball bat. I rapped the surfboard with my knuckles.

"That's Danny's," she said. "He's at Harvard. And Arthur Junior is living on a commune in Oregon, bless his heart."

She took a wooden ladder from a hook on the wall —I helped her as soon as it became apparent what she was doing—and set it so it led up to a trap door in the ceiling.

"Let me go first," she said. "The door's a little tricky."

Reaching the top, she pushed the door in and slid it over to one side. I handed her a powerful flashlight and she disappeared into the square. I was halfway up the ladder when I heard her gasp and say, "Oh my God," in the most hopeless, pathetic voice. I hurried up the last few rungs, pulled myself through the door and, by the broad beam of the flashlight, saw what had disturbed her so. Five gray file cabinets were over-turned, the drawers pulled out, the contents scattered across the floor. In addition numerous cardboard cartons had been emptied of letters and file folders, and the accumulated mass of paper had been soaked with some thick, sticky, sweet-smelling liquid— molasses, I think.

As we stood there, surveying the destruction, Mrs. White began to sob.

"It's too much," she gasped. "I try to be strong, but sometimes it's too much."

I helped her back down the ladder and through the back door into the kitchen. Fortunately Cupcake sensed something was wrong and decided not to eat me for trespassing. I sat her down at the kitchen table—kitchen tables are always comforting in times of crisis—and went into the living room where I found some brandy. After taking a swallow myself, I brought a glass to Mrs. White and held it to her lips. Soon she looked better.

"It was probably the same boys who've been knocking down the mailboxes," she said. "When you're young you don't understand the value of things. I'm sure if they had known that those were Arthur's papers . . ."

She wouldn't let me see her cry. She excused herself, went to the bathroom and came back about fifteen minutes later, smiling as though nothing had happened.

"How would it be," I said, "if I sorted through that mess up there. I'd throw out anything that was ruined beyond saving and try and make some order out of what was left. At the same time I can look for the information I need."

"I'd appreciate that very much. I don't think I can go back up there. It's so humiliating."

If Mrs. White was speaking the truth—if she really hadn't been up in the attic since the day she stored away her husband's files—then the damage might have dated from that time. The only clue I had was the number of insects and the quantity of dirt that had been picked up by the sticky liquid. Mrs. White had supplied me with a yellow plastic bucket of sudsy water, some mops and sponges and two rolls of paper towels. All afternoon I sat on the floor, sorting through the sticky mess. I tried soaking the pages and then pulling them apart, but they only shredded; I tried prying them gently from the corners, but more often than not I'd end up tearing away the print. Finally I had to satisfy myself by throwing away the sheets that had been permeated and salvaging what remained. Fortunately the blanket of papers was several inches thick, and the liquid had soaked through only a few layers.

Mrs. White was in the kitchen preparing her dinner when I came in to tell her that I'd finished; the file cabinets were in some sort of order; the cardboard cartons had been filled and labeled; most of the sticky goo had been wiped up; and I had found three objects that, with her permission, I would take home with me and return to her within a month at the most.

"I really should be mad at you," Carol said when she opened the door and saw me standing there. "I don't hear from you for days. And then there you are on my doorstep with your pant leg torn and that maniacal look in your eye, and all I can think about is how much I love you. But really, Louis, what would you do if you popped up here one night and found me with another man?"

"Propose a ménage à trois!"

"You're impossible."

"And you're the most terrific woman I've ever met." I kissed her and went inside. "Now listen. Do you still have that reel-to-reel tape recorder I bought you for Christmas?"

She nodded.

"Good. After dinner we're going to listen to a tape

that will blow this whole Tony Valenti thing wide open."

"Tony Valenti. Tony Valenti. That's all you ever talk about anymore."

"Carol, I have evidence! I just spent four hours going through Arthur White's papers . . ."

"Who's Arthur White?"

I explained and continued: "So I went through his papers and I found these. Exhibit A, one file folder marked 'Rosalee Romain'—empty."

"What's that sticky stuff all over it?"

"Pay attention. Exhibit B, one reel of tape marked 'Interview with Mary Spivack,' who, in case you haven't heard, was Rosalee Romain's maid and the last person to see her alive. It must have rolled into a corner when they were tearing up the files, and that's why they missed it. What an incredible piece of luck."

"Louis, wait a minute! You sound like a crazy. What does any of this have to do with Tony Valenti?"

I explained and continued: "And finally Exhibit C." I held up an ancient yellowed clipping, a photograph of a man laid out to rest in a coffin. He wore a broad tie, a broad-lapeled suit, and pencil-line mustache, and his hair was as smooth as patent leather. There were enormous floral arrangements all around him.

"Who is he?" Carol asked.

"I'm not quite sure, but look closely at his tie clip— you see where someone's circled it in pencil?"

Carol took the clipping over to a lamp and squinted at it.

"What is it?"

"A little clay man with a skull's head. Tony Valenti

was wearing a charm just like it when he was laid out for visitation."

"Far out," she said. She gazed at it a moment longer. "So what?"

I shrugged. "I don't know so what. But maybe I will after I listen to that tape."

Everyone in Los Angeles harbors a secret desire to be in the entertainment business, the same way anyone stationed at an army base would sooner or later want a taste of war, and Carol was no exception. She had a low, breathy voice, she could carry a tune, and she was a fair hand at the guitar. So for Christmas I bought her a tape recorder, my head filled with visions of the two of us cruising up Wilshire in a Rolls-Royce Corniche, guzzling champagne and munching pâté de fois gras. And here we were, a year and a half later, eating bean sprouts in Toluca Lake. After dinner I took down the tape recorder from the top of the closet and threaded the reel I had salvaged from Arthur White's garage. I switched on the machine and settled back, sipping my coffee.

"*When was the last time you saw Rosalee Romain alive?*" The voice was a man's, froggy with cigarette smoke.

"That's Arthur White," I said.

"*It was the night of June fifth*"—a woman's voice, high, reedy, nervous—"*Saturday. We were spending the weekend at the Malibu house.*"

"*Can you tell me what happened that night?*"

"*Well, I made dinner for Miss Romain, veal parmigiana, that was her favorite dish. She was very de-*

pressed about her marriage breaking up and all the trouble they were giving her at the studio."

"What happened after dinner?"

"We sat on the screened-in terrace, watching the waves break. Rosalee was reading a book and I had some needlepoint. Rosalee liked me to sit with her— she didn't like to be alone, if you know what I mean. She kept on putting down the book, getting up and pacing. Then she'd try and read some more. She must have finished two or three bottles of wine, trying to relax. Then she said to me, 'You'd better call Dr. Kellerman. I don't think I'll be able to sleep tonight.' "

"And who was Dr. Kellerman?"

"Miss Romain's psychiatrist. The dearest little man. I think, aside from myself, he was the only one she trusted. On nights when Miss Romain couldn't sleep, he would drive all the way out to Malibu to give her a sedative. Frankly, I think he must have been a little in love with her. After all, every man was."

"And did Dr. Kellerman come out that night?"

"He did. I called him and a little less than an hour later he was at the door. Just the sight of him made Rosalee relax. Then he gave her the injection . . ."

"Now wait a minute. Did you tell him about all the wine she'd been drinking?"

"I mentioned it. He said it didn't matter—"

I switched off the tape recorder and shouted triumphantly. "There! She told him they were drinking and he went ahead and gave her a sedative anyway. That's murder! I've got the son of a bitch cold."

"What if," Carol interrupted, "the injection wasn't a sedative?"

"But it was a sedative! The next morning she was dead from a barbiturate overdose. That's what the death certificate said."

"Play some more of the tape," Carol urged. She was getting excited too.

I switched it back on.

"*. . . and sent her to bed. Dr. Kellerman was very tired, so I fixed him a cup of coffee before he left.*"

"*Did he give you any special instructions?*"

"*He told me to call him if Miss Romain had any trouble during the night. He made me swear not to let any other doctor see her because his treatment was very special and if another doctor didn't know about it, he might accidentally kill her.*"

"*And did Miss Romain have trouble during the night?*"

"*It was awful. It was so awful. About three o'clock in the morning she started screaming. I put on my bathrobe and ran to her room, and she was having spasms, jerking around on the bed, her face all contorted and her hands like claws almost.*"

"*What did you do, Mary?*"

"*I called Dr. Kellerman. He said he'd be right over and in the meantime I should put hot towels on her face and chest and arms. Dr. Kellerman arrived about fifteen minutes later—*"

"*Excuse me, but didn't you say that it took Dr. Kellerman an hour to drive to the Malibu house?*"

"*Oh, I forgot to mention: When he saw what kind of shape Rosalee was in, he decided to stay with a friend in Malibu Colony so he'd only be a few minutes away. He gave me the phone number there.*"

"*Do you know the name of the friend he stayed with?*"

"*No.*"

"*What happened after Dr. Kellerman arrived?*"

"*He ran into Miss Romain's room and closed the door. I was so nervous! I did my needlepoint and turned on the television so I wouldn't have to listen to the sounds.*"

"*What sounds?*"

"*Miss Romain was screaming. About an hour later he came out of her bedroom. He was sweating and wiping his hands with a towel. He looked like he would cry. He shook his head and said, 'I'm sorry, she's dead. There was nothing I could do to save her.'*"

"*What happened next?*"

"*I suggested we call the police. Dr. Kellerman said we didn't have to. Since he was her physician, he could make out the death certificate himself, and that way we could save her from a lot of bad publicity. Wasn't that thoughtful of him? So instead of the police, Dr. Kellerman called some friends from the hospital to come and take away the body. He was so considerate to go to all that trouble. In all my days I've never seen anyone handle a tragedy with such taste and efficiency.*"

"*Thank you very much for answering my questions, Mary.*"

"*The pleasure was mine, Mr. White.*"

Click.

The tape continued to roll, unwinding off one spindle, winding onto the other, slipping between the sensitive heads that read the magnetic impulses, but those impulses gave no more answers, only a steady hissing.

Carol and I sat where we were, too stunned to say a word.

"I don't understand," she said after a minute. "Why would Dr. Kellerman want to kill Rosalee Romain?"

"Let's make up a scenario." I stood up and began to pace the living room, my hands clasped behind my back. "A young lawyer named Marty Rubin works in the legal department at Fox. He's smart and he's hungry. He spots a beautiful starlet on the lot one day and it occurs to him that with a few alterations—like a bleach job—and a little hyping to the studio executives, this girl could be a star. The trouble is, she's already under contract to Fox and our young lawyer, as an employee of that same studio, won't be allowed to take a cut for his services.

"As for Rosalee, she's even hungrier; she came here six month ago and she's got six months left on her contract, and all she's done so far is pose for publicity stills. As a matter of fact, she's desperate, she'll agree to anything. Our young lawyer approaches her with an offer: He'll guarantee her a juicy movie role in return for her signature on a secret agreement giving him a percentage of her earnings in perpetuity. Somehow he figures out a way to disguise the income so nobody can trace it, not even the IRS. He also arranges it so that in the event of the starlet's death he comes into a good piece of her estate.

"Slow dissolve: five years later. Our little girl is no longer a starlet. She has her own production company and she's produced three films, each of them grossing in the tens of millions. She's worth a bundle, her stock is at an all-time high. But she's a high roller; any day now she may piss it all away in bad investments. So our smart young lawyer decides to make his move. He gets in touch with her psychiatrist and offers him half the loot if he'll murder her. They'll make it look like suicide.

"They pull off the murder without a hitch—at least that's what they think—but then they find out that a journalist named Arthur White is beginning to piece together the clues. So they hire two goons to get rid of him and make it look like a mugging. Now they're in the clear; in fact they're so successful they decide to try it again. But remember, they're smart and they're patient. They wait ten years—time enough for everybody to forget about the starlet's death—before they sign a hot young actor named Tony Valenti to the same sort of agreement. And so forth and so on. Well?"

I stopped pacing and faced Carol, whose pretty face was screwed up in thought.

"It doesn't sound right to me," she said finally.

"What do you mean it doesn't sound right?"

"Don't get angry. I'm just telling you the truth. You want me to tell you the truth, don't you?"

"Of course I do. Now why doesn't it sound right?"

"Well, first of all, I don't think you'd be able to disguise the transfer of so much money—even if you were a lawyer. Don't all wills have to be made public? The other thing is, well, maybe Marty Rubin murdered Rosalee Romain when he was hungry, but today he's really rich. He paid that huge hospital bill of yours without blinking. Would he risk murdering somebody else just to get a little richer?"

"Okay, what's your theory?"

"I'm not going to tell you," Carol said.

"Why not?"

"Because you'll scream at me."

"I never scream at you," I said. "Now tell me!"

"I think it was like Fritz Uhler said. They were sacrifices."

"That's the stupidest goddamned thing I ever heard."

"You're screaming at me."

"I'm not screaming at you. I am just racking my brains trying to unravel the most important multiple murder of the decade and your Theosophical twaddle isn't helping."

"You are the most condescending person . . ."

"And the baldest," I added.

She laughed.

"I'm sorry," I continued. "I don't want to put you down. But I don't think the solution lies in the realm of the metaphysical."

"Well neither do I. If you ever let me finish a sentence . . ."

"Okay. Okay."

"I was going to say that it sounded like cult murders, like Charlie Manson stuff. The *Inner Circle*. And the funny little pendant Tony Valenti and the man in the clipping were wearing. It could be sacrificial dressing."

"Like Russian dressing, or French dressing. Or Thousand Island."

"Louis, stop it."

"Sorry, sorry. But I find it difficult to believe that Abraham Kellerman, one of the leading psychoanalysts in the United States, is a cult murderer."

"Maybe they're forcing him to cooperate," Carol

said. "Maybe he has a teen-age daughter and they're holding her hostage . . ."

"Since nineteen sixty-seven?"

"What I mean is, they might have a way of controlling him."

"It's possible," I admitted, humoring her. "I think my next move is to contact Mary Spivack and introduce her to a cop I know named Perez. Then maybe the police will be able to get Dr. Kellerman to talk."

"Tell me one thing, Louis."

"Anything, my love."

"How did you rip your pant leg?"

"I went to see Arthur White's widow and her dog took an instant dislike to me."

"Are you sure you didn't try to molest her?"

"Me? You must be kidding. Here's all that happened. I sat down next to her on the couch"—I sat down beside Carol to demonstrate—"and I put my right hand *here*."

"Yes."

"Then I put my left hand *here*, and I squeezed gently."

"I see."

"Then I slowly massaged her from here to here . . ."

"Louis, I have to go to work tomorrow."

"It's all right, this will just take a minute. So then I did this . . ."

"Ahhhh."

"And this . . ."

"Mmmmm."

"And this . . ."

"Oh! No wonder the dog bit you."

7
DETECTIVE
LESTER PEREZ

Getting in touch with Mary Spivack wasn't going to be as easy as I thought, not unless I employed Fritz Uhler. Mrs. Spivack had been killed by a hit-and-run driver on June 11, 1967—six days after Rosalee Romain's death, one day before Arthur White's. That was what Shenky Andreevna told me when I called her next morning. Apparently the Inner Circle was a remarkably thorough organization.

When I got off the phone with Shenky, I called Lieutenant Perez at the Beverly Hills Police Department and told him that I was fully recovered and would like to have a look at his short stories. He said he was free for lunch; he would go home to pick them up, then meet me at Nate 'n Al's Delicatessen.

At noon I locked the tape of Mary Spivack and the

clipping of the mystery corpse into the glove compartment of my Honda and drove to Beverly Hills.

Lieutenant Lester Perez would never get promoted for his taste in clothes. When I found him sitting at a corner table, poring over the menu, he was wearing a pink leisure suit, the heavy Navajo jewelry, all silver and turquoise, and dark glasses. He smiled, rose and shook my hand. Standing, he towered over me, a giant, good-natured grizzly bear.

When we were both seated, he pointed to the menu.

"Isn't it odd? I'm Mexican, but I can't stand Mexican food and I adore Jewish cooking. My wife is Jewish and her mother cooks the most fabulous banquets when we go back East. Noodle kugel, blintzes, gefilte fish. Marvelous."

"I always figured," I said, opening the menu, "that Jewish cooking was a plot by Jewish women to murder their husbands. What other excuse could there be for a food like stuffed derma? Intestines filled with chicken fat—*yechh*. It's no mystery why Jewish men die of heart attacks at the age of sixty. Personally, I prefer a nice chicken enchilada."

"We all grow up with contempt for our surroundings. And when we are second-class citizens, like the Mexicans in Los Angeles, relegated to cleaning swimming pools and keeping house, the contempt increases. Recently, however, I have discovered Mexican poets such as Octavio Paz, and I am experiencing a new pride in my heritage."

"How did you get to be so interested in literature, Lester— May I call you Lester?"

"My parents were wonderful people, kind and intelligent, but because they spoke English poorly, they were treated like fools. When I was a very small child, only five or six, it occurred to me that speaking proper English was a prerequisite to any sort of success in this country. They tell the blacks in our public schools that there is a Black English, a language with its own grammar and syntax, but I say that until the day blacks speak English as educated whites do, they will be second-class citizens and likewise for Mexicans. Americans judge people by their speech every bit as much as their English ancestors did. So I studied English, I read it, I wrote it . . ."

"And now you're the youngest detective on the poshest police force in the country. What are your plans, Lester? Captain? Chief?"

"I think," Lester said, "it's time this city had a Mexican mayor."

"You've got my vote."

Lester ordered a pastrami on rye with a side order of cherry blintzes and, on my advice, a Dr. Brown's celery tonic, a beverage entirely new to him. I ordered the cherry blintzes, too, and a roast beef with Russian dressing.

"There's something I have to talk to you about," I said after the waiter had left. "I didn't tell you the whole truth about the two goons who beat me up. It wasn't any coincidence; they were looking for me."

"I suspected as much."

"I think I've uncovered one of the strangest multiple murders in history. The trouble is, nobody will believe me. It's that bizarre."

"Why don't you try it out on me," Lester said. "I've

seen so many strange things within the confines of this
rich little ghetto that I'll believe almost anything."

I started my story with the night Tony Valenti came
to my apartment and I finished it—the cherry blintzes
were no more than a smear of red on my plate—with
the revelations of Mary Spivack's tape. Perez examined
a saltshaker and avoided my eyes. I couldn't tell what
his reaction was.

"I'm not a private detective," I said, "and I'm not
a cop. There's a limit to the amount of information I
can gather. But if you went in, you could make Kellerman talk. You could subpoena his files. If you exposed
these guys, you'd be a national hero. You'd be mayor
in five years."

Lester laughed and shook his head. "You're very
persuasive, Louis. But even if everything you say is
true, we would have no basis for arresting Dr.
Kellerman."

"Couldn't we bring him in for questioning?"

Perez spread his hands in a gesture of helplessness.

"On what grounds? All you have is a little circum-
stantial evidence and a great deal of conjecture."

"What about the tape?"

"Mary Spivack is dead. Without her testifying to
the validity of the tape, it's meaningless."

The frustration must have shown on my face. "You
can't imagine," he continued, "how many times I've
tracked down some heroin dealer or child molester,
only to have the case thrown out of court for lack of
evidence or a technicality. And compared with what
you've just told me, those cases looked like airtight
convictions."

"What if . . ." I thought for a moment. "What if

you took him in for another crime; then could you question him about Tony Valenti's murder?"

Lester nodded. "What crime?"

"Attempted murder—of me."

Lester's eyebrows went up. "Have they attempted to murder you?"

"Not yet. But they will. I'm sure they're planning to right now. They've already murdered Rosalee Romain and Mary Spivack and Arthur White and Tony Valenti and who knows how many others. Why should they hesitate about me? The only thing I don't know for certain is when they'll try it, and with a couple of phone calls I think I can arrange that too. But first I want to know that you'll be there to stop them."

He shook his head. "I can't allow it; it's too risky. Furthermore, there's something called entrapment and the law is none too fond of it."

I pointed to a leatherette binder stuffed with dog-eared pages lying on the seat beside him.

"Are those the short stories?"

He nodded shyly.

"Ever have any of them published?"

He shook his head. Gone was the self-assured cop and in his place sat a fidgeting child.

"I have great magazine contacts," I said. "The fiction editor at *BonHomme* magazine is a close friend of mine. If the stories are good I'll show them to him."

"That would be wonderful."

"But in return I'd like you to be there when the time comes and make sure this attempted murder is just that and nothing more."

The waiter returned and we ordered cheesecake and coffee while Lester thought about it.

Finally, grudgingly he said, "Louis, I'll go along with you on one condition. If you set a trap and nobody comes, I want you to agree to give up investigating Tony Valenti's death."

"Why should I?"

"Because the police are better equipped to handle it. Because most people don't like to be investigated and one of them may knock your teeth in. And because when you search hard enough for a crime you may wind up creating one."

"In other words, you don't believe me either."

"I'm withholding judgment. Now what about it? You accept my conditions, I'll accept yours."

I went to the phone booth at the back of the restaurant and called Kellerman's office. His secretary said he wasn't available. I went to the cashier, got a whole handful of dimes, and began calling the poor girl over and over again. Each time she sounded more agitated. At the eighth call she gave in and connected me with Kellerman.

"Why are you harassing me, Mr. Pinkle?" His voice was icy.

"I've got a tape, a tape made by Mary Spivack, that just about names you as the man responsible for Rosalee Romain's death." It was easier to talk back to him when I didn't have to look at his face. Thank God for telephones. If I was in his office, I'd probably be on my knees by now, begging forgiveness. "She says that she told you Rosalee had drunk a couple of bottles of wine and you injected her with barbiturates anyway. Now, I know it's not going to be much use in court, but I can give it to the tabloids and smear your name until none of your celebrity clients will go near you. Or I can give you the tape in exchange for some information about the Inner Circle."

After a short silence he said, "Mr. Pinkle, I should call the police and have you arrested for blackmailing me. But I promised a young lady named Bini Valenti that I would try to help you. So I'm going to tell you that I believe you are suffering from a paranoiac psychosis. The secret organization, the conspiracy of murders. It is classic. Listen very carefully and I will try to explain. Tony Valenti came to you for help. You believe that he committed suicide because you denied him this help. You feel that his death was your fault. But, Mr. Pinkle, if you can prove that Tony Valenti was murdered, then the fault is no longer yours. On the contrary, you become the hero, you have brought justice to him. All this is simply a need to save face. You will not cure yourself of this delusion, Mr. Pinkle, until you can see that you were not the cause of the suicide. Even if you had taken him in that night, he would still have killed himself, if not on the freeway, then by some other means. You are not guilty, you are not responsible. Tony's death was not your fault, do you understand?"

"Right, Kellerman, a very nice performance. Very convincing. Now you can be there at eight tonight if you want the tape. My Honda will be parked on Mulholland between Benedict and Beverly Glenn, on the shoulder overlooking the valley. I'll have the emergency flashers blinking."

"Mr. Pinkle," Kellerman said, "you are badly in need of help."

"You're the one who's going to need help," I said and hung up.

After lunch Perez went back to work and I visited a shop called The Bead Brujo, across the street and several doors up on Beverly Drive. The Bead Brujo was owned by a friend of mine named Alex Kotsky, whom I first met in the summer of '68 in Berkeley.

I had driven to California with some friends to check out all I'd been hearing about a Summer of Love and a Revolution in Human Consciousness. When we arrived on Telegraph Avenue the air was clouded with tear gas, and the police (or "pigs," as we called them at the time) were charging down the street, waving their nightsticks in a most menacing manner. As I stood there weeping and wondering what to do, a man ran past me, grabbed me by the arm and shouted, "Follow me." He was forty-five, with beady eyes, oily black hair and beard and an enormous belly. He was wearing overalls, a Fidel Castro cap and a black arm-band. He looked like a politicized Santa Claus and he sounded savvy, so I followed him.

When the police reached us they all converged on the two of us like a pack of dogs running after a rutting bitch. They handcuffed us, put us in a paddy wagon and took us to jail. As it happened, Alex was the organizer of that day's demonstration, a demonstration for some terribly important cause, although what the cause was, I can't recall. He was also the secretary of the SDS, a member of the Socialist Labor Party and a close personal friend of both Mario Savio and Allen Ginsberg.

The next time I met him seven years had passed. I was staying at the Hilton in Albuquerque, New Mexico, where I had been sent by *BonHomme* to do a story on Clint Eastwood, who was shooting a movie in the area. I went down to the cocktail lounge one evening and there was Alex Kotsky, surrounded by three luscious teen-age girls. He urged me to join them, bought me dinner and afterward took me outside to show me his custom Mercedes Benz, fully equipped with metallic paint and cassette player and a telephone under the dash. Several years earlier, Alex explained, he had set up a "factory" using the cheap local Indian labor to manufacture jewelry—the rings and bracelets, fetish necklaces and squash blossom belts that have become so popular now that the American Indians have become almost extinct. By using Indian labor he could honestly claim that the pieces were "Handmade by Indians." In addition to wholesaling all across the country, he had a large retail shop downstairs from his "factory," a second retail shop in Santa Fe and a third on Beverly Drive in Beverly Hills. The shop in Beverly Hills allowed him to write off the private plane in which he commuted between here and Albuquerque and the apartment he kept at the Sunset Towers on the strip. He also owned real estate in Mill Valley, a house in the Berkeley Hills and a geodesic dome in Taos. This last structure housed his publishing company, The Labor Press, which specialized in Marxist pamphlets and feminist tracts.

Inside, The Bead Brujo looked like a stable. The walls and counters were paneled with old barn siding and the ceiling beams were rough oak. The floor, however, was carpeted, and the only smell was the perfume of the salesgirls who were, without exception, gorgeous. Bosomy redheads—they were Alex's favorites, and that specification was nearly his only criterion for hiring.

Of course there's never any shortage of gorgeous girls in Los Angeles—gorgeous boys too—and a friend of mine has a theory to explain it. After World War II, he argues, every man and woman in the country who had any kind of beauty decided that they could make it in Hollywood as a movie star. It's true that millions of good-looking kids flocked here in the forties, starry-eyed and broke, looking to be discovered sitting in Schwab's or driving a mail cart around the studios. After a couple of years, when they realized it wasn't going to happen, they married one another, settled in the valley, and got jobs in the aerospace industry or the like, thereby creating the world's first "beautiful" gene pool. Pretty soon they were having kids who looked like Greek gods.

Anyway, the salesgirls were so beautiful they made you sigh. One of them, Peggy Crabtree, who managed the store while Alex was away and also served as his girl Friday, was helping some rich hippie types pick out a silver necklace. She had cinnamon skin and crooked teeth, and she wore big round glasses with pink lenses. Alex had picked her up hitchhiking down the coast and hired her instantly.

"Hi, Peggy," I said when she was free. "Is Alex in town?"

"He's in Salt Lake City wheeling and dealing."

"Really? What's the action?"

"It's secret. Can I help you?"

"Okay, but pay attention. This is of the utmost importance."

I removed from an envelope the clipping I had found in Arthur White's attic, the picture of the man laid to rest, and showed it to her.

"See the tie clip he's wearing?" I said.

"Oh, it's some kind of fetish, isn't it?"

"Have you ever seen anything like it?"

She held the clipping closer and chewed on her lower lip.

"It's not Navajo and it's not Hopi. I don't think it's American Indian at all. You know what it reminds me of? The things they dig up in South America and Mexico, the pre-Columbian stuff."

"You think Alex will know?"

"Alex," she said worshipfully, "knows everything."

"Tell him to get in touch with me when he comes back—and don't forget! Lives hang in the balance."

Mulholland Drive snakes along the very top of the range of hills which separates southern Los Angeles from the valley, twisting along cliffside turns all the way to the Pacific where it finally tires out and expires not far from the water's edge. At night it's virtually deserted except for teenagers who park on the dirt shoulders to fornicate and stare out at the galactic lights of Hollywood and dream of contracts in six figures. I wouldn't have minded some fornication myself, or at least a little company, sitting there alone in my Honda in the chill California night, listening to the coyotes howl and imagining rattlers crawling in through the air vents.

If I craned my neck I could just make out the dark silhouette of Lieutenant Perez's car blocking out the stars. He was parked across the road—his car partially concealed by a clump of bushes—watching me with a dandy little gadget called an "infrared viewing scope" which looks like an overgrown pair of binoculars. You stare through the right tube while the left tube projects a beam of infrared light. If you were being watched, as I was then, you could detect nothing; but if you were peering through the scope, the scene would appear brighter than an overcast afternoon and eerily tinted blood-red. Perez had let me try it when we had arrived to set up our trap nearly an hour before. I looked at my watch—no, an hour and twenty-two minutes, that's how long we had been sitting there, waiting, while all the time my mind had been playing with the same question: What if nobody came?

For the first time since Tony Valenti's visit it occurred to me that Kellerman and Rubin might be no more than what they claimed: a top-notch Hollywood lawyer and a psychiatrist to the stars, two hardworking men being driven out of their minds by a busybody journalist named Lou Pinkle who ran around town accusing them of homicide and who was presently occupied in something that bore a suspicious resemblance to extortion. Not a pretty picture. Was I determined, as Kellerman had suggested, to show that the two of them were guilty simply to free myself of responsibility for Tony Valenti's death? It was certainly possible. My unconscious was as dark a cave as any other man's.

Eight thirty, still no sign of them. A coyote howled and somewhere in a warm living room his domesticated cousin yapped a reply. If nobody appeared by nine o'clock I would admit defeat; I would give up the story and go back to doing an occasional short piece while I tried to peddle my screenplay; such was the agreement Perez and I had made.

My screenplay was called *The Climber*. Remember Frank Lloyd Wright's idea of compressing an entire city into two mile-high skyscrapers and turning the rest of the land into parks and meadows? The story begins in the year 2077 when such a city, New Los Angeles, had just been completed. Now, in this year 2077 everything has been streamlined and homogenized and made so safe and efficient that life has become a terrible bore. There are no new frontiers for the human spirit; adventure is a thing of the past; excitement is sitting in front of a ten-foot television screen and watching a version of *The Gong Show* where the losers are fried with laser beams.

Our protagonist (who is played by Robert Redford) decides to make his own adventure. He will scale the outside wall of one of the towers, a sheer one-mile vertical ascent. He says good-bye to friends and family and one sunny morning, armed with ropes and spikes and a pickax, he begins his climb.

The first night he stops outside the window of a poor black family (you see, the higher you get, the higher the rents: the lower floors are slums, the middle floors middle class, and the upper floors belong to the rich) and there he falls in love with the daughter (Diana Ross). She decides to climb with him and the following day they set out together, happy as kids. But she gets tired, she starts to slow him down. And when they reach the middle floors, the people discriminate against them, withholding food and water. It's a terrible choice, but finally he decides to go on without her.

By the time he reaches the upper floors he has become world famous. Helicopters fly alongside videotaping his progress. Men offer him executive positions in their companies, film producers want to buy his life story, beautiful women throw themselves at his feet. Now the top of the building is in sight, only a couple of hours away. Redford passes the penthouse where a mad party is in session and the revelers invite him to spend an hour or two with them before he finishes his climb. The wealthiest, most glamorous people in the world are present; they give him drugs and booze and involve him in an orgy.

The first light of dawn finds him passed out on a sofa. Despite a splitting headache he hurries to dress and resume his climb. But when he looks out the window he is amazed to see another man standing at the summit of the building, being interviewed and photographed and celebrated by one and all. Apparently this other man was climbing the opposite side of the building during Redford's ascent.

Back inside the apartment Redford is ignored. The man who last night offered him a seat on the stock exchange pretends not to know him, the woman who pleaded to be his mistress won't speak to him. He realizes that once again he is nobody, that fame is fickle and transitory. The only person who ever mattered to him, Diana Ross, he sacrificed for the sake of his climb. But on his way down in the elevator he meets her by chance and she admits that she still loves him despite everything. They walk away together into the sunset. Fade out.

All right, it's not Bergman. But it's at least as good as half the garbage produced in this town and better than most. My problem is not so much the writing, I think, but the selling.

Granted I have nerve; when I'm doing a story I can talk my way into somebody's home and ask them just about anything. But the minute I set foot in a producer's office with intentions of peddling a screenplay, I turn into a bashful virgin. I'm so filled with doubts about my own work that by the time I leave they wouldn't hire me to write aphorisms for fortune cookies. Even if somebody wanted to buy *The Climber*, one meeting with me would talk him out of it.

I once discussed this problem with a screenwriter I know, a pro with a lot of credits, and he admitted to doubting his own work too; that's why at meetings he keeps his mouth shut and lets his agent do all the talking. He says that the natural condition of the artist, even screenwriters (about whom the word "artist" is used with caution), is self-doubt. Anyone who has absolute certainty about his work is not an artist, he is an engineer.

I was startled by a sharp rap on the window and saw Lieutenant Perez standing beside the car, smiling at me sympathetically. I rolled down the window.

"Fall asleep?" he said.

"No, I was just thinking."

My watch dial glowed in the darkness: 9:12 P.M. With a sick feeling in my stomach, I realized that I had lost the deal; we had waited twelve minutes longer than agreed on and no one had made an attempt on my life. And now I was pledged to give up the story. I felt that I was giving up some of myself, so much a part of my thoughts had the murder become these past few weeks. I felt a horrible sense of loss, of deprivation, the way I imagine an alcoholic feels when he decides to go on the wagon, or a devout Christian, when his faith is destroyed. I felt that I had nothing.

"Let's go have a beer," Perez said, "and I'll tell you about the time I arrested an innocent man on three counts of robbery and a manslaughter charge."

I sighed and nodded and twisted the ignition key, but the engine was silent, as if the Honda, too, were reluctant to give up the vigil.

"I must have killed the battery running the blinkers and the heater together for so long."

"I've got jumpers in the trunk," Perez said.

He turned toward his car; then he stopped and snapped his fingers.

"Crap. I lent them to the captain. Tell you what, I'll drive down to Santa Monica and borrow a pair from that garage on the corner, all right?"

"Sure," I sighed. I felt so weary. I didn't really care about anything.

Perez drove away and I sat slumped on the steering wheel, mulling over my fate.

Now, my car was situated on the shoulder of the road; ahead of me was a stretch of level road, about a hundred feet of it, and beyond that, a steep incline curving around a hillside beneath somebody's wall-in mansion. If I could push my car—the Honda was light as a feather—onto the level road, it would be simple to roll it along to the hill, jump in as it gathered speed, slip it into gear, and jump-start the engine. Anything would be preferable to sitting here bored and depressed.

I put her into neutral and let out the brake. Then I went around behind the car and started to push, rocking her back and forth. It wasn't easy, but the Honda finally rolled up onto the road. I sat down on the back bumper to catch my breath.

Just then I heard the roar of an approaching car. Two blinding headlight beams came around the corner. I stood up and waved my arms in a semaphore signal in case they didn't see me. They didn't seem to be slowing down, although it was hard to tell with the car coming straight at me.

At the last instant it occurred to me that *I* was the target—they were going to crush me like some offending insect—and I leaped out of the way, rolled to the shoulder and lay there breathless, the sounds of shattered glass and crushed metal lingering in my ears.

The bastards had rear-ended (as they say out West) my Honda at 40 mph! They must have been insane. As I crawled to my feet I saw my beloved little car, what was left of it, rolling slowly down the road, driverless. Meanwhile the other car, a battered red Cadillac, screamed into reverse and backed up for another try.

Can I explain the emotions I felt in that fraction of a second? Fear for my life, certainly; anger at Perez for not being there when I needed him; a great sadness about my Honda—I still owed the bank nineteen payments; yet also elation: My story had been returned to me, and I was on my way to avenging the deaths of Tony Valenti and all the others—or else adding my own name to the roster.

I didn't have much time to reflect. The red Cadillac

was preparing to charge again. I ran for the Honda hoping to jump inside and start it now that it was moving. It was either that or outrunning the bastards on foot.

I had just reached the door when the headlights of the Cadillac swung in my direction and bore down on me with frightening speed. I scurried onto the roof of the Honda in time to avoid having my legs flattened like drinking straws.

The Cadillac rammed the Honda, backed up and rammed it again. The impact of the second collision knocked me from my perch and I landed belly down on the hood of the Cadillac, clutching the louvers for dear life, staring into the windshield at the drugstore cowboy, who was wearing the most demented grin I've ever seen, and the Oriental, grim behind the wheel.

Now they had me where they wanted me and they made a game of it, trying to shake me off. They jammed the car into forward and reverse, they stomped on the gas and slammed on the brakes, they raced along the side of the road making hairpin turns so fast that two wheels spun in the air. I dug my fingers into the louvers—the metal felt like knife blades—and wedged my right foot under the hood ornament for support.

After three or four minutes I had just about had it; my fingers were numb and the hot liquid running down my hands must have been blood. They rammed a boulder at the side of the road and I tumbled off, striking the blacktop with my shoulders and head. For a second I was stunned. Then I heard a sound like a mechanical man on a trampoline.

Some three hundred feet to the north my Honda had

rolled over the side of the hill and was bouncing merrily down an eighty-degree incline. As I watched, it struck a hillock and exploded in a lovely fireball, a little early for the Fourth of July. Acetate recording tape burns beautifully, and I knew that part of the flame was Mary Spivack's tape, my one piece of real honest-to-God evidence, which I had locked in the glove compartment for safekeeping. Schmuck.

I said a fast farewell to my Honda, the car that had served me so well on amorous outings to Toluca Lake and business trips to the *BonHomme* building and everywhere else my fancy took me, with nary a busted fan belt, not to mention terrific mileage. No goddamned pair of punks were going to total it without paying the price!

With a fresh burst of energy I got to my feet and began to run in tight circles, teasing the car the way a toreador does a bull, letting them think they had me, then sprinting out of the way. The more I teased them, the more reckless their driving became; and I was counting on that.

The rains in Southern California are always washing away big chunks of hillside, and as I was running I noticed that the earth under the boulder—the one they had rammed to knock me off the hood—was almost gone. It looked like one good shove would send the rock toppling over the cliffside.

I pretended to fall in front of the boulder and they rammed it, just as I had hoped. I rolled out of the way with a second to spare. The boulder teetered.

I ran them around again, and again I stopped in front of the boulder. This time when they rammed it the stone moved a whole foot. I had to make them come at me faster.

I ran them around and I ran them back, and I let them come so close that I caught my pants leg on the bumper and nearly fell. When I knew the instant had come—I could almost feel their blood-lust like a stench in the air—I fell against the rock, pushing it backward with all my weight. The Cadillac came at me fast and I fell out of the way and they hit the rock.

For an instant everything hung in the balance; then a whole chunk of earth came loose, and rock and car tumbled down and down and down. Headlights disappeared into the darkness. The final crash echoed from the hills. I brushed off my hands and sat down at the roadside, breathing deeply. Then all of a sudden I started to shake.

I was hiking back along Mulholland Drive when a car slowed down opposite me. I was ready to leap into the bushes when I saw that it was Lieutenant Perez.

"Louis," he called, "I had a hell of a time finding the cables. The garages were all closed and I had to go back to the station house. But I finally found a pair."

"Now all we need is a car," I said and started laughing like a crazy man.

8

ALEX KOTSKY

"You're always saying," Carol pointed out, "that you don't believe in miracles. Well, you're still alive after last night—that's a miracle."

"I don't mean that kind of miracle," I said, shifting my body so the jets of water played across my lower back. I was soaking in the back-room spa, and she was standing by the door, chatting with me and watching for customers. "I want to see stones turned to loaves, and water turned to wine. I want to see the Pacific Ocean part so I can drive to Japan—assuming I still had a car—and I want to see a plague of locusts visited upon Bel-Air."

But she was right, it was a miracle of sorts. Aside from scraped knees, my encounter with the goons on Mulholland Drive had left me unharmed, physically at least. Mentally I was still shaking. But my beautiful

Carol, my angel of mercy, was once again nursing me back to health, letting me feed on her strength and peace, and soak in her soothing spa.

"Those are pretty spectacular requests," she said.

"I'm a pretty spectacular person. All right, here's a humble miracle. If there is a God, and He is good, let Him give me a set of wheels."

"Oh Louis," she sighed in mock despair.

The sleigh bells hanging over the front door jingled.

"Customer," Carol said. "Don't overcook." She went out, closing the door behind her.

As far as Carol was concerned, every little co-incidence is a major miracle. If you're walking down the street and you run into someone you haven't seen since ninth grade: miracle. If you go out to buy a quart of milk and find that you have exactly the right change: miracle. She saw the touch of God every-where. It was part of her Catholic upbringing, I sup-pose, as was her appetite for peculiar sexual practices (thank God for that) and her predilection for smart Jewish men (that too). Whenever I mentioned all the things that happen that are totally meaningless—like when you walk down the street and you don't meet anybody you know, or when you go to the store and don't have the right amount of change—she would sigh and shake her head and look at me as though I were something pitiful. Ah faith. It must be fun to think the world has some sense to it.

The door opened and Carol returned, grinning.

"You won't believe who's here!"

Then in walked Alex Kotsky, all beard and belly, and Peggy Crabtree carrying a swag bag and a bucket of champagne.

"Surprise!" they both yelled.

"Surprise indeed," I muttered. "A man can't even bathe in peace anymore."

Peggy peeled off her clothes and climbed in the tub with me while Alex began wiggling the cork out of the champagne. Carol went out front to lock the door and put up the CLOSED sign, and came back with paper cups and a plate of organically grown raisins and raw cashews.

"What are we celebrating?" I asked as the cork ricocheted off the ceiling.

"My new career," Alex said.

"What happened to your old career?" Carol asked, unzipping her jeans. She pulled her frilly white blouse over her head and joined Peggy and me in the spa.

Alex had stripped to his jockey shorts; gross and hairy, belly hanging over the elastic waistband, he went around pouring the champagne and passing out the cups.

"Indian jewelry is passé. Indians are old hat. Nobody's buying the stuff. So I sold off all my jewelry-related industries and I purchased . . ." He paused dramatically, opened the swag bag, and brought out three wooden boxes. We crowded to the edge of the spa to see. Inside the first box was a flintlock pistol with a maple stock and shiny silver and brass inlays, resting on a cushion of purple velvet.

". . . an antique firearms factory! We're manufacturing replicas of antique firearms identical to the originals in every detail. They even fire! This one's a Kentucky flintlock pistol by Beeman, eighteen twenty, and this one's an eighteen sixty-two Colt with Tiffany grips, like they used in the old West . . ."

The second box contained a silver six-shooter engraved from barrel to butt with floral designs and eagles and rosettes, and the third box an enormous black .45-caliber automatic with the appropriately evil name of Savage. Alex said it had been developed in 1906 for government trials to determine which automatic was best suited to military needs. Colt won the trials, but the few Savages that survived were coveted collector's items.

"I'm telling you, man," Alex went on with boyish enthusiasm, "this is the next big craze. You hang them on the wall—but then if somebody comes monkeying around the house in the middle of the night, you pull one down and *BLAM!*"

He held up the Savage and made a motion as if to fire. Carol shrank back in terror.

"It's okay, the safety's on."

He thrust the gun at her, to show her, and she turned her head away as if he were offering her rancid food. Carol's always had a thing about guns.

A little deflated, he continued: "The factory in Salt Lake can turn out a couple of hundred of these a day, and I'm going to start another factory in Albuquerque, soon as I can retrain my Indians. Then I'll turn all my Bead Brujo shops into Fabulous Firearms. Well? What do you think?"

He looked back and forth between us, but we were silent.

"You've become a Munitions Maker," I said finally.

"Hey man! I've become nothing of the sort. These aren't weapons, these are pieces of art. They're cultural artifacts. Why, do you know you can trace the whole ascendancy of Western civilization in terms of firearms?"

"Guns is guns," I said.

"Look, when the revolution comes, these will be handy things to have around."

Carol turned away from him.

All Alex's enthusiasm was gone now, and his tone was almost apologetic. "Ninety-nine percent of the guys who buy these are collectors, *I swear*—and the other one percent just shoot at beer cans. Don't hate me, please. I had to do something to stay in business. Indian jewelry's had it, and I just couldn't lay off all those Indians. Some of them do terrific leather work, and I'm going to have them make holsters. And I'll let the really good silversmiths do engravings on the Colts."

"Oh Alex," she sighed. She patted him on the cheek and he smiled with relief.

Although Alex was about fifteen years older than either Carol or me, he occasionally cast us in parental roles and begged for approval. Particularly Carol's. He never really had the guidance we all need as children. Both his parents died when he was very young, and he was raised by a widowed aunt in Washington Heights who already had five children and who was so busy keeping body and soul together that she rarely noticed his existence unless he set off a bomb under her chair. He's been setting off bombs of one sort or another ever since, I suppose.

Anyway, Alex was delighted when Carol forgave him. He packed up the guns and climbed into the spa, and we all soaked together, hardly saying a word.

"Did you get a chance to look at the clipping?" I asked ten or fifteen minutes later. "I want to know about the funny little sculpture the guy is wearing on his tie tack."

Suddenly Carol was staring at me, furious.

"Isn't it enough that you are practically killed twice? Do you have to get yourself completely killed? Louis, you may not give a damn about yourself, but I do; I love you—I love your wisecracks and your obsessions and your funny hats—and I won't let you get yourself murdered! I won't allow it! I need you, damn it!"

And then she was crying.

"Hey," I whispered, "take it easy." I put my arm around her and rocked her gently against my chest while Alex and Peggy watched with concern.

"Promise you'll stop trying to find Tony Valenti's murderer," she sobbed, "promise me, Louis . . ."

"Sure honey," I whispered, "whatever you want. I didn't realize you were so anxious about me."

"I don't want to look uptight. When I worry about you, you say I'm like your mother, and I don't want to be like your mother . . ."

"You're not a bit like my mother. You're one of the kindest, most beautiful people I've ever met, and it makes me feel good to know you're concerned about me. Now let's dry the tears, okay?"

She sniffled a little; then she smiled.

We had some more champagne and by the time we crawled out of the spa we were puckered up like geriatrics and stinking of chlorine. We dried and dressed. While the girls were off brushing their hair, Alex whispered, "What's this stuff about you almost getting killed?"

"I'm doing a story about Tony Valenti's murder—"

"Murder?"

"*Murder*—and certain people would be happier if I was reclining under several feet of dirt. So two nights ago they ran my car off the side of Mulholland Drive and then they tried to print tire tracks on my face."

As I spoke I couldn't help notice Alex's eyes spark with interest. Any kind of adventure, particularly something involving a person or an ideal in jeopardy, attracts him like a moth to a flame.

"If you need a car," he said, "I'm going to be in LA for the next couple of weeks while I'm getting rid of inventory; I can drive you around in the Mercedes."

"You're not going to try and find out about the tie tack?" Carol said, overhearing Alex's offer. Her voice was filled with anxiety. "Honestly, Louis, I can't bear it, knowing that people are trying to kill you. If this goes on I don't want to see you anymore. I'm serious. I simply can't take the strain."

For the first time I noticed the rings under her eyes, the creases in her forehead. Had they been there a month ago?

"You have my promise."

I kissed her on the forehead, and she threw her arms around me and clung to me as if I were going away forever.

Alex drove his silver Mercedes back to The Bead Brujo where we dropped off Peggy Crabtree. Then we drove east on Santa Monica, past the stone spires of the Beverly Hills City Hall and the sweet-smelling Wonder bread factory. Alex lit up a joint and slipped a cassette into the tape deck. Country Joe and the Fish. They were singing:

Come on all you brave young men
Uncle Sam needs your help again,
He's got himself in a heck of a jam
Way down yonder in Vietnam . . .

He passed me the joint and I took a deep drag and settled back into the leather seat. I closed my eyes and it was 1968 again.

"Where'd it all go?" I murmured. "Hippies. Haight-Ashbury. Peace and love and good vibes . . ."

"Look man," Alex said, "it was co-opted by the media. The media tamed it and sanitized it and sold it to Middle America. That's what happens to every revolution in America. Look man, here's the Black Panthers. Next thing you know, there are Black Panther fashion boutiques and Black Panther soul food franchises. The Black Panther comedy hour on the tube. That's the way this country maintains the status quo. That's why Marx missed the boat on the ascendancy of the working class. Know what I mean, man?"

"The question," I replied, "was rhetorical."

"Whatever. Now tell me what the hell's going on here with people trying to kill you."

I told him and by the time I finished he was gripping the wheel with his fists, squinting his beady eyes at the road and muttering, "Those scumbags, those twisted cocksuckers. I loved Rosalee Romain. I would have died for that woman. Remember her in *Sweet Inno-*

cence? I must have seen that movie two hundred times. We got to make those bastards pay."

"Wait a minute, I promised Carol—"

"Come on man, what do you think? You're going to let these fuckers go because your chick's worried about you?"

"Alex, she said she'd leave me if I didn't."

"Look man, they always say they'll leave you. But you know what she'd think if you did what she said?"

"What?"

"She'd think you were a faggot. Pussy-whipped. She wouldn't have any respect for you. Look, here's the thing about chicks. They say one thing, they mean something else."

"I don't know . . ." I said.

"Well, I do."

He lowered his foot on the gas pedal in emphasis and didn't raise it again until he came to a parking place on La Cienega near Melrose, an area of West Hollywood known for its fashionable art galleries.

New Yorkers are always saying that Los Angeles is a cultural wasteland (I don't care—I never use culture myself), but in fact the city has a surprising number of galleries, museums and concert programs, and Los Angelinos pursue "culture" with frightening gusto, probably to compensate for the feeling of Philistinism which, as New Yorkers have brainwashed the rest of the country into believing, increases in proportion to one's distance from that dirty, overcrowded eastern city.

"What are we doing here?" I asked.

"Going to see a guy named Ruckhauser, probably the numero uno authority on pre-Columbian art in

Los Angeles. Sometimes we help each other out, like when one of his customers wants Hopi stuff, or one of my customers wants Olmec or Toltec. Wait till you meet this guy, he's really too much. Part German, part Egyptian, full of that European charm bullshit. He used to teach anthropology at the University of Mexico in Mexico City until the *federales* got after him. Something about smuggling national art treasures out of the country. Now he's got one of the richest galleries in town."

We left the air-conditioned coolness of the car for the dry heat of the sidewalk and strolled down the block—Alex slackening pace to ogle some overripe California sun babies—until we came to a gallery called J. W. Ruckhauser. Two objects were set on black pedestals in the window: one an obsidian mask partially covered with a mosaic of sea-green turquoise and red-pepper coral, with mother-of-pearl eyes and an expression both serene and timeless; the other a crude stone wheel carved with a skull in the middle, a hollow-eyed horror that seemed to hark back to the nightmares of my childhood.

Inside, the shop was small, cool and elegant. No more than seven pieces were displayed on pedestals and perhaps ten more in a wall cabinet, but each piece was breathtaking. Having always thought of pre-Columbian art as crude statues of red clay, I was amazed by the subtlety and variety of the display: a lump of basalt made, with only a few lines, to represent a coiled snake; a bowl of midnight obsidian, thin as porcelain and polished to a mirror finish; a shaggy coyote chipped from rough rock, sitting as a human child would sit, legs out straight.

"Is Joe around?" Alex inquired of a refined young woman.

She went to a door at the back of the gallery and returned a minute later with an older man. He was tall, thin, aristocratic and silver-haired, impeccably dressed in a gray suit and a silk tie. He had hooded eyes and a hawklike nose with flaring nostrils, and he spoke with a Middle European accent I could not place.

"Alex, my dear, it's been too long! Why don't you ever come and visit a lonely old man like myself?"

"Lonely!" Alex said. "You old fraud, you've got more pussy than you know what to do with. This is my buddy, Lou Pinkle."

"Alex has the most remarkable assortment of friends," Joe Ruckhauser said, shaking my hand. "Now you, Louis, you are an artist, am I correct? You have the sensitive expression—so soulful—and yet there is also the uncompromising intellect."

"I didn't know it showed," I said. "Actually, I'm a journalist. I write for the 'Calendar' section of the *Times* and for *New West* and *BonHomme*."

"So then you *are* an artist, one who paints life on a canvas of newsprint!" He turned back to Alex. "And how is the shop?"

"I'm phasing out the jewelry and bringing in replica antique firearms. I bought a gun factory in Salt Lake."

"Isn't he remarkable?" Ruckhauser said to me, slapping Alex on the back. "Like a Howard Hughes, always buying and selling." He said to Alex, "I hope you will help me out when I'm too old and feeble to run my shop."

I couldn't tell if he was kidding, but I noticed the refined young woman crack a smile.

"Come on," Alex said, "everybody knows you're worth a couple of million."

"No! Never. I can hardly afford the rent on my little shop. Now, what can I do for you gentlemen? You are interested, Mr. Pinkle, in Mexican antiquities? They are an excellent hedge against inflation. If you were to buy this Olmec head of gray jade, for example —an exquisite piece, I assure you, and fully authenticated—you could arrange to have it donated to a museum after your death and enjoy the full tax deduction now."

"You old crook," Alex interjected, "they disallowed that one in 'seventy-four."

"It's beautiful," I said, running my fingers over the smooth melon shape. "What do you want for it?"

"Two hundred and seventy-five thousand dollars."

"I'll think it over," I said.

"We didn't come to buy," Alex said. "I wanted your opinion about the fetish in this picture."

He took the envelope out of the pocket of his denim jacket and removed the yellowed clipping.

Ruckhauser glanced at it; then he beckoned us to follow, through the door in the back of the gallery, into a small office crowded with furniture, a desk, an easy chair and a daybed. The walls were covered with bookcases from top to bottom, and many of the books were oversized, with beautifully bound spines and gold filigree.

He switched on a green-shaded student lamp, sat down at the desk, placed a pair of steel-rimmed glasses on his nose and spread out the clipping on the marbleized desk blotter. We stood behind him, leaning over his shoulder, mostly through interest but partly because there was nowhere else to stand. Next he took out a huge magnifying glass and, hunching forward, passed it back and forth between his nose and the clipping. First he nodded, then he smiled, then he said, "Ah-hah, yes, yes, very good."

"What?" I said.

"Come on," Alex agreed, "don't keep us in suspense."

"First of all," Ruckhauser began, "it's a fake. Or perhaps I should say a 'copy-in-the-style-of' for reasons I'll explain in a moment. You must understand that most of the pre-Columbian art sold in this country are fake; it's difficult to distinguish a forgery because the techniques used by Mexican artisans today differ only slightly from those of their ancient ancestors. Even an experienced dealer like myself is fooled occasionally. Ah, the stories I could tell you about fortunes I've lost on forgeries." He sighed and shook his head ruefully.

"I know this is a copy," he continued, "because I know the piece it's copied from, a statue from Cozcatlan, Puebla, presently in the collection of the Mexican Museum of Anthropology and History."

He took a big art book down from the shelf, laid it open on the desk and ruffled through the pages. Then I was staring at the exact duplicate of the fetish in the clipping, the same fetish Tony Valenti was wearing when they laid him out for visitation: a rigid stone man with a skull's head and cat's claws.

"The difference," Ruckhauser said, "is that this statue is six feet tall and your tie tack is no more than a few inches. So it is not technically a forgery."

"Who is he?" I asked.

"Do you know anything about the Aztecs?"

I shook my head.

"The Aztecs were nomads through most of their history; they only settled down in the last few centuries before their demise. During their wanderings they encountered—and conquered—many other tribes, often adopting their deities and adding them to their own pantheon. As a result, they accumulated a staggering number of gods. Huitzilopochtli, their own tribal god; Xipe-Totec, the god of spring planting; Quetzalcoatl, the god of life and fertility; Tlaloc, the god of rain and thunder; Xilonen and Coatlicue, Tlazolteotl, Cihuateteo, Chantico, Itzpapalotl, Ixtlilton, Mayahuel, and Xochipilli—ah, the list is endless. And what makes it all the more confusing is the variety of guises in which each of the gods appeared as his role changed within the society. Huitzilopochtli, for example, was the hummingbird, but he was also the sun, and war, and hunting, and later his symbol became the eagle! Fortunately Mexican archaeologists have already identified this figure for us."

He pointed to the caption on the page opposite the photograph.

"Tezcatlipoca the god of night, of the stars and the moon, of night monsters of destruction, of sorcerers and magic. I believe you can tell by the cat's claws. You see, he often took on the shape of a jaguar. Quite a sinister fellow. He was the eternal rival of Quetzalcoatl, the plumed serpent, the traditional favorite of Mexico. Quetzalcoatl represented life and fertility. Once he knocked Tezcatlipoca out of the sky with his staff, and in revenge Tezcatlipoca knocked him out of the sky with his jaguar claw. While Quetzalcoatl was in the underworld, in the form of Xolotl the monster, he found some old bones and created man from them. Not quite as tidy as the Greek mythology, is it?

"Tezcatlipoca owned an obsidian mirror in which he could view everything that went on in the world, past, present and future. At certain festivals the Aztecs would scatter cornmeal on the floor of the temple and Tezcatlipoca's footprint would appear in the cornmeal, proving that he had attended. On other occasions he would appear on earth in grotesque human form, meeting warriors alone at night and doing battle with them, testing their courage. A warrior who wasn't frightened and who seized Tezcatlipoca could demand anything he desired."

"What sort of grotesque form?" I asked and was surprised to hear my voice quavering.

"A headless body with two doors in its chest that opened and closed with a noise like an ax on a tree."

"Is it possible," I asked, "that there are still people around who believe in Tezi—?"

"Tezcatlipoca."

"Right. Could there be Tezcatlipoca cults in existence today?"

"It's certainly possible," Ruckhauser said. "In Mexico Indians still sacrifice animals and bury them in the fields before they plant their corn, while others make sacrifices to the rain gods. There is still wide belief in shamanism, in curing sickness by magic, and in the Nahual, each man's totemic animal. You've read Castaneda's *Teachings of Don Juan*? He discusses it there—although I must say the book strains credibility in other respects. Then, of course, there is the fascinating syncretism with Christianity. The pilgrimage to the earth and moon goddess Tonantzin at Tepeyac is still practiced, only today they call her Our Lady of Guadalupe. All these practices date back to Aztec times and earlier.

"Remember, Aztecs were not so ancient as most people think. They reached the apex of their culture, the construction of the fabulous city Tenochtitlan, in the fifteenth and sixteenth centuries. That's only four hundred years ago, scarcely a heartbeat in the history of mankind. Before that they were farmers and vassals to the Toltecs, and before that they wandered, semi-barbaric, through northwestern Mexico and what is now the southwest of our own country."

"Didn't they cut out human hearts?" Alex asked. "Or something like that?"

Ruckhauser nodded. "Human sacrifice existed in Mexico since the preclassic period, but it was never practiced on a mass scale until the fifteenth century. The tribal god of the Aztecs was a fellow named Huitzilopochtli, whom I mentioned earlier. One year, sometime in fourteen fifty according to most authorities, the Aztecs had a particularly terrible winter and all their crops were destroyed. Four years of famine followed—so severe that women sold their children into slavery in return for food.

"Now, the Aztecs decided that the winter had been so severe because the sun—Huitzilopochtli—was weak from lack of food. Food in this case meant blood, human blood, and hearts that were still beating. So the Aztecs started warring with their neighbors for the sole purpose of having sufficient prisoners to sacrifice. The priests would dress the prisoners in the garb of the god to whom they were making the sacrifice. They would carry the prisoner to the altar, where the executioner would smash in his chest with a stone knife, pluck the heart, still beating, from within and place it on the priest's plate. The priest would carry the plate around to all the idols, smearing the hot blood on their stone faces. During the four-day dedication of Huitzilopochtli's temple, *eighty thousand men, women and children were sacrificed.* Charming fellows, the Aztecs."

"Did they ever make human sacrifices to Tezcatlipoca?" I asked, feeling rather proud of myself for getting the name right.

"Certainly—when there were problems relating to his domain, the night sky. Comets, for example, or meteor showers. But he was never fed so lavishly as Huitzilopochtli."

Another question occurred to me: "You said they dressed the prisoners like the gods they were sacrificing them to. Did they ever simply pin a little figure of the god to the prisoner instead?"

Ruckhauser raised his eyebrows with interest. "A sort of shorthand method, you mean? I don't know if it was ever done. It does sound like a logical extension of the idea, however."

"Thank you for answering all these questions," I said. "I really appreciate it."

"Let me ask you a question. Why are you so interested in the ornament Francis Hertzel is wearing in this picture?"

"Francis Hertzel?" Alex and I asked almost in unison.

Ruckhauser regarded us curiously. Once again he

spread the clipping on the desk and held the magnifying glass an inch or two above it so we both might see.

"The man in the picture," he said, "is Francis Hertzel. You mean you didn't know?" He looked back and forth between us with amazement; then he shrugged philosophically. "Of course, you're both children, why should you remember him? He died before either of you was born. It surprises me because when I was a boy, Francis Hertzel was the most famous movie star in the world. He made a film called *The Silver Hawk*. Women fainted with passion when they saw him on the screen."

"Do you remember *how* he died?" I asked with growing excitement. "Was it a natural death or a suicide?"

"I apologize, Mr. Pinkle, but I am an authority on Mexican antiquities, not on movie stars."

"Chester," I gasped, running into The Great Spectacle and grabbing him by the arm. "Did Francis Hertzel die of natural causes?"

He looked at me with the confusion of someone who is suddenly asked, with a roomful of people listening, to name all the presidents in order or find the cube root of sixty-four.

"*Francis Hertzel,*" I said, speaking more slowly, "*the silent movie actor. Did he die of natural causes?*"

"Think hard, man," Alex said, "this is really important." He had driven me there straight from Ruckhauser's gallery.

Chester began to stammer. The little blond girl, his singing discovery, who was in the back of the store polishing glasses with a chamois, put down her work and ran to his side.

"How dare you talk to Chester like that! You come running in here, shouting at him and shaking him like he's some kind of—" The metaphor eluded her. Instead she huffed at us and helped him to a chair. "Chester is an artist," she continued, "a sensitive soul."

"It's all right, Ellie," Chester said, and to us: "You surprised me, rushing in like that."

"I'm sorry, Chester," I said.

"He's really sorry," Alex agreed.

"You know," I said, "sometimes when you're working on a story, you get so caught up in it you forget that anything or anybody else exists. It's a blissful condition, a kind of neurotic nirvana. The trouble is, it makes you blind to the feelings of your friends; suddenly they're not people anymore, they're tools to help you pursue the story. And once the story's done, it's all over and people are themselves again and you can't remember why you ever treated them so badly."

"Forget it," Chester said. "My little baby likes to take care of me, that's all." He put an arm around her hip and squeezed her. She ran a hand over his head, straightening his hair, glaring at us. "Now what do you want to know about Francis Hertzel?"

"Did he die a natural death?"

"Let's see. I don't know if you'd call it natural or not. I'd say the press killed him. See, he was the great lover of the silent screen, but he was also a pansy. Half the men hated him because he made their wives swoon; the other half hated him because he made homosexuality chic. Talk about your gay lib. In 'twenty-six, I believe it was, a dance hall opened in Chicago called the Silver Hawk, after Hertzel's biggest hit. The clientele was exclusively male, like at that bath club in New York. And in the little boys' room they had a cosmetic dispenser with lipstick and rouge and a gimmick that squirted powder on your face for a quarter.

"But I guess the main reason the press hated him was because he was so damned popular! They hate success, you know. I've seen it time and again. First they build you up and then they shoot you down. And then they come to the funeral and talk about what a terrific guy you used to be.

"One day Hertzel collapsed. They took him to Cedars of Lebanon and it turned out he had a perforated ulcer. He would have been fine, but something went wrong with his treatment—somebody gave him the wrong medication or something—and the poor son of a bitch died.

"And if that wasn't enough, there was trouble at the funeral. Nobody could agree where to bury him, so in the meantime they put him in the Grand Mausoleum at Forest Meadows. About three months later his brother Rudolph got a court order saying he could move the body back to the family plot in Vienna. But when they opened the crypt the body was missing and a wax dummy had been put in its place. The theory was that one of his lovers had stolen the body."

"Jesus, you're great," I said. "You're a walking encyclopedia of the movies."

"That's what flacks get paid for," he said. "Keeping up with scandals and making new ones."

"You wouldn't know who his doctor was at Cedars of Lebanon?"

"That much of a genius I ain't."

"I'll bet it was a young man named Kellerman," I muttered. "And what about his agent? Who was his agent?"

"I don't know, but I remember he had a business manager, a guy named Penny. Wallace Penny, I think."

"Sure," I said, "Penny. Weston, Rubin, Weiss, and Penny. Penny must have been the senior partner. When he retired he passed his duties along to Rubin. It makes perfect sense."

"Not to me it don't," Chester remarked.

"Excuse me," somebody said.

We all turned around, and a young man in a USC T-shirt was standing by the door. He was tall and lanky, with sandy hair and a droopy mustache, aviator glasses and a rucksack over his shoulders. He had the guileless, puzzled look of a just-hatched chick, viewing the world for the first time and not sure just what to make of it.

"Could I see those silver frames in the window," he said, "the ones with the double wire across the nose?"

"For Christ's sake," I said, "can't you see we're busy? Sit down and Chester will get to you when he has a chance." I turned back to Chester. "What year did he die?"

" 'Twenty-seven, 'twenty-eight."

"They kill one every ten years," I said. "Valenti in 'seventy-seven. Rosalee Romain in 'sixty-seven. Who was it in 'fifty-seven?"

"Who was what in 'fifty-seven?" Chester asked, still more puzzled.

"Who was killed in 'fifty-seven? What movie star died an unnatural death?"

"Dean Jamison."

"Of course! Jamison. He shot himself in the head. Look, he was in psychoanalysis, wasn't he?"

"I think so," Chester said. "He sure should have been."

"And who was it in 'forty-seven? Who died in 'forty-seven?"

"Let me think," Chester said.

"John Barrymore?" the little blond girl suggested.

"Nineteen forty," Chester said.

"What about—" Alex thought for a moment. "Montgomery Clift?"

"No, no," I said. "He died in the fifties."

"Excuse me for interrupting," the young man in the USC T-shirt said, "but Dory Grayson disappeared in nineteen forty-seven. Does that count?"

"Right you are," Chester said, "Dory Grayson. Vanished in a plane over Baja. The wreckage and the body were never found."

"Nineteen thirty-seven?" I said.

"Jean Harrold," Chester snapped back. "Came down with uremic poisoning from using so much bleach on her hair. That sounds like a joke but it's the truth. She died in Cedars of Lebanon from complications."

"Complications," I whispered. "Nineteen twenty-seven, Hertzel. Nineteen seventeen . . .?"

"Sorry." Chester shrugged. "Can't help you, that's before my time."

"Nineteen seventeen," the young man in the USC T-shirt began, "was the year Virginia Nightingale disappeared from William Randolph Hearst's yacht, somewhere off the coast of Mexico. She and Lance Carlyle took a dinghy into shore early one morning to sun and swim off the beach. Lance appeared a week later in Los Angeles and told the press that the dinghy had been caught in a strong offshore current and capsized. Lance had tried to save Virginia; then, realizing the hopelessness of it, he had made for shore himself. Lance's wife, comedienne Mabel Edmonds, who was also on the yacht that weekend, accused Lance of spending the week with Virginia in Mexico and sued for divorce."

He almost laughed at our incredulous expressions. "My name's Bob Goldman," he said, "and I'm doing graduate work at USC film school. My dissertation happens to deal with this period."

"Beautiful," I said, "you can take it from here. Nineteen seventeen, Virginia Nightingale. What about nineteen-o-seven?"

"There weren't any movie stars in nineteen-o-seven," Bob Goldman explained. Now that he was the center of attention his manner became professorial; he began to pace, taking off his glasses and using the stems to chew on and occasionally to emphasize a point. "There were movies, but the Patents Company—that was a trust made up of the big studios, Biograph and Vitagraph— refused to release the names of their actors. They were worried that if the public knew them, then the actors could demand more money. At that time actors rarely earned more than five or ten dollars a day. Naturally the public had their favorites, but they knew them as the Biograph Girl or the Vitagraph Girl. So the identi- fication was with the company rather than with the individual."

"Man, it's such a typical capitalistic ploy," Alex

interrupted, "I can't believe it. The exploiter buys his villas while the artist is content to work for only a few crumbs. Didn't they realize that they were only aggravating the class struggle by—"

"Alex, will you shut up and let him finish!"

"Okay, okay. Be cool."

"As I was saying . . ." Goldman cleared his throat. "The identification was with the company. However, in nineteen ten Carl Laemmle—he was one of the independent producers who was always warring with the Patents Company—hired Florence Lawrence, formerly the Biograph Girl, to star in his own films, promising to feature her under her own name. That was the beginning of it. By nineteen fourteen stars like Mary Pickford, Douglas Fairbanks, Charlie Chaplin, and Fatty Arbuckle were making as much as two thousand dollars a week. By nineteen sixteen Chaplin's salary had hit a record high of ten thousand dollars a week. From then on the sky was the limit. Today it's not unusual for big stars to earn a million dollars a picture plus a percentage of the gross."

"Really?" the little blond girl asked.

"Listen," Chester said, "you'll be making half a million a week when you play Vegas."

"Oh come on," she said, tugging at a strand of hair with embarrassment.

"But why all the interest?" Bob Goldman insisted. "You don't think there's some pattern to all these deaths, do you?"

"I can't explain now," I said, "but pretty soon you'll be able to read the whole story in *BonHomme* magazine. As a matter of fact, if my suspicions are right, you'll be seeing it in every newspaper in the country, sprawled across the front page in two-hundred-point type."

"What an intriguing idea," Goldman said. "Now I hate to get mundane, but could somebody please show me the silver frames in the window, the ones with the two wires across the nose?"

AUTHOR
LESTER PEREZ

I was just opening a can of tamales for dinner when Carol called. I barely had time to say hello before she started in on me:

"You promised you were going to stop investigating Tony Valenti's death. You *promised*!"

"What makes you think I haven't?" I asked.

"Lieutenant Perez called the 'office.' He said he had to speak to you—it was urgent."

"Oh Carol," I laughed, "that's got nothing to do with murders. Perez is a writer; he gave me some of his short stories to criticize. Like any writer, he can't wait to find out what I think of them. Gee, you really don't trust me, do you?"

"I trust you, Louis"—her voice was level and serious—"but I also know you. And I know that once you get your mind stuck on something, you'll lie and cheat and maybe even kill for it. That's what I love about you, Louis; but it's also what I hate."

"Terrific. So now I'm a liar and a cheat. Why didn't you ever mention that before? I mean it's great to have a relationship with somebody where you think it's terrific and suddenly you find out the other person thinks you're a liar and a cheat, that's really great."

"I didn't mean it like that . . ."

"How else could you mean it? You said, and I quote: 'You'll lie and cheat.' I mean, it's plain old English, there's no misunderstanding it."

"Louis, you're twisting around my words. I said—"

"You said what you said. You said I'm a cheat and a liar, and you said you wouldn't be surprised if I murdered somebody. It's nice to know you think I could murder somebody."

"You're being completely crazy." It sounded like she was crying. "Won't you please listen to me for a minute? What I meant was—"

"Oh, so now I'm crazy too. Well, there's no point in trying to be rational with a crazy man, is there?"

And I hung up. We've had scenes like this before, and I knew that if I gave her a while to cool off she'd be fine. So I went back to cooking my dinner.

I stirred the tamales, started a saucepan of Minute rice and stuck some potato puffs in the oven. Then I took the ice cream out of the freezer so it would be soft enough to pour over the cheese Danish I had discovered hidden under a piece of waxed paper in the vegetable bin. While I was waiting for everything to be ready, I opened a bottle of Coke, sat myself down at the Formica table in the kitchen, and emptied the manila envelope containing Lieutenant Perez's literary efforts.

For years I have been bombarded with the writing of friends and relatives who seem to believe that once a writer has been published he can magically get his friends and relatives published, much the way one who has gained membership in an exclusive country club can then nominate whomever he likes. They want me to act as their agent, for no fee naturally, and they expect sudden, large cash payments. They seem to think of writing as a sort of get-rich-quick profession, even the ones I've been borrowing money from for years. And invariably their writing is lousy.

You wouldn't expect to pick up a violin cold, climb on stage at Carnegie Hall and have people pay to listen. Yet that's precisely what happens when people decide to write their article, short story or—heaven help me—nine-hundred-page novel. Without even learning the basics of style and technique, without analyzing the work of others, or at least choosing a model to imitate, they sit down at their typewriters and bang away. There's good reason why this sort of amateurism is more common in writing than in the other arts. Music must be learned; likewise sketching from life or performing the difficult movements of modern dance. But English we write and speak from the time we can toddle. From this long companionship we assume we are her master.

Then imagine how surprised and delighted I was by the professional quality of Perez's work. No, it was more than professional, it was brilliant. It turned my mood from condescension to envy. Beginning writers—fiction writers, that is—usually think their own lives are boring and write about what they've never experienced; ergo they don't know what they're talking about and the writing sounds false. But Perez's stories were so real I knew they had actually happened —even if they hadn't, if you know what I mean.

One story was about a terribly sensitive Mexican kid growing up in East Los Angeles, torn between trying to make something of his life and peer-group pressure to join a street gang. Another story described a day in the life of a Mexican cop on the Beverly Hills police force, the racism he suffered, the small rewards and the awful frustration of police work.

By the time I finished the third story the tamales were burning and I didn't care. I ran into the bedroom and phoned Jack Murphy, the fiction editor at *BonHomme*, at his home number and told him that I had just discovered one of the most important new writers of the decade. I would be sending the stories to him posthaste and if he didn't buy every one of them, then I would have to assume that he had lost all powers of discrimination.

Then I called Perez.

"Louis, where have you been?" he said. "I've been trying to reach you for days. The second number you gave me was some sort of spa showroom in the valley, but the girl who answered the phone seemed to know you."

"That's my girl friend, Carol," I said. "She gave me the message. Now here's the good news. Your stories are sensational. I love the low-key realistic style. I sent them all on to the fiction editor at *BonHomme* along with my strongest recommendation."

"Louis, that's wonderful, I can't thank you enough. But that's not why I'm calling. The car that crashed on Mulholland Drive? *It was empty*."

"But how could that be? The punks were in it when it went over the edge."

"They must have jumped out while it was falling. I just thought I'd warn you that they may still be after you. Should I call the sheriff and have him send a deputy to watch your apartment?"

(West Hollywood, where I lived, was part of unincorporated Los Angeles and therefore under the jurisdiction of the sheriff's office.)

"That's not necessary," I said. "I can take care of myself. Did you find out who they were?"

"The car is registered to the Burbank Wax Museum Corporation, which is run by a man named Wendell Grimmer. I haven't been able to get in touch with him by phone so I thought I'd drive out tomorrow. You're welcome to come along if you like."

"I'd love it," I said, "but you have to pick me up at my house. My car was in a little accident."

Perez chuckled. "Is nine o'clock too early?"

"Nine o'clock is fine."

"And Louis, please be careful about those two punks. If they tried to murder you once, they'll try again."

"It couldn't bother me less," I said, rushing to get off the phone so I could bolt the doors. Aside from the fags having their lovers' quarrels, West Hollywood is a reasonably safe, peaceable place to live, and when I'm home I always leave the doors off the latch. I love being able to come and go without having to undo fourteen different locks. That was one of the reasons why I left New York; I couldn't stand living in a state of guerrilla warfare.

But no sooner had I hung up when I thought I heard the faint, familiar squeak of the front door opening. Was it my imagination? I froze—didn't make a sound, didn't even breathe. Outside on La Cienega a wave of traffic passed, leaving me in silence. Yes, there it was again, the door being closed. Footsteps. Slow, cautious. One man alone, I could handle that. Big man from the weight of those footsteps—must have been the Oriental. If only I had a weapon, a pistol or even a baseball bat. Buy a pistol tomorrow; tonight I'd improvise. Improvise, improvise. That heavy wooden lamp on the dressing table would make a good bludgeon. Pulled off the shade, tore out the plug. Now the room was pitch black. Footsteps closer. Careful to get him off guard— I'd only have one chance. Tiptoed to the door, stood behind it waiting, waiting while the footsteps came closer, the knob turned, the door swung open . . .

"Louis?"

"Oh my God, Alex, is that you?"

"Yeah man. What are you doing in here with the lights out?"

"What are you doing sneaking into my apartment?"

"I was going to surprise you. I thought maybe you'd like to watch *Dolores*."

"What's Dolores?"

"It's my favorite TV show. Look." He held up a brown paper bag. "I brought Burritos and Milky Ways. We can sit in front of the tube and get high and eat."

"Alex," I said, breathing deeply, "do me a favor? No more surprises?"

When I came out of my apartment early next morning, Mr. Scheuermann was watering the garden around the driveway. On any other day I would have popped back inside and waited until he was gone, but this morning I was too preoccupied with Aztecs and movie stars and wax museums; I felt like I had opened two or three different jigsaw puzzles and gotten the parts mixed up, and that was why I couldn't make a whole of it. I didn't realize it was Scheuermann until I was nearly at the street and by then he had spotted me and it was too late to hide.

"Mr. Pinkle," he called in his thick German accent, "I would like a word with you."

He was a small, burly man with gray hair and blue eyes, a moon face and a nose like a mushroom. He and his wife had an apartment in the next building, the white stucco Spanish-style apartment house on the corner. Mrs. Scheuermann was a fanatical housekeeper and a devout member of the Jehovah's Witnesses. You couldn't leave her apartment without a copy of *Watchtower*. Mr. Scheuermann was a passionate gardener, a facile handyman and the manager of both his building and my own. Manager, by the way, is California parlance for superintendent.

"How are you today, Mr. Scheuermann," I said in my most ingratiating tones, "and how is your lovely wife? My, it certainly is a beautiful day, isn't it? Your garden looks terrific! I'm amazed how you get things to grow in this desert climate."

"The rent, Mr. Pinkle."

"I know I'm a little late . . ."

"Four months."

"The fact is, I'm getting a check for an article any day now. If you can just hang in there . . ."

"Next Monday, Mr. Pinkle. If we don't have all the back rent—"

"*All* the back rent? Now wait a minute, that's not fair. There's no way I can get—"

"If we don't have *all* the back rent by Monday, it will be my unpleasant task to have you evicted."

"You can't do that to me! I'm in the middle of the most important project of my life! I need my files and my typewriter, and—and—"

"Louis!" somebody yelled.

I turned around and saw a brown Ford pull up at the curb. Perez smiled and waved from the driver's seat.

"Monday, Mr. Pinkle," Scheuermann threatened.

"Jesus Christ," I pleaded, "give a guy a break."

"We've given you breaks. These buildings are a business, not a charity. If you want charity, go to the Salvation Army."

"Spare me the philosophy," I said.

I strolled over to Perez's car and climbed in next to him. Mr. Scheuermann followed me with his head, allowing the garden hose to stray from the marigolds. The water splashed against the hot concrete, making steam.

It was one of those days when the heat and the pollution combine to make the air almost unbreathable. As we came over the hills on the Hollywood Freeway, the valley appeared to be filled with a foul green-colored vapor, like a bowl of old pea soup. We turned east on the Ventura Freeway, where the temperature must have been 110 degrees. Perez removed the jacket of his lime-sherbet leisure suit and rolled up his shirt-sleeves. A big black revolver was strapped under his arm.

When the valley is bad, Burbank is worse, the temperature always a few degrees hotter, the air a wee bit murkier. Once the city of Burbank even considered blasting a giant tunnel through the wall of mountains that mark the northern boundary of the area and installing a giant ventilating fan; but like all revolutionary ideas, it was vetoed by men of little vision.

After getting lost a few times, we found the Burbank Wax Museum sandwiched between a dry cleaners and a sandwich shop. A marquee flashed "WAX MUSEUM" in red and green neon, and a smaller sign underneath it said "See the Stars in Person/ So Close You Can Almost Touch Them/ So Real They Almost Breathe." Sonny and Cher were posed in one window as though they had been frozen midchorus by some kind of Buck Rogers paralysis gun; likewise Charlie's Angels, who occupied the other window, dressed in clinging T-shirts. The sculptures were surprisingly good, realistic flesh tones and delicate features; they didn't have those blank, glassy stares that dress mannequins have.

An old woman with platinum blond curls and smeared lipstick sat at the ticket window just left of the entrance, engrossed in the *National Enquirer*. Adults $3.50, $2.00 for Students, Children and Senior Citizens. It occurred to me that the Catholic Church

lets people view their wax effigies for free, and the
Catholic Church was losing converts left and right. Yet
the Burbank Wax Museum seemed to be doing a pretty
good business. It didn't leave much doubt about which
was the more popular religion.

Perez nodded to me. He strode up to the window,
and in a second his wallet was out and open under
the woman's face.

"Police," he said. "We'd like to speak to Wendell
Grimmer."

She folded the paper—I caught a glimpse of "Amazing new cancer cure from apricot pits . . ."—and,
regarding us with frightened eyes, spoke into an intercom on the desk:

"Wendell, there's some people to see you. Police."

"Send them right on up," said a jovial voice.

"Go inside, all the way back," she directed us.
"There's a staircase at the right of the Beatles."

We crossed the lobby, where souvenirs were available, and popcorn from an old-fashioned machine with
a glass top, and entered the museum itself, musty-
smelling corridors dark as velvet. At intervals tableaux
glared with a harsh light: stilted figures in stage sets,
actors, pop singers, politicians. JFK smiled toothily
from a lectern draped with American flags; W. C.
Fields leaned over a pool table with a cue that bent
like a dog's leg. Dorothy, the Tin Woodsman and the
Cowardly Lion began their trek down the yellow brick
road.

I caught a glimpse of something and asked Perez to
wait. In a side corridor stood Tony Valenti cast in the
stuff of soap and candles, wearing a chef's hat and holding up his hands to catch a circle of pizza dough that

hung in the air mystically. A neon sign said *Dino's Pizzeria*. I stared at it for a few seconds, marveling at the authenticity, which was of course the fun of wax museums, while also feeling slightly ghoulish at the display of death in life; then I rejoined Perez.

The sound of the Beatles reached me, "A Hard Day's Night," and then I saw the four of them open-mouthed at their microphones yet eerily still-lipped. Perez was walking so fast I almost had to run to keep pace. He bounded up a dark stairway to the right of the Beatles exhibit, two stairs at a time, and pounded on the door when he reached the top.

We were ushered into a bright workroom with ply-wood tables and plaster dust everywhere. A huge old crystal chandelier hung overhead, and gathered against the walls were storage bins filled with hands of different shades of wax—black, yellow and red—and more storage bins stocked with legs and torsos of burlap and plaster. Heads were lined up on the shelves like melons in a fruit market.

"Come in, come in," Wendell Grimmer said, smiling. He was in his fifties, plump and pale and jovial, with lively blue eyes and white hair that puffed out on either side, almost clownlike. He wore a plaster-caked denim apron and rimless spectacles with half-moon lenses. There was something exceedingly nervous about his jollity, like a blade concealed in a birthday cake.

"Excuse me if I don't shake hands," he said while Perez was showing him the badge, "but I'm covered with clay." He wiped his palms on the apron, examined them, wiped them again, and gave up. "I assume you've come about those two young criminals I employ. Well, I haven't seen them in five days and as far as I'm concerned they can go to blazes. What have they done this time? Robbed an orphanage? Raped an old woman?" He laughed nervously.

"Speeding, reckless driving, destruction of property. Attempted murder."

Grimmer sighed and shook his head.

"Do you own a nineteen fifty-eight Cadillac with plates JBL twenty-eight?"

Grimmer nodded. "The museum owns it—or should I say *owned* it? I haven't seen the car for days."

"Why didn't you report it to the police?"

"It's happened before. Billy and Franklyn, the boys who work for me, go off on a joyride sometimes, but they always come back in a day or two. Billy's on parole—he's trying to rehabilitate himself—and I don't want to be the one responsible for sending him back to prison. What's the difference as long as they do their work? Speaking of work, give me a moment. I must cover the head I'm working on or the clay will dry out." Grimmer returned to the plywood turntable where an egg of gray clay was beginning to take on human features.

"Hey, that's pretty good," I said. "Jimmy Carter, isn't it?"

"That's correct," he said, swathing it in wet towels and clear plastic. "And very difficult it is when you have to work from photos." He waved at the magazine clippings of Carter pinned on the wall. "Most celebrities will agree to have lunch and let me photograph them and measure their face with calipers. Streisand even let me take a cast of her nose because I couldn't get the bump right. Of course she was promoting *Star Is Born* at the time and she was very cooperative.

Does that surprise you? My dear sirs, it's a great honor to have a place in the Burbank Wax Museum. We're one of the few museums left that make their own sculptures. Yes, it's true. Most of them buy from Tussaud's in London. The complete figures are too expensive so they usually order the head and the hands and fit them onto a dress dummy." Grimmer snorted with disgust. "That's why they all go bankrupt in a few months. No quality, no pride in their work. But *we've* been in business seventeen years!"

"Where's the vat of bubbling wax?" I said, looking around. "I thought every wax museum had to have one."

Grimmer's smile turned to the merriest grin. "As in the old Vincent Price movie? I don't use it, although Tussaud's does."

"What's it for?" I asked. It had suddenly occurred to me that this might make a very interesting article.

"It will take me a few minutes to explain. If the lieutenant doesn't mind . . .?"

"Keep it short," Perez said.

"Very well. When I finish sculpting Mr. Carter's head, I will make a plaster mold and cast the head in wax."

"That's where the vat comes in?" I guessed. "To melt the wax?"

He shook his head. "No, we use a plain old coffee urn." He led me to a five-gallon coffee urn covered, like everything else in the studio, with plaster dust and chains of beaded wax. "Into this we mix beeswax"— he held up a milky-white slab a little larger than a Hershey's bar— "and pigments, acrylic paints most often. We cast several heads to season the mold; then we make the final casting and, when it's cooled, sculpt in the fine details."

"Now the vat?"

"Patience," Grimmer said, smiling. "Makeup is applied to create lifelike gradations in skin tone, and the eyes are hollowed out so that eyeballs can be inserted. These eyes come from Germany."

He opened a box shaped like an egg carton, and inside were eight eyeballs in assorted colors.

"They are very expensive," he continued, "—made by the same company that makes glass eyes. Another reason why our figures are so lifelike. Still, they sometimes send us a set where the pupils are improperly matched, and then we have to return them. Now that the head is completed, a layer of clear wax is applied over the makeup to give the skin a lifelike sheen and translucency. At Tussaud's they dip the head into a vat of clear wax—and that is the vat we see in the movies. Personally, I prefer a spray gun. It's less dramatic but more efficient." He showed me the spray gun and the compressor which he used, and explained how hot wax was loaded into the jar and then applied in a thin, even coat.

Meanwhile Perez was clearing his throat, growing more and more impatient. Finally I said politely that it was getting late and while the making of wax figures was fascinating, it was not what we had come to learn about.

"Of course," Grimmer said, "excuse me. You want to know about Billy Chou and Frank Pollacek."

Grimmer gave a description of the two men and I corroborated it; they were, without a doubt, the ones who had attacked and tried to murder me. He had needed two boys to do carpentry, run errands and work as night guards, and his lawyer had recommended them, explaining that Chou, a surf bum from Hawaii, was a gifted artist who might one day learn wax sculpture; and that Pollacek, an ex-hustler and ex-addict from Hollywood, had had some experience as a fighter. But from the day he had hired them they had been nothing but trouble, irritating the neighbors with midnight brawls, committing petty thievery, now this.

"With a lawyer like that," I said, "you don't need enemies."

"They'd been paroled in Marty's custody and I owed him so many favors . . ."

"Marty?" I said. "That wouldn't be Marty Rubin, the theatrical lawyer?"

Grimmer looked surprised. "That's right. Do you know him?"

While I mulled over this new information, Perez asked more questions about Chou and Pollacek, their ages and addresses, mundane details. He noted everything on his pad and when he was done he asked, "Mind if I look around?"

Grimmer tensed. His eyes snapped toward a door in the corner, then back to us. "Not at all," he said casually.

While Perez poked around I asked Grimmer about his life. Something here fascinated me, and I think it was the idea of someone being so skilled in such an antiquated, bastardized craft, an art that appealed to few, offered limited rewards, and was about as permanent as a bar of soap. How had he gotten involved in it? Certainly no boy ever told his third-grade teacher that he wanted to be a sculptor of wax figures when he grew up.

He told me he was born on a farm in Iowa and started working in clay as a child, urged on by his mother, who taught art at the local elementary school. After the war he went to New York to pursue a career as a serious sculptor while supporting himself working in the Ripley's museum on Broadway. Soon it became apparent that his "serious" occupation was no occupation at all, and he devoted himself fully to wax sculpture, traveling around the country from museum to museum as one after the other went bankrupt (apparently most wax museums were short-lived). At first he felt that he had sold out; he began to despise himself. But after many years he came to realize that anything done with care and love became an art form of the highest order, and wax sculpture was no exception. Now that he owned his own museum, and business was good, and he could work when he wished, doing what he wished, he had found a certain peace. He was happy —happier than most men, he supposed.

Perez interrupted us. "What's in here?" he called from across the room. He was standing in front of the door in the corner.

"Nothing," Grimmer said quickly. "Storage, that's all."

Perez tried the handle. "It's locked. Open it."

"I—I don't have the key."

Perez put his ear to the door and frowned. "There's something in there, something's moving around. Open it."

"I can't."

Perez pulled the gun out of his shoulder holster and aimed it at the lock.

"Stop!" Grimmer shouted. In his excitement his voice cracked, like an adolescent's. "Don't you dare. It's search without warrant. I'll sue you. I'll call the police."

Perez remained frozen for the longest moment, his finger tightening around the trigger. The tension in the room grew and grew as we waited for the crack of the bullet, the ripping of wood. It never came. Perez jammed the gun into the holster, turned on his heels and strode out of the studio, silent and furious.

10
MABEL EDMONDS

"The list of murder victims," I told Flora McReese, "is as long as your arm. Remember Dean Jamison? *Tomorrow Never Comes. Exiles from Paradise.* Shot himself in the head, nineteen fifty-seven." I ticked them off on my fingers: "Valenti, 'seventy-seven; Rosey Romain, 'sixty-seven; Dean Jamison, 'fifty-seven. Suggest something to you?"

Flora sat at her desk, her hands folded primly before her, her eyebrows rising and falling with appropriate interest. She thought about it a moment before replying.

"More people commit suicide in years ending in seven?"

"Ten-year intervals, Flora! They kill a movie star every ten years. It's part of a ritual worship of Tezcatlipoca, the Aztec god of night and magic and sorcery. And it didn't start with Dean Jamison, either! Remember Dory Grayson, lost in a small plane over Mexico, nineteen forty-seven. Nineteen *forty-seven*! And Jean Harrold, died of 'complications' at Cedars of Lebanon Hospital, nineteen thirty-seven—the same hospital where Dr. Abraham Kellerman might have been her physician."

"Might have?"

"I'm still checking that one out. Nineteen twenty-seven, Francis Hertzel also died at Cedars of Lebanon, once again of 'complications'—a convenient euphemism for murder at the hands of our friend Kellerman. But it doesn't stop there . . ."

"Where does it stop, Louis?"

"Nineteen seventeen! The day Virginia Nightingale disappeared from William Randolph Hearst's yacht, somewhere off the coast of Mexico. And those are just the stars; I'm not counting the people they killed keeping the thing covered up, Arthur White and Mary Spivack and who knows how many others? They've tried to get me twice now, and it's only dumb luck that I'm standing in your office today.

"Flora, you're a woman of vision, you can imagine how big this story is. It's a mass murder with nine victims—nine of the most talented, celebrated actors that ever graced a movie screen—spread over a period of sixty years and perpetuated by a secret organization of wealthy, respected professionals. This is the kind of story that will establish *BonHomme* as a first-rate news magazine, not just a purveyor of tits and ass and sophomoric college humor. That's why you have to advance me another thousand bucks." I stared at my feet. "My landlord's going to evict me."

"What about the money we gave you to be psycho-analyzed by Kellerman? You told me you only had one session."

"I used it for the back payments on my car."

"Louis," Flora said, "we can't advance you any more money. Furthermore"— she hesitated uncomfortably —"I'm not sure we can use the article."

"What?" I said, leaping to my feet.

She raised a hand. "Hear me out."

I sat back and she continued:

"When you first described it to me, it sounded as though Tony Valenti might possibly have been murdered. Frankly, Louis, even at the time I didn't fully believe it, but you're such an entertaining writer I assumed the article would be of interest, convincing or not. But over the past few weeks I've watched this article grow from a small, slightly sensational—yet reasonably plausible—idea to what sounds like the rantings of a paranoid schizophrenic."

"Thanks a lot."

"Oh Louis, you know how much I respect you; that's why I'm trying to be completely honest. If you were somebody else I'd wait until you submitted the article and then I'd send you the kill fee along with some excuse about the style being wrong for our readers. I think you are one of our best regular con-tributors. But sometimes the world gets to be too much for us. The pressures of earning a living, of dealing with people we love. We begin to lose perspective . . ."

"Flora, I am not cracking up!"

"I never said you were, Louis." Her voice was soft, filled with sympathy. "What I said was, sometimes the emotional pressures of life can be enough to make us

lose perspective. Let me give you an example. A man's
store burns down. The police find a rag soaked in
gasoline. Other buildings in the neighborhood have
been victimized by arson in the past months. Furthermore, the man is Jewish and the neighborhood is
notorious for its anti-Semitic youth gangs. Now we
also learn that the man's business was failing. He has
been trying to sell the store for several years, but
because of the deteriorating neighborhood he can find
no buyers. He is heavily insured for fire damage.

"If we are Jews, and we are particularly sensitive
about anti-Semitism, then it might appear to us as an
obvious case of arson. On the other hand, if we are
insurance investigators, we would prefer to view the
incident as an insurance swindle. And if we are determined, let's say, to write the greatest murder story of
all time, we might be tempted to string together events
with only the most tenuous relationships, such as
people born under the same astrological sign or people
whose names begin with the letter *M* or people who
happened to die in years ending with the digit seven.

"Now, Louis, I know you've been under great personal strain. I'm going to give you the name and
address of a psychiatrist I know. He's extremely warm
and sensitive, I'm sure you'll like him. As for the
money, I have two assignments for you, one on the
Van Phenomenon—you know, the customized vans
the kids are driving—and how it's altering the patterns
of adolescent sexual behavior; and another on Mabel
Edmonds, the silent film actress. Do you ever watch
the situation comedy *Dolores*? Well, Mabel Edmonds
plays Dolores's grandmother, and I understand she's
quite a crusty old girl. The van article will serve for

the advance we've already paid you. If you can get it to me by Friday, we'll advance you an additional thousand dollars for the Mabel Edmonds article. I haven't spoken to Fletcher about it yet, but I'm reasonably sure he'll agree."

She held out the slip of paper with the psychiatrist's name and address.

"Jesus Christ, Flora, I thought you were on my side!"

"I *am* on your side. That's why I want you to get help."

"Well, if you think I'm going to write an article on adolescent sex or some washed-up movie actress, you're the one who needs psychiatric help."

Saying this, I got up and left her office. I passed the reception desk where the foxy black girl was doing her nails, and I rang for the elevator. While I was waiting it occurred to me that someone had mentioned Mabel Edmonds during the past few days; idly I tried to recall the specifics.

Then I remembered. I turned around and dashed back to Flora's office, rushed inside without even knocking.

"Do you mean Mabel Edmonds who used to be married to Lance— What was his name? Lance Carlyle. Mabel Edmonds who used to go yachting with William Randolph Hearst?"

"Why, I don't really know," Flora said, taken off guard by my sudden reappearance. "I believe—yes, I believe she was once married to Lance Carlyle. I'm not really much of a silent-film buff. Louis, does this mean you'll take the assignment?"

She looked at me so hopefully; and suddenly it

occurred to me how much she cared about me. That's a rare thing. Oh, people fall in love every day and care for each other, and when people think you're in a position to do them some good, then they pretend to care about you—that's the normal mode of behavior in Los Angeles, Hustle City; but for somebody to care about you with nothing promised in return, neither sex nor security, nor employment nor status, nor any of the other carrots that dangle in front of our noses, merely to care about you because you are their friend—that is something rarer than a clear day in Burbank.

"I'll do the Mabel Edmonds article," I said, "but I'm not going to write about vans and adolescent sex. All I remember about adolescent sex is jerking off six times a day."

"Louis—?" She held up the slip of paper with her psychiatrist's name and address.

I hesitated; then I sighed and took it.

"Understand, I have no intention of going to see this guy. But I think you're beautiful for trying."

Leaning over the desk, I pecked her on the cheek.

I called The Bead Brujo from the corner phone box, hoping that Alex might be in the mood to chauffeur me around this afternoon. As luck would have it, he had just gone out to lunch, no one knew where. I left word for him to call me at Schwab's, and I began hiking along Sunset in the direction of that fine drugstore, where I intended to grab a bite to eat. The distance from the *BonHomme* building would be no more than a mile or two; in New York I wouldn't have thought twice about it, but here in West Hollywood it seemed perverse, moving by foot in the noonday sun. The poor, the crippled, the old people and the children whizzed by me, all driving their Porsches. I alone was without a car, I alone was bald. Furthermore, everyone thought I was crazy and things were getting worse, not better.

By nature I'm a happy, easy-going guy. I'm not very introspective and I'm certainly not given to fits of depression. Yet I was experiencing a profound sense of desolation; I even, for an instant, considered stepping out into the traffic on Sunset. The cars were coming fast; they wouldn't have time to stop. A head-on collision at forty miles an hour and it would be all over. Let's see Scheuermann collect back-rent from a dead man. Oh, those damn debts. I tried not to acknowledge them but they weighed me down like a lead vest. To be out of debt was almost worth being dead.

I thought about my father, who was born in poverty and worked his way up to Scarsdale manufacturing cheap dresses. Like all Jews he worshiped education and the written word. I guess that's a holdover from the old days in Russia, when the men who studied the Torah were the gentry. So he convinced his son to be a writer. "You'll never starve if you know a craft," he said, but he neglected to mention the numerous intermediate stages between starvation and earning a good living, some of which were dismal enough to make you want to step in front of a car on Sunset Boulevard.

I should have gone into his dress business, but he discouraged me. "Leave the business to your brother Walter; he's the businessman. You're the artist."

Actually Walter was a thief. As a kid he used to buy the bubble-gum packs with baseball cards—six cards and a slab of gum for a nickel—chew the gum and resell the cards individually for a penny apiece to other kids who were either too lazy or too stupid to compute his profit margin. I liked to stare out the window and help my mother bake cookies; that's what, to my father, constituted "artistic temperament."

Walter loved sports. At summer camp he was chosen Best All-Around Athlete. I was fat—"husky" was the euphemism they used at the clothing store—and un-coordinated, and I can only remember once that summer when I wasn't picked last when we chose up teams.

I despised Walter until high school, when my endo-crine glands decided to make me slim and fatally attrac-tive to women, while Walter's pitted him with acne until his face was like Swiss cheese.

We both went to NYU (Walter was one year my senior). I was the editor of the college paper, a heavy-weight politico, the hippiest of the hippies, with hair down to my shoulders, if you can believe it. Walter was still wearing button-down collars and pants with buckles in the back, still trying to figure out why he couldn't get laid.

Ah, how the great mandala spins out our fates. Today Walter was comfortably ensconced on Seventh Avenue, pulling in a hundred grand a year, and I was wearing out my shoe leather on Sunset Boulevard, figuring out how to pay back a three-thousand-dollar advance.

He had an apartment on Manhattan's Upper East Side, a closet full of everything in Bloomingdale's men's department, and a summer house on Fire Island that he rented with three friends. He still didn't know how to seduce a woman, but the women no longer seemed to care; his assets made him sufficiently attractive.

In 1975 Pop had a heart attack and died within a few hours, Walter and Mom at his bedside. I flew in from California but by the time I arrived his body had already been removed to the funeral home. I haven't seen the family since, although we have long long-distance calls during the holidays when we all try to get something from each other—I don't know what, a sense of family, a sense of being together, or maybe even something as simple as love—and we all inevitably ring off unsatisfied.

I felt better when I got to Schwab's. A few terminally unemployed actor friends of mine, who were sitting around drinking coffee, waiting for casting calls, saw how depressed I was and did funny bits to cheer me up. I had a cheeseburger and a Coke, and one of them even offered to pick up the check, but there I drew the line. I wasn't so far gone that I needed to accept charity from an unemployed actor.

I went to the pay phones and dialed NBS in Burbank. The operator connected me with one of the producers of *Dolores*, a man named Jerry Rosenberg. I told him I was a great Mabel Edmonds fan; I would write a puff piece on her for *BonHomme* if he could arrange a meeting for us that evening. He was agreeable ("as long as she doesn't have to pose nude for the centerfold, ha-ha-ha") and told me to come by the studio at seven that evening. I could watch the show being taped and meet with Mabel afterward. He'd leave a pass at the rear gate.

While I was on the pay phone, Shirley, who works at the cash register, signaled that I had a call on the house phone. It was Alex, just back from lunch. I asked him if he felt like driving me to Burbank that evening to watch a taping of *Dolores*. Alex, in addition to his other virtues, was a tube freak. He loved television and often sat for hours, stoned, in front of the flickering gray screen, eating ice cream and cupcakes and popcorn. As it happened, *Dolores* was one of his favorite shows. He would meet me at Schwab's in an hour or two, have an early dinner with me, and drive me out to the taping. From the enthusiasm in his voice, you'd think I had just invited him to hear Marx lecture in person. Ah Kotsky, what a collection of contradictions. But who isn't?

Dolores was a situation comedy about a woman of forty, just divorced, who moves from the suburbs to New York City to pursue a career in publishing and raise her two teen-age children. In line with the network's characteristic opportunism, it had been developed as a women's-lib program; but thanks to the network's characteristic loginess, by the time it had reached the air, the women's movement was no longer chic. Not that it mattered much: Because of the network's characteristic timidity, it wasn't really a women's-lib show at all. True, the woman was divorced. True, she had a job and she was supporting herself without alimony. The trappings were all right, but the ideology was all wrong.

For example, in the show Alex and I watched being taped that evening, Dolores learns that she will get a raise if she can convince a handsome best-selling author to sign up his next book with her publishing company. Her strategy involves donning her sexiest evening gown, taking the author to an expensive restaurant for dinner and giving him the unmistakable impression that she will be dessert. Yet afterward, when he invites her to his apartment for a nightcap and bed appears to be imminent, she calls a halt to the proceedings. She cannot go through with it! She must tell him the truth, even if it means losing her raise. It has all been a ploy, she confesses, to make him sign up his book with her company (although she must admit, she does find him attractive). Well, he is so impressed by her honesty that he decides to sign with her publishing company anyway. Dolores gets her raise and the handsome author takes her out to celebrate.

"What precisely is it," I asked Alex during a commercial break, "that you like about this show?"

"Her tits," he replied.

Aside from this dubious asset, the program's saving grace was Mabel Edmonds as Dolores's grandmother, a woman of eighty-nine living in sin with a younger man of seventy-two, "a mere child," as she is fond of saying. The joke is that Mabel is a geriatric swinger while her granddaughter Dolores is rather more conservative at half the age. The joke wears thin quickly; then the interplay is kept alive only by Mabel's sparkling eyes, unclouded by age, her rubbery face, her marvelous comic timing. No wonder the network was considering giving Mabel a spin-off, a series of her own.

After the show Alex and I filed down the steps along with the rest of the audience, mostly tourists, judging from snippets of conversation I could overhear. The studio was like a legitimate theater, only smaller—it seated no more than a hundred and fifty—and without a proscenium. The sets—the office, the restaurant— stopped just beyond the range of the camera and gave way to cream-colored cinder block, decorated with bunches of colored cables and light stands and booms, video-prompters and other things mysterious and electrical.

We waited outside the third exit where Jerry Rosenberg had agreed to meet us, and he appeared within minutes, a man a little older than myself with curly hair, a mahogany tan and more than twice the normal number of teeth. I introduced Alex and lied about how much I had enjoyed the show.

"Hey man," Alex grunted as Rosenberg led us through the labyrinthine corridors of NBS, "do you think I could meet Dolores? I'm a heavy fan. I've got a little present I'd like to lay on her."

The "little present," which Alex had been clutching in his sweaty hand all evening, was a silver bracelet with a lump of turquoise the size of a hen's egg, hand-made by one of the best of the Navajo silversmiths. This, plus the fact that he was dressed in his finest ruffly silk shirt, gold cowboy boots, fringed calfskin jeans and matching vest (a twelve-hundred-dollar outfit from Longbeach Leather), led me to believe that he was intending to make time with Dolores, although it was difficult for me to imagine this—well, let's be frank—gross person with a woman who was virtually a symbol of American purity, an updated Shirley Temple.

We walked through twisting corridors of cream-colored cinder block, past windows that opened into

darkened rooms—rooms filled with banks of TV
monitors, rows of bull's-eye test patterns, of housewives selling soap, of cop shows and song stylists, of
newsmen and superstars, all pouring entertainment into
the airwaves, radiations that would someday reach
distant galaxies and puzzle the hell out of green-
tentacled Earthologists.

It's not that I look down on television; I see it for
what it is, an advertising medium. You don't have to
be a Marxist to know that any art medium that is paid
for in full by the great corporations of America is not
going to be entirely without censorship. Would
General Foods sponsor a show about famine in India?
Would Mobil Oil give us the true story about
political repression in Iran? On the other hand, a show
wholly without new ideas or controversy, a show
where every character is cliché and every plot pre-
dictable—in other words, a show just like *Dolores*—
is a show that soothes and reassures us, and if we feel
that way about the show, then we will feel that way
about the product we associate with it.

A friend of mine who writes for television loves to
illustrate the network mentality with what he calls the
Pumpernickel Analogy. It seems that there are only
three big bakeries in the United States and they all
produce an identical loaf of white bread. And every
year the executives of each bakery hold a meeting, and
the president says, "All right, we've had enough of
this white bread! It's time we gave the American
public something they can sink their teeth into, something with a rich flavor, something with texture and
aroma. By God, let's make a pumpernickel!" At which

point all the other executives jump to their feet and begin to cheer.

Now the president goes out and hires the finest baker in the land, a man who still remembers how to stone-grind grain. At first he refuses; he's worked for the big bakeries before and he knows the frustration involved. They offer him more money and creative control, and finally he agrees.

Six months later the executives meet again and this time a fabulous loaf of pumpernickel sits in the middle of the conference table. "Beautiful! . . . Splendid! . . . Fragrant! . . ." They all congratulate one another. "Now," the president says, "with a couple of minor alterations we'll be ready to market it. First let's get rid of all these seeds. Then we'll need to bleach it a lighter color. And see if we can't soften it up a bit . . ."

Rosenberg stopped in front of a black door with Mabel's name on it and rapped shave-and-a-haircut.

The dressing room was not much bigger than a walk-in closet and sported the same motif of cream-colored cinderblock and hard neon lighting. The furnishings consisted of a couch covered in green corduroy, a small vanity table and makeup mirror bordered with light bulbs, a clothes rack of aluminum tubing upon which hung several costume changes. I also noticed a stuffed panda with "MABEL" embroidered on its belly, a cigar box with press clippings shellacked to the top, a congratulatory telegram from the network president, and a photograph of Mabel Edmonds, a half century younger, standing on the old Santa Monica pier arm-in-arm with Charlie Chaplin in his tramp outfit.

Mabel Edmonds, a half century older, sat at the vanity table wearing a white terry-cloth robe, removing her makeup with cotton balls dipped in cold cream. Where the matting powder had been taken away, the skin looked raw and pink. She was a small woman—petite, I guess you'd say—with delicate features. Her hair was as white as cotton, cut short and curly, and her face was wrinkled like a walnut shell; yet I felt it was nothing more than a mask behind which a little girl was hiding. Occasionally she would flash a smile at me, a smile of heartbreaking charm, a smile of disarming naiveté, a smile I could tell she had practiced for years in front of mirrors and audiences and movie cameras.

"I hope you're not going to ask me to pose nude for the centerfold," she said with a big wink when Rosenberg introduced us. "Fifty years ago," she continued, "I just might have done it." She laughed. "I wish I'd met you then, Mr. Pinkle. I always liked bald men. Max Von Weber, my third husband, he was bald as a baby's bottom. I used to tell him if he polished it, I could use it for a mirror!" She laughed some more, and her laughter was as light as sleigh bells.

Seeing that we were hitting it off together, Rosenberg excused himself and took Alex along to meet Dolores, leaving the two of us alone—alone except for the crew members and fans who stuck their heads in the door every half minute or so to make a joke or compliment Mabel on her performance. Apparently she was everyone's favorite. Finally, harumphing with annoyance—that is, as much annoyance as an actress can summon over being too popular—she locked the

door and the interview proceeded without inter-
ruptions.

"Well, Mr. Pinkle, where shall we begin?"

"Why don't you tell me about the early days in the
movie business?"

"But don't you need a tape recorder or a note pad?"

"It all goes up here," I said, tapping my dome. "I'll
call you to verify any quotes."

She thought about that for a moment; then she smiled
and nodded and began.

"I started to work in the movies in nineteen ten—I
was only fourteen years old!—but I looked like twenty.
A friend of mine introduced me to Mack Sennett, who
was working at the Biograph Studios in New York.
He liked my looks and hired me to play in a comedy
he was directing. I remember, it was called *A Rube
Comes to the Big City*, and it was awful! Mack wanted
to do fast-paced, lively stuff, but Mr. Griffith—he was
running Biograph at the time—Mr. Griffith made
Mack do the old-fashioned-style comedies.

"Finally Mack borrowed some money from his
bookies, and we all took the train out to Los Angeles.
My goodness, how this city has changed! You wouldn't
have recognized it in nineteen twelve, just orange
groves and farms. Mack set up his Keystone Studios
and he was the boss! He made the kind of films he
wanted to and the public loved 'em! You know how
we'd work? He'd be reading the paper and he'd see an
article about a lake being drained. And he'd say, 'You
know, Mabel, wouldn't it be funny if Fatty'—that was
Fatty Arbuckle of course—'wouldn't it be funny if
Fatty dived into a lake and while he was swimming
around, all the water disappeared?'

"And the next thing you know we'd be bouncing along in Mack's Model A, out to that lake where they were going to drain the water. We'd shoot Fatty diving into the lake and swimming around. And then when the lake was emptied, we'd shoot Fatty lying in the mud, trying to swim . . ."

She started to giggle and I could tell she was seeing it all vividly in her mind's eyes.

"Then," she continued, "we'd go back to the studio and make up a story to go around it. Oh, Fatty, he was such a dear, funny man. Dead now, they're all dead. Ford Sterling, Fred Mace. Fatty and Ben and Mack Swain. Charlie Chaplin. He wrote music, did you know? And he was frightfully serious about it. I remember a party at Pickfair when Charlie was playing the piano and Doug Fairbanks came over, roaring drunk, and told him he sounded like—but I'm rambling, aren't I? What was I telling you about? Yes, of course, how we made the movies.

"Well, a lot of it was improvising. If one of us thought of a funny bit during shooting, well, we'd go ahead and do it. It wasn't like now, when every minute of film costs a thousand dollars. We could afford to make mistakes. Everything was so lively! Everybody was experimenting all the time. It was all such fun. I was the first to throw a custard pie, you know. I was doing a scene with Ben Turpin—it needed something to liven it up. So I picked up a custard pie and tossed it in his face . . ."

She was giggling again.

"It seems like yesterday," she mused. "I can't remember what happened ten minutes ago, but those early days are so bright and clear. You know what I

think, Mr. Pinkle? I'm not a religious person, but sometimes I think that life is a circle, that the beginning and
the end are linked together, and as I come closer to
death I am also coming closer to my own birth. Oh,
I know it doesn't make any sense, but it's a feeling I
have. And that's why the old memories are so clear.
I'm glad you're writing this article because once I'm
gone there won't be any more memories of the silent
days. I'm the last of the lot. The last of the dinosaurs."

Her voice trailed off and she seemed to be gazing
into the distance. After a minute or two I said, "Why
don't you tell me something about your first husband,
Lance Carlyle."

"Oh, Lance." She pressed her lips together and shook
her head. "He was the cruelest, most ambitious man
I've ever met. Do you know how people sometimes
pretend to be the opposite of what they are? Well,
Lance seemed to be so mild and sweet. That's why I
married him. We had just begun making movies in
California when Lance came by the studio—of course
his real name wasn't Lance, it was Herman Butsky—
looking for work as an actor. He was a real cowboy,
with muscles out to *here* and that kind, gentle manner
I mentioned. I fell in love with that man the moment
I laid eyes on him. But he was no good. The night of
our marriage I found him with one of the bridesmaids
—my niece, as a matter of fact. Now, I'm no saint—I
had my fun too, but I was always discreet. Lance used
to arrange it so I would catch him in the act, just to
hurt me. He'd pick up a couple of girls and have them
in bed, all drunk and giggling, when I came home from
the studio. He enjoyed humiliating me in public."

"Tell me about the weekend on William Randolph

Hearst's yacht when Lance disappeared with Virginia Nightingale."

She hesitated. "So you want to reopen that old can of worms? Well, why not? We were close friends with William and Marion. He was an oaf, but she was delightful. And I'll tell you something else: She could have been a first-rate comedienne if he had only let her career go its own way. She had a great comic gift and a certain sweetness . . . Well, we would all go weekending on his yacht, and the booze and the drugs would flow, and before you knew it there would be a disaster. Poor Bill Ince, the director, the man who made those marvelous westerns. Charlie Chaplin was—well, I don't know if he was, but he certainly had eyes for Marion. Willy tried to shoot him with a pistol but he hit Bill Ince instead and killed him. That sort of thing happened all the time. We knew it would happen, yet we kept on going.

"Lance had been seeing Virginia Nightingale. In a way they were meant for each other. She was his match in ambition and cruelty—but she was also a very great actress. If you ever have the opportunity, see her in *Blue Violets*. No, they don't show the silents on television, do they? I don't know where you would go to see it. Perhaps at one of those film societies or at UCLA. I remember when I spoke at UCLA a few years ago, they showed some of my early Keystone films. Then they gave me a plaque. If you live long enough, Mr. Pinkle, everybody starts to honor you."

"The weekend on the yacht," I reminded her.

"Yes. Well, I knew Virginia would be on the yacht that weekend, but Lance wanted to go and I agreed because I didn't want to give him the satisfaction of knowing how much he was hurting me. We sailed down past San Diego, down the coast of Baja, and we anchored for the night. The next morning Lance and Virginia were gone along with the dinghy. Frankly, I expected something like that. It wasn't unusual for someone to take a dinghy into shore when the sea was mild, for a picnic or a swim. But then they didn't come back. He had humiliated me so many times before; that was the straw that broke the camel's back. When he turned up in Los Angeles, I sued him for divorce."

"He claimed that Virginia Nightingale drowned when the dinghy capsized, didn't he?"

"He claimed a lot of things," Mabel said.

"You don't think he could have killed her?" I asked.

Perhaps her eyes opened just a hair wider. "He had no reason to," she said. "They were lovers."

"Not unless he was part of the Inner Circle," I said.

That did it. For a full minute she just stared at me, dumbfounded.

"After all these years," she whispered.

"That's right," I said. "They're still around. They murdered Tony Valenti."

She sucked in her breath at the mention of his name. "That wonderful young actor. I thought somehow the chain would break . . ."

"It won't break," I said, "unless you help me break it. What is the Inner Circle?"

"Then you don't know?"

"I know they're conscienceless murderers. I know they span three quarters of a century. I know they have something to do with an Aztec god named Tezcatlipoca."

At the mention of that name her eyes clouded with terror; then a membrane seemed to pass over them, like shades drawn over a murderer's evil deed. Her gaze became opaque, impenetrable.

"What is the Inner Circle?" I pressed, with the terrible, sinking feeling that I had blown my advantage.

"Oh, it's a secret," she said casually. Her manner was light, carefree. She gazed at herself in the mirror, avoiding my eye. "But if you really want to know, I suppose it wouldn't hurt to tell. As long as you promise not to write about it."

I promised. I would have promised anything.

"Do you know how certain unions have burial plans —you put away an amount every month and when you die your funeral and plot are already paid for? Well, the Inner Circle is a sort of burial plan for the stars. But instead of insuring a plot and a pleasant funeral, it insures that you'll look decent when they cart you away. Oh, it's horribly vain, really. That's why no one likes to talk about it. You see, when a member of the Inner Circle dies, Forest Meadows calls in a special embalmer, a master embalmer, a man who will make sure that we're beautiful for our final performance. Actors worry about that. They really do. And that's all the Inner Circle is. As for Aztec gods and conscienceless murderers, well, frankly I don't know what you're talking about. Now, if you have no further questions, I'd like to be left alone. I'm quite tired."

I thanked her, promised to send her a tear sheet of the article—if I ever wrote it, which seemed doubtful —put on my hat and let myself out the door.

"Good night, Miss Edmonds," I said, "and thank you."

She said nothing, she didn't even look up from her makeup mirror, but while I stood out in the corridor, wondering how I would find Alex in this labyrinthine maze, I heard a strange noise from inside. I was about to knock to see if she was all right, since it sounded like she might be choking. Then I realized that it was the sound of an old lady crying.

Rather than try to locate Alex within the building, I decided to go out to the parking lot and take a nap in the back of the Mercedes until he arrived. I seemed to remember his having left it unlocked. A guard directed me to an exit and I found the night air especially cool, the parking lot especially spacious after the dressing room with its tense, oppressive atmosphere. Arc lamps, taller than the maples back East, illuminated the black-top parking area; beyond, the sky was red with reflections of supermarket marquees, or possibly the light from a brushfire. It hadn't rained in weeks.

I didn't have much trouble finding the Mercedes, and it was unlocked. As I opened the door I noticed, out of the corner of my eyes, a dark shape in the back seat.

"Don't make any fast moves," I said. "Come out slowly with your hands up and nobody will get hurt."

"Louis, for shit's sake," the dark shape said. A corner of the shape rolled back—it appeared to be a blanket—and Alex's head popped out. From what I could see, he was naked; his gross form, pink, hairless and covered with rolls of fat, was wedged in beside a fairer one, slim and tan. A rosebud nipple peeked at me from under a corner of the blanket.

"Alex, who's there?" the slim form demanded sleepily. "Make them go away."

With a shock, I recognized the voice. It was Dolores. He had done it; he had seduced the foremost symbol of American purity. The ramifications of this were mind-boggling. If only I could have photographed the event for posterity; but having no camera, I apologized and strolled around the parking lot until they had finished.

"According to Mabel Edmonds," I explained to Alex as he chauffeured me over the Hollywood Hills, weaving his way perilously through the light, late traffic, "the Inner Circle is a burial plan that ensures actors of being beautifully embalmed. That sounds crazy, doesn't it? Wipe that shit-eating grin off your face and pay attention—I need your feedback."

"Sorry," Alex murmured, smirking despite himself.

"When she thought I knew what the Inner Circle was, she wanted to talk about it, as though it were some awful weight on her conscience. Particularly when I told her they murdered Tony Valenti. But when she found out I didn't know, she tried to cover her tracks. She was conflicted; part of her had sworn to keep the Inner Circle secret and part of her wanted to see an end to the killing."

I looked to Alex for a response and he said, in a far-off voice, "It was great. It was just like I always imagined. Better."

"Alex, try to pay attention."

"Remember in high school," he went on dreamily, "there was always one girl, one gorgeous chick who looked like she was made out of porcelain? She was always so neat and pretty and sexy, but she'd never let any guy get past second base with her. And she wore those little sweater sets and there was never a wrinkle in her skirt. And you used to go home and jerk off dreaming of all the sick things you'd like to do to her? Well, tonight I did them all—and I feel terrific!"

He stuck his head out the window and let go with a whoop of joy that left my ears ringing.

"Suppose it really is a burial plan," I said a few minutes later, "—not to have actors beautifully embalmed, but to stop anybody from finding out that they've been poisoned. Mary Spivack said that Rosalee went into convulsions a few hours after Kellerman gave her the injection. I don't know what kind of poison he was using, but when Rosalee died she was grimacing and her hands were like claws."

I illustrated, tensing my hands, curling my fingers.

"Obviously," I continued, "they couldn't bring her into the mortuary looking like that when she was supposed to have died from an overdose of barbiturates. So after Kellerman administered the poison, some friends of his arrived in a phony ambulance and took the body to the master embalmer's house. He made it look like she had died a peaceful death. Then they carted the body over to Forest Meadows for services and burial. They have an arrangement: Forest Meadows knows they'll be getting the body already embalmed; it's a little out of the ordinary, but it's been going on for years and it assures them that the top movie stars will be buried there. Good publicity."

"If Kellerman wants the murder to look like a barbiturate overdose, why doesn't he just shoot her up with barbiturates and save himself the hassle? Why does he use this poison that leaves them looking like they've had a run-in with the Boston Strangler? And what about the death certificates?"

"Well, I don't understand about the poison either. But Kellerman is a psychiatrist, which means he's also an MD, and by California law, if any patient who's currently in his treatment dies, he can write out the death certificate. Nobody else needs to see the body."

"Okay," Alex conceded, "that makes sense for Rosalee Romain, but what about Tony Valenti?"

"Of course I'm just guessing, but—maybe that collision with the concrete piling didn't kill him. Maybe he was still alive when Kellerman came driving up (he'd been following the goons in his own car). Kellerman pretends his arrival is coincidence and pushes his way through the crowd, saying, 'Let me through, I'm a doctor. I may be able to help him.' Tony sees that it's Kellerman and tries to scream for help, but he's only half-conscious and feeling too much pain to be able to express himself coherently. Kellerman reaches for his black bag, takes out a hypo and fills it from a little bottle. The onlookers think it's Adrenalin, but Tony knows it's the poison. He struggles, but he has no strength. Kellerman slips the needle into his arm. The drug takes a while to work, and before he goes into convulsions the ambulance arrives—not a real ambulance, a phony one, complete with phony attendants. They take the body to the embalmer's and from there it becomes worm food."

"I thought these actors were supposed to be sacrifices to that Aztec god, Tez-catty-what's-his-face? You can't sacrifice a body *and* bury it. And why do they use the funny poison?"

"Alex, you're absolutely right. There's only one way we're going to get to the bottom of this. We've got to take Tony Valenti's body to a coroner and find out just what the poison is. There's bound to be traces of it in the tissue. And if we can show that he was poisoned, they'll have to begin an investigation."

"Yeah man, but Tony Valenti's in his final resting place."

"Ever hear of disinterment?"

"I saw a TV show where they tried to get a body disinterred. The cops had to arrange a hearing and convince the judge to give them permission. How are you going to convince a judge when you can't even convince me? It's no good trying to work within the legal system in this country. Justice is for the rich. It's just another product of the capitalist system that gets sold to the highest bidder. Look at Nixon, the biggest crook of them all and he's living like a king in San Clemente. None of these California Republican judges are going to give you permission to dig up Tony Valenti's body."

"Then we'll have to do it ourselves," I said.

Alex turned and stared at me, running the light at the corner of Fairfax and Sunset. Cars screamed to a halt only inches away from us, drivers stuck their heads out the windows, screaming insults.

"Hey man," Alex said slowly, "you don't think I'm going to help you rob a grave . . ."

I smiled.

11
THE GHOULS

Alex picked me up the following day around four and drove me to Carol's apartment in the valley. He waited in the car while I ran inside, since I intended to be only a minute or two.

It was Saturday and all the divorced mothers were sitting by the pool watching their little darlings try to drown each other. Two kids on tricycles tried to run me down as I walked to the stairs.

I rapped on Carol's door and she opened it a minute later and stared at me like I was some stranger.

"Louis," she said. Her voice was flat and her eyes were red.

"Honey, I'm really sorry I haven't called, but I've been so damned busy."

"Have you caught Tony Valenti's murderers?"

"Not yet, but we will! The evidence is piling up so

fast I don't know what to do with it. Yesterday I interviewed an old actress named Mabel Edmonds and she admitted that she knew all about the Inner . . ."

I stopped short, remembering that I had promised to give up the investigation, and I tried to back down.

"Carol, I promise you, I'm not taking any risks. I've changed it around so that ninety percent of the article is a character sketch and ten percent is speculation about his murder . . ."

"Louis . . ."

"And it's not even my main project anymore! I've got two new assignments, a profile of Mabel Edmonds and—"

"Louis . . ."

"—and an article on the van phenomenon and how it's affecting teen-age sexual mores. Now, can you imagine anything safer than that? The worst thing that can happen is I can get arrested for doing too much research on fourteen-year-old chickies . . ."

"Louis!"

"What?"

"I don't care. Do the article. Find out who murdered Tony Valenti." Her voice was quiet and weary.

"You mean that? Seriously? You don't care if I do the article?"

She shook her head. "I've had a lot of time to think this over. And I've decided that you are who you are and a hundred years of my nagging isn't going to change you."

"Hey Carol, that's great, that's really great. Now I've got to run because Alex is waiting down in the car. I wanted to ask you the name of that doctor who's into all the criminal stuff. You remember, the guy in

Watts, the one who sold the cocaine to your friend Alice?"

Carol offered to call Alice to see if the doctor was still in business. While she was in the bedroom phoning, I noticed that she had taken the posters off the walls and emptied the contents of her bookcases into nine or ten cardboard supermarket cartons.

Carol returned to the room. "Here's his name and address," she said, handing me a slip of paper. "Alice said please don't mention her."

"I won't. Hey, what's with the books and the posters?"

"Redecorating."

"Well, thanks again," I said, opening the door.

"Louis . . ."

"What?"

"Nothing. Good luck. And—" She hesitated; then she said quickly, "Knowing you was one of the happiest times of my life"; and she kissed me and shut the door.

I stood on the landing for a minute, trying to figure out what the hell she was talking about; then I shrugged and jogged down the stairs, past the pool and out to the car.

We parked outside the black iron fence that surrounds Forest Meadows cemetery. Through the bars I could see the Memorial Mausoleum, a massive gray building, separated from us by no more than a mile of tombstone-studded greensward. There Tony Valenti slept the final sleep. We would break into his tomb, cut a slice from his liver, then escape across the lawn, climb the fence, return to the car. We would drive the tissue sample to the home of our doctor in Watts; an old, grizzled ex-abortionist, he had supplied me with scalpel and specimen bottle and instructed me on how to locate the organ, how to cut the flesh. Apparently, during embalming, most of the blood was removed from the body and replaced with preservatives. However, any trace of poison, he assured me, would remain in the liver.

But I worried about the fence. It was eight feet high and every bar ended in a sharp little arrowhead.

"Alex," I said, "are you *sure* you can climb it?"

He looked at me disdainfully. "Maybe I put on a little fat around the middle, but I'm still in shape. Look at this."

He made a fist and pulled back the sleeve of his coat. An egg bulged beneath the skin.

"Nice," I said.

We had to walk several blocks to reach the main gate. I told the guard at the kiosk that we were friends of Tony Valenti and we wished to visit his gravesite. He handed me the familiar green map, having first sketched our route in ballpoint pen.

"When you come to the end of Heavenly Rest Drive," he said, "you'll see the Cathédrale de Notre-Dame right across from the Memorial Mausoleum. Ask the guard at the door and he'll direct you further. It's a pretty long walk—don't you want to take your car?"

"We're in it for the exercise," Alex said.

The guard looked curiously at Alex's long leather coat—the temperature was in the upper seventies—shrugged, and wished us a pleasant day.

Alex began to pant and sweat almost immediately. By the time we reached the grand cathedral, perspiration was running down the sides of his neck and he was cursing me under his breath. From the look of his shirt he might have just been swimming. The end of a fine friendship, I thought regretfully. I stepped up to the booth at the entrance to the cathedral and rapped on the glass. The guard was an old-timer with a blotch of purple pigmentation on his face, as though someone had crushed a handful of grapes against his cheek.

"You better hurry along," he said, "if you want to see the Sistine Chapel ceiling."

I explained that we had come to pay our respects to Tony Valenti.

"Go across the drive to the Memorial Mausoleum," he said, "then around to the far side, and take the third entrance on your left. You'll see a little intercom by the door. Press the buzzer and I'll let you inside. You better hurry up, boys, the grounds close at six."

We followed his directions, arriving finally at a peaked oak door set in an alcove in the stone, one of three that penetrated the rear wall of the mausoleum. A small barred window gave a view of a chapel, a long room of white marble, a stained-glass rose window high above.

I pressed the button beneath a perforated speaker plate and the guard's voice came out, tinny and faint:

"*Hello?*"

"We're here."

"*What?*"

"WE'RE HERE!"

"*You the boys I just spoke to?*"

"YES!"

"*All right, I'll buzz you in. When you get inside*

*turn left, walk about forty feet. Mr. Valenti will be
on your right, about waist level. Buzz again when you
leave."*

Buzzing. Alex pushed the door and we stepped inside, letting it close behind us; and all the sounds that
permeate our hearing until we no longer notice them—
the bird whistles, the whining of the crickets, the distant cars and low-flying jets—all those sounds suddenly
ceased, plunging us into a silence so profound that my
nervous stomach sounded like a factory in comparison.

We were standing in the chapel we had viewed
through the door. The rose window reminded me of
the designs I used to make with a compass when I was
a kid. The floor was a darker marble veined in white
and the absence of pews gave the room a peculiar,
half-finished appearance.

Alex started to take off his coat. I told him to wait.
He scowled at me, hiking it back onto his shoulders.

The walls of the hall on the left were massive plates
of bronze into which were set "drawers" containing
the caskets, laid horizontally, feet first, so as to take
up as little space as possible. The drawers appeared
to come in two sizes—two prices, most likely—one
so narrow it hardly seemed possible that a coffin was
squeezed inside, the other, twice as large. Tourist and
First Class. There was row after row of them, all the
way from floor to ceiling. The drawers were bronze
too, with plaques featuring the names and dates of the
deceased, and a little motto like "A beloved father" or
"Always in our memories." The smaller drawers had
one bronze flower vase on a little arm; the larger
drawers, two.

I should mention here, for the benefit of those who

have never visited Forest Meadows, that despite its impressive size, there is a real space problem. You realize this when you notice that outside of the mausoleum they bury people standing up. It makes sense: A reclining body requires at least three feet of width and six feet of length, or eighteen square feet of surface area; a standing body, on the other hand, can make do with three feet by two feet, or six square feet—one third the surface area (although standing up doesn't seem to me a very restful position for eternity).

"Here he is," Alex whispered, leaning over a drawer to read the plaque:

Anthony Valenti

1948–1977

The Angels Shall Guard His Peace

A vase on either side of the plaque held a bouquet of waxy white lilies. Without disturbing the flowers, Alex crouched in front of the drawer, gripped one vase in each hand, and tugged experimentally. The drawer didn't budge.

"Suppose it's welded closed?" he asked.

"Doesn't look welded."

"Suppose it's cemented?"

"It seems to me they'd use something neater, like a hidden bolt or a clip. Do the vases unscrew?"

Alex tried rotating one; he shook his head. He started to take off his coat and I stopped him again.

"But I'm going to pass out," he protested.

"We've got to wait till closing. How would it look if somebody wandered in here and found us hammering away?"

"Why didn't *you* wear the coat?"

"All I've got is a skimpy little ski parka."

"I don't know how you ever talked me into this," Alex grumbled.

"Simple. Despite all your twisted desires for financial and sexual conquest, you cannot stand injustice. You're a champion of the underdog. That's what makes you a beautiful person."

"Hey man, do me a favor? Cut the bullshit—I feel stupid enough."

I checked my watch; ten minutes had passed since we entered the mausoleum. We waited another ten, then we walked to the exit. The door had a working handle on the inside (as the great Houdini once said about safes, the idea was to keep people out, not in). As we stepped into the sunshine, I wedged my toe between the door and frame, keeping it open an inch, and stretched my arm to press the buzzer on the intercom.

"We're through now," I said when the guard answered. "Thank you very much."

But then, instead of leaving, we ducked back into the mausoleum and closed the door behind us.

Just beyond Tony's drawer a small corridor opened to the left; this too was lined with drawers. Since it was out of view of the main corridor, it seemed like a good place to wait. We sat on the cool floor, resting our backs against the wall.

Alex sighed deeply. "*Now* can I take off my coat?"

I nodded.

With visible relief, he stood up and began unbuttoning. He slipped it off, folded it in half and put it down on the marble. He was wearing two belts underneath, one around his waist, the second around his chest. They held in place a four-foot crowbar, a sledgehammer of almost the same length, two chisels and a flashlight. In addition he removed from the pockets of his overcoat the .45-caliber Savage automatic, a bottle of chloroform, some gauze, the scalpel, the specimen bottle, four Milky Way candy bars and a little tin box. He tore the paper off a Milky Way and bit into it; then he removed a joint from the tin box and started to light up.

"Alex!" I hissed and grabbed it out of his mouth.

"Hey, come on! You can steal bodies, why can't I get stoned?"

"For Christ's sake, I am not stealing bodies, and the propriety of the act has nothing to do with it. I just don't want anybody to smell the smoke."

"My head's clearer when I'm stoned."

"Do me a favor? Don't smoke it?"

"All right, all right. What a drag. How long do we have to sit here anyway?"

"The grounds close at six and it's almost six now. We'll wait another hour to determine if there's a guard and how frequently he comes by . . ."

"What if the guard finds us?"

"Then we'll use the chloroform."

"And if that doesn't stop him?" Alex asked.

"Then we've got your forty-five."

"I never shot anything bigger than a beer can with that gun and I'm not going to start now."

"We'll threaten him with it."

"What if he threatens back?"

"Alex, relax."

"I'm trying."

"Tell me about Dolores Wintergreen," I said, to take his mind off where we were and what we were doing.

"She wants to see me again." He grinned, his gold tooth flashing. "Her husband's some big-time movie producer. He's going to London on a midnight flight tonight. She's got to drive him to the airport but she wants me to meet her afterward. I told her I had to help out a buddy, but I'd give her a call when I got done."

"Such loyalty. We'll be out by eight, I swear it."

"We better be. I'll tell you man, she's got the nicest little . . . what the hell?"

Quite suddenly the lights went out. The blackness was so complete that I couldn't see Alex, who was sitting less than three feet away from me.

"Don't worry," I said, "they probably turn them off at closing to save power."

"Who's worried? I'm not worried. I dig it, being stuck in the dark with a thousand dead millionaires and one living lunatic. Where's the flashlight?"

"Leave it off, someone will see."

So we sat there in the dark and the only thing I could perceive was the glowing green dots on my wristwatch, counting away the minutes until we could begin to open Tony Valenti's tomb. Now, for a while I must admit I was uneasy. All the nightmares of my childhood came back to me, all the ghost stories from summer camp, all the Poe tales of people buried alive, all the Sunday afternoon horror movies about corpses rising from the grave, skin peeling from their ivory skulls, eyeballs hanging by a thread from the sockets. But after a time all the old fears went away and it occurred to me that a dead body was nothing but compost. What made flesh into a man had departed and what was left was no more than a few dollars' worth of chemicals. What remained frightening, though, was the veneration given the body after death: the massive stone tomb, the bronze walls and drawers, the zinc-lined mahogany coffins. The relatives returning to leave flowers year after year—did that really help keep the memory alive? Or did it exchange the memories of a living, breathing human being, with all his foibles and ticks and eccentricities, for the memories of these oversized safe-deposit boxes with their rotting contents? Wouldn't it be better, instead of visiting the grave, to look through a photo album or go to a place they and the deceased often visited together?

A friend of mine, a Zen Buddhist screenwriter—one of the best in Hollywood—has made this peculiar provision in his will: In lieu of a funeral, his business manager is to arrange dinners for all his friends at the very best restaurants; during these dinners the friends are to reminisce about him, toast him and tell funny stories about him while they get totally sloshed on Dom Perignon.

"Alex," I said, "if something happens to me tonight, will you make sure that I'm cremated?"

"Sure. What should I do with the ashes?"

I thought about that for a minute.

"Smoke them."

At seven o'clock I roused Alex and we went to work. I turned on the flashlight and propped it in the corner so it illuminated Tony's drawer like a tiny klieg light. Then we tried pulling the drawer out with our hands.

I took one vase, Alex took the other, we braced our feet against the wall and we tugged in unison. Nothing. We tried again and again; the drawer was steadfast. I was reluctant to use the tools for fear of defacing the bronze and leaving clues of our visit, but I had no choice. I fitted the claw of the crowbar into the crack between the drawer and the wall and leaned against it with all my weight. Nothing. Alex added his weight, a considerable amount. Now, the power of the lever is not to be underestimated. A four-foot crowbar will open almost anything. As Archimedes said, "Give me a fulcrum and a lever long enough and I will move the Earth." But all those Greeks were big talkers.

I put down the crowbar and wedged the smaller of the two chisels into the crack.

"Hold it in place," I said to Alex, "while I get the sledgehammer."

But he pulled away his hand when I lifted the over-sized mallet in the air.

"I won't hit your fingers," I said. "Promise."

"Why don't *you* hold it and I'll hammer?"

"Alex!"

"All right, all right."

I raised the mallet again and brought it down squarely on the head of the chisel. The entire bronze wall reverberated like a Chinese gong. It was literally enough to wake the dead. We grabbed up all our tools, hurried back to our hiding place in the small corridor and crouched there, hardly daring to breathe for fifteen minutes while we waited to see if anyone would come to investigate.

"You know what I think?" I whispered. "I think

this place is soundproofed. Remember how quiet it got when I closed the door?"

"Hey Louis, let's get out of here, huh? We can go up to my place and get stoned and watch Johnny Carson. I got a homemade blueberry pie in the fridge. You can stay when I go to pick up Dolores."

"I'd be delighted—just as soon as we pry open this drawer."

I was happy to see that the small chisel had widened the crack a millimeter or two, room enough to substitute the larger chisel. I hit it a thunderous blow and the crack opened even more, nearly a quarter of an inch. But then, hammer as I might, the crack would grow no wider.

"We've got to use both chisels at once," I told Alex.

He put the two of them in place, holding the handles level (although the heads were different widths, they were about the same length); but this time when I lowered the hammer I knocked the chisels out of the crack and nearly crushed Alex's hand.

"Oh my God, I'm sorry," I said, "are you all right?"

"Ohhhhhh," he groaned, holding his pinkie, rocking back and forth.

"Let me take a look." I knelt beside him and pried open his hand. "There's nothing wrong with your hand."

He shrugged. "You can't blame a guy for trying."

Soon he had the two chisels back in place. I swung the hammer with all my might, and something went "*Twaaaaang!*" like a tuning fork being cracked in half, and the drawer slid open half a foot.

Alex gripped one vase, I took the other, and together we pulled. Inch by inch the drawer came out of the wall, the squeal of metal against metal raising the hair on the back of my neck. Soon we could see the dull-gold coffin in the beam of the flashlight. Now the drawer protruded seven feet into the corridor and the coffin was entirely exposed.

I reached for the lid.

"Tell me when it's over," Alex said, covering his eyes with his hands.

I took a deep breath and lifted it. The lid was heavy, smoothly hinged, held closed by nothing more than its own weight.

"Well?" Alex said after a minute.

"Take a look. There's something weird going on here."

Alex made a space between his fingers and peeked. Then he took his hands away from his face. Then he took the flashlight off the floor and shined it directly at the body.

"I don't get it," he said. "Shouldn't there be some rot or something? I mean, shouldn't it smell? The skin looks perfect. It looks like . . ."

I knew what he was going to say because I was thinking the same thing. I gouged Tony Valenti's cheek with the point of the chisel and the skin came off easily, leaving a notch with a texture like the inside of an apple. I rubbed some of what I had removed between my fingers, feeling the consistency.

"*Wax.*"

Gingerly Alex reached out and touched the skin too. He scraped a hole in Tony's hand with his fingernail, rolled the scraping into a ball and sniffed it.

"I'll be damned," he muttered. "Why would they want to bury a wax dummy?"

"Because—" I tried to think, but my mind was half frozen with shock. Then, one by one, the conclusions started coming, like tumblers falling into place. "Because they needed his body for something else—for the sacrifice to Tezcatlipoca! Sure, that explains it, that's why Kellerman gave them a special drug."

"Why?"

"To make it look like they were dead. Slow down the heartbeat and breathing, lower the body temperature. *Catatonia*, it's called. They took the real body away in an ambulance and they brought back one of Grimmer's wax dummies."

"Remember what Ruckhauser said about those Aztec sacrifices? They liked to tear the hearts out of *living* people."

"Living sacrifices . . ." I murmured.

"That's right, keep him alive until the time comes. You see what I mean? Tony Valenti might still be . . ."

"He might still be alive!"

"Exactly." The revelations were making Alex feverish. "But where have the bastards got him?"

"At Kellerman's house? Rubin's house?"

"Too dangerous," Alex said.

"At their offices?"

"That's worse."

"You're right. They must have rented a place somewhere— Oh no, I've got it: the door in Grimmer's workshop. He panicked when Perez wanted to go in there. Sure, that's it. Dear God, I hope we're not too late."

Quickly we closed the coffin, slid the drawer back in place, belted the tools under Alex's overcoat—all except the flashlight, which we kept to find our way in the dark—and filled his pockets with the remaining paraphernalia, including various Milky Way wrappers with which he had littered the floor.

Cloaked by a moonless night, we jogged silently down Mausoleum Slope. We had gone no more than a hundred yards when we saw a flashlight beam round the corner of the cathedral some distance ahead.

"Alex!" I hissed, beckoning for him to follow. We crouched behind a large gravestone near the side of the road and waited in silence. Gradually the flashlight came closer. Soon we could make out the details of the figure, a security guard, a fellow of at least seventy. In his right hand he held what appeared to be a bottle of Scotch, and his weaving step confirmed the identity of the liquid. When he was closer we could hear him singing:

> *You take the high road,*
> *And I'll take the low road,*
> *And I'll be in Scotland before ye . . .*

I glanced at Alex and saw that he was holding the Savage in his right hand, raising it to eye level.

"Alex, don't!" I hissed.

"Of course not," he whispered. His voice grew distant. "I was just wondering how it would feel." Then: "Give me a hand."

To my relief he tucked the Savage under his belt. He took off the leather coat and turned it inside out so the quilted red-silk lining was showing; then he put the coat back on, backward, like a strait jacket. He inserted the flashlight into the collar so the beam of light illuminated his face from the bottom, giving it an eerie, ghoulish quality which he enhanced by baring his lower teeth.

When the guard was no more than ten feet away, Alex stepped out from behind the tombstone, staggering stiff-limbed, groaning and growling in a low animal voice. The guard stood facing him for a moment, his mouth half opened, jaw slack, eyes glazed; then the poor man turned and ran and ran and we made our way to the fence, and Alex's Mercedes parked beyond it, without further incident.

The ticket booth at the Burbank Wax Museum was empty, the neon sign was dark, and Charlie's Angels were only shadows in the light from the street lamp; yet the front gate had been left open. Alex and I leaped over the turnstile and ran silently through the lobby on the balls of our feet. It was difficult to see our way in the darkness but after a time our eyes adjusted and the pale-red lights of the exit signs were like beacons. Figures seemed to leap at us every time we turned a corner, wax figures brought to life by our excited imaginations and raw-edged nerves. We crept up the stairway to the right of the Beatles and at the top we crouched by the door, listening. Silence, dead silence.

Alex pulled the huge .45 Savage out of his belt. "Ready?" he whispered to me, and then he leaped forward and kicked at the door. It opened, revealing the workroom empty, the gaudy crystal chandelier blazing light. We entered the room tentatively, Alex holding the revolver at his waist, sweeping the barrel back and forth. The tension was palpable.

"What the hell?" he whispered.

"Look . . ." I said. The red indicator light at the bottom of the coffee urn was shining. A plaster mold lay open on the table nearby, the inside surfaces dark with shellac, and right beside it I saw the head of Jimmy Carter, hairless and pink and empty-eyed, still fresh from the pouring.

"Somebody's here," I whispered.

"Look . . ."

From beneath the corner door came a trickle of blood, a black stream that seeped between the floorboards. *Tony's blood*, I thought with a sinking heart. We were too late. But then Alex threw open the door and I saw that it wasn't Tony's blood after all.

The door led to a storage room with shelves along each wall, rows of chemicals in gallon cans, slabs of beeswax, rags and paints and piles of pornographic magazines. The room smelled of turpentine and dust and death. There was a folding card table with a half-eaten sandwich in a nest of wax paper, and three folding chairs. And there was a man lying on the floor, curled up like a bundle of old clothes, arms crossed over the deep wound in his stomach as if to stem the awful tide of blood. I knelt beside him and lifted his head by the chin. I looked at his face and experienced an awful sadness and disgust at human life so capriciously wasted, a feeling like a rock in the pit of my stomach. I wanted to be away from here, I wanted to be with Carol in Toluca Lake, making love and having babies and affirming life.

It was Perez.

His breath made a gurgling sound. His eyes opened and he squinted at me.

"Louis?"

"Christ I'm sorry," I whispered. "I'm sorry I dragged you into this."

"I'm a cop," he said, as if that were sufficient explanation for everything. "I came back with a warrant . . . to find out what was in the room. Tony Valenti . . ."

"Forget it. Save your strength."

"No, I've got to tell you. Tony Valenti is . . . he's still alive. I was humoring you. I thought you were crazy but . . . you were right. They had him locked up here. They took him to the airport, to Van Nuys . . ."

"There's no airport in Van Nuys."

"Yes there is," Alex said. "It's noncommercial. That's where I keep my plane."

"Yes, a private plane." Perez gagged and a bubble of blood formed at his lips. I wiped his mouth with my shirt-sleeve.

"Did they say where they were going?"

"San . . ." The gurgling in his throat grew worse. "San Ignacio."

"That's in Baja," Alex said, "near Guerrero Negro. I've flown over it. How long ago did they leave?"

"Minutes . . ."

"Hush," I said, "we're going to call an ambulance."

"Too late," Perez gasped, grabbing my arm as I rose. "Louis? Thanks—for the stories."

"Thank *you*. They were terrific stories and you're going to write a lot more."

"No. Tell Sandy I love her."

"Who's Sandy?" Alex whispered.

"I don't know. His wife?"

Another bubble of blood formed over his lips and he started to choke. It was mercifully fast; a spasm passed through his body, and then another, and then he was still. I closed his eyelids while Alex phoned for an ambulance. When he hung up he said, "Let's go. If we move fast we can catch them."

"What are you talking about?"

"We've got to get those bastards."

"Alex," I said patiently, "they've flown away in an airplane. What are we going to do, follow them in a car?"

"No man, we're going to get in my plane and fly them down."

The thought had never crossed my mind. "Really? Can we do that? I mean, don't you have to have the plane prepared. Preflight checkout and stuff like that?"

"Not if you're in a hurry," Alex said, dragging me to the door, "and you're willing to take a little risk."

"A little risk?"

"Come on, man!"

I took a last look at Perez, whose life I had glimpsed like a window seen from a passing train. *Tell Sandy I love her.* Was that his wife whose mother cooked the fabulous Jewish banquets? Or was it some secretary at the station house? Even the hearts of our closest friends are secret to us.

Alex and I started for the door and stopped short. Billy Chou and Frank Pollacek were blocking our way.

"Nice to see you again, Baldy," Pollacek said, opening his switchblade.

Alex went for the .45 tucked under his belt, but Billy Chou saw the move and knocked the gun out of his hand. That same instant I made a grab for Pollacek's knife. He held on tight, and we fought over it, circling around and around in a funny, nervous kind of waltz. Pollacek was wiry but strong; I outweighed him, but I hadn't been in a fight since I was a kid: I didn't know the moves. He forced me down on my knees and pushed me toward the table where the hot coffee urn was bubbling its waxy brew. When he had my head under the spigot, he turned the valve. I squirmed out of the way, getting just a few drops on my shoulder—they stung like hell—and rolled onto my back, kicking him in the shins until he fell. Then I jumped to my feet, grabbed a plaster leg out of one of the bins and, before he could get his bearings, clobbered him with it. He staggered like a drunk.

Behind me Alex and Chou were circling the gun on the floor, each waiting for the other to make a move. I broke the stalemate—and the leg—by smashing it over Chou's head. Alex leaped for the gun, but Chou was hardly stunned; the guy had amazing stamina. He kicked the gun out of Alex's hand so it slid across the floor and under one of the bins. Then he leaped on top of Alex and they rolled away, wrestling.

I turned back just in time to see Pollacek come at me with the switchblade. I grabbed the bust of Jimmy Carter off the work table and held it over my heart, and he sunk the blade into the president's smiling mouth, where it struck. Then I let go and while he was shaking the knife, trying to free the blade, I kicked him in the groin, hard enough to get even for the time he'd done the same to me. With him doubled over, it was easy to remove the knife from his grip, but I couldn't get the wax head off it either. While I was trying, Pollacek's hand hit my chest like a piston; his other hand grabbed the knife handle which suddenly came free, throwing him off balance. He staggered backward, twisted and fell over, his arm under him. I waited a second for him to get up again but he didn't. I rolled him over with my foot and I saw the knife sticking out from between his ribs.

Chou was on top of Alex, banging his head against the floor. I jumped on the Oriental and tightened my fingers around his throat, but he didn't seem to notice. When I started punching him in the back of the neck with both fists, he just picked me off with one hand, flung me across the room and went back to murdering Alex. Alex's face was blue and his cheeks were puffed out, and I knew I had better do something fast if I wanted to see him walk out of there alive.

So this time I grabbed both of Chou's ears—it was hard to get a hold on the right one—and twisted as hard as I could. He howled with pain and, lumbering to his feet, started after me, his eyes red with rage, his fingers grasping and closing. I ran to the other end of the room. No help from Alex—he was rolling on the floor, gasping like a fish on land. My hands reached for anything and seized on a box of imported eyeballs. Opening it, I scattered the eyeballs on the floor. They rolled away like oversized marbles. Then I dumped a second box and a third. The floor was covered with eyeballs. Chou stepped on one and started to slide. He skated across them, his feet slipping out from under him, falling one moment, regaining his balance the next. His weight collided with the table holding the coffee urn and the table overturned; Chou fell and the coffee urn fell on top of him, covering him with hot wax. The shrieks of pain made my hair stand on end. Meanwhile I could hear ambulance sirens coming closer and closer. I helped Alex to his feet and led him toward the rear exit.

"Wait . . ." he said.

"For God's sake, they're going to be here any second!"

But he broke away from me and, staggering to one of the bins, pushed it aside. The bin rolled easily—it had wheels on the bottom—and there was the .45 automatic where Chou had kicked it during the scuffle. Alex stuck it into his belt and we made for the exit just as footsteps were sounding below.

"You don't look so good, buddy," Alex said as he steered the Mercedes through the streets of Burbank.

"I never saw anybody murdered before. Except on the tube, and there it always looks so clean and simple. They don't bleed much, they don't make those awful sounds. And no matter how good the story is, in the back of your mind you always know that once the director shouts 'Cut,' those corpses are going to get to their feet, brush off their pants, and have a cup of coffee and a smoke. Not Perez, though. He's gone for good. You would have liked him, Alex."

"I like anybody you like. What about the guy who runs the museum? What do you think happened to him?"

"Grimmer? He probably took off after Perez got suspicious. Changed his name, left LA. I suspect that in a couple of months a new wax museum will open somewhere in Southern California or maybe Nevada this time. And it will stay open, even if business is rotten, because it'll be subsidized by an organization called the Inner Circle. Hey, where are you going?"

Alex had turned north onto the San Diego Freeway.

"To the airport," he said.

"You're not still serious about flying to Mexico?"

"Now more than ever, man."

"But what about your head?"

There was a lump the size of a pigeon's egg on the back of his cranium and red finger marks on his neck. Furthermore his voice sounded raspy and constrained, as if his larnyx had been damaged. But no matter how hard I pressed, Alex refused to go to the hospital.

"This is all the medication I need," he said, opening a little tin box he was carrying in his pocket. He took out a flat joint wrapped in wheat straw, pushed in the cigarette lighter and grinned at me. One gold tooth gleamed madly in the beam of a passing headlight.

"You can't get stoned now—not if you're going to fly!"

"Why the hell not? I always fly stoned. I do everything stoned. It clears my head."

"Yeah, but flying . . ."

"Listen man, I'm rich and happy and I get all the pussy I ever wanted. *You*—you hardly ever smoke grass and you're broke and miserable and so busy running around you never get a chance to screw." He lit up, took a deep drag and exhaled, coughing violently. When he had recovered he said, "Shit, that reminds me. My rendezvous with Dolores—I'm not going to make it." He looked at the dashboard clock. "Nine-o-five, too early to call—her husband will still be home. She's going to think I forgot. Now how the hell can I reach her?"

I thought about it for a minute and then I suggested calling Carol. He could leave a message with her and she would relay it to Dolores later, after the husband in question had left for London (we would meanwhile be incommunicado in the air or, more likely I feared, in the ground). Good old Carol, she never minded doing these little favors.

Alex approved. He picked up the phone bolted onto the transmission hump and gave the radio operator Carol's number. It took about a minute for the call to go through. I watched with amazement, wondering how anybody who has just had his head smacked against a wooden floor at least ten times could simultaneously drive on a Los Angeles freeway, smoke a joint and carry on a coherent telephone conversation. When he had finished explaining the message to Carol, he waved the receiver at me and said, "She wants to talk to you."

I took the phone. "Hello?"

"Louis? Listen, I was having dinner and the doorbell rang and it was a chauffeur and he gave me an envelope. It has your name on it. He said it was from Mabel Edwards—"

"Mabel Edmonds?"

"That's right. And he said it was urgent that you read it immediately. I don't know what's in it, but it's pretty thick. I thought it might be a script they want you to rewrite . . ."

"Carol, do me a favor?" It felt weird, talking on the telephone in a speeding car. "Open the envelope, read it to me. If this is what I think it is, it could be the key to everything."

"All right, hold on." She was gone a minute. "Now let's see . . . it's not a script, it's a letter. First there's the date—today's date—and then it starts: 'Dear Mr. Pinkle, When I spoke to you yesterday it reopened wounds which I prayed had healed forever. All night long I lay awake struggling with my conscience. Dean Jamison and Rosalee Romain and all the rest came to my bedside. The voices of all those dear dead actors called to me. They told me I must make a clean breast of it. And so I have put down the whole story here on paper for you. This is the truth and you must believe it no matter how amazing and astounding it may sound. . . .' "

"Go on."

"Louis, it's twenty pages! I'm not going to sit here and read the entire thing to you over the telephone. I've got things to do."

"Carol, please, it's a matter of life and death."

"It's always a matter of life and death with you."

"Listen, don't go anywhere. We'll be there in twenty minutes."

"Fifteen," Alex interjected.

"Fifteen," I said.

She sighed. "Oh, all right."

"Thanks, honey," I said, "you're a sweetheart," and hung up.

Alex was grumbling. "Shit, it's going to be awful hard catching those fuckers if we lose another half hour."

"I know, but we've got to do it. This letter is the key."

"You're the boss."

There was a space in the concrete road divider, the kind left for roadwork, a space hardly wide enough for a car. The NO U-TURN sign seemed unnecessary.

Alex looked quickly right and left. He stood on the brakes and wheeled the car around and slipped it neatly through that space in the road divider without letting our speed drop below forty.

"You're crazy," I said.

"I'm not crazy, I'm an anarchist."

"Then you're a crazy anarchist."

"That might be," he admitted.

12
THE FLYBOYS

I opened the wrought-iron gate and jogged across the courtyard of Carol's apartment building. The pool was still and smooth, illuminated by one underwater floodlight, and skateboards and tricycles lay abandoned on the pink concrete apron. As I ran up the stairs I could hear television shows, one fading into the next.

I rang Carol's door bell and impatiently rang again.

"All *right*!" she snapped, opening it almost instantly. Her expression softened when she saw me. She was wearing a red kimono which set off her blond hair, and slippers with bunnies on them. She handed me the letter, a small pink envelope bulging with pages.

"I hope it's everything you want, Louis."

"This has got to be the key to it all, I'm positive. Hey, what are those for?"

Three suitcases were lined up near the door.

"I'm going on a little trip."

"Not too far away, I hope. I want you to be here when I get back from Mexico so I can explain this whole crazy thing to you. Carol, you wouldn't believe what's going on! When I'm done with this, I'll be the most famous journalist in the country. But there's no time to talk now, got to run . . ."

I kissed her quickly and raced down the stairs.

Van Nuys Airport appeared on our left, bounded by a tall playground fence. Spotlights picked up hundreds of small planes parked in tidy rows along the edge of the runway. I also noticed some big-bodied planes that looked like converted army trainers, and a row of huge cargo planes still wearing the harlequin camouflage of World War II. After we passed a hanger with "Great Atlantic and Pacific Airplane Company" written on the side in stylish art-deco lettering, Alex drove through a gate, into a parking lot. I thought he'd stop there but instead he kept on going, out onto the airfield, down the aisle between the planes, finally parking beside a neat black and silver twin-engine craft. He jumped out of the car, ran over to the plane, and immediately began opening the various gas caps—that's what he told me they were—and sticking his hand into the tanks to determine whether we had enough fuel. It seemed like a very unsophisticated technique, but he swore that was how you did it. There were four tanks, a pod-shaped one attached to the end of each wing, and another inside each wing, enough gas to take us all the way to San Ignacio according to Alex. The news didn't impress me. I had come to grips with the fact that I was going to die. I was going up in an airplane—a very pretty airplane, granted, all streamlined and shiny—but an airplane not much larger than a Volkswagen with two surfboards sticking out of the windows, an airplane that was to be piloted by a drug-crazed, overweight Marxist whose idea of caution was to honk loudly before running a red light.

Now he was unfastening the chains that anchored the airplane to the runway, one under each wing, one under the tail. Now he was removing the "chocks"— prism-shaped blocks of wood that stopped the wheels from rolling—and now he was climbing up on the right wing, opening the door and slipping inside, beckoning for me to follow. Despite his weight, he moved as gracefully as a ballet dancer. When I stepped on the wing I could feel the plane rock; this was no 747. I was sure my foot would rip right through it.

"Come on," Alex shouted from inside the cabin, "what are you waiting for?"

I climbed into the seat next to him and fastened my seat belt.

"What's the movie?" I said.

Alex grinned. "We'll have enough to keep us busy."

The cabin was too low for standing and barely wide enough for two to sit abreast, although there were seats for additional passengers behind us. Four very small, very brave additional passengers.

Alex had a notebook open on his lap, and he was running his finger down some sort of checklist, pausing now and then to adjust a dial or pull a lever on one of the thousands of clock-faced instruments recessed into the black, crinkled panel before him.

Presently he reached across my lap to slam my door and latch it; then he opened a little window on his left and shouted, "CLEAR!" He pushed buttons and pulled levers until the left engine sputtered and caught, then he did the same with the right. The whole plane was shaking and the noise hurt my ears.

Then we started to roll.

"What about the radio?" I said. "Don't you have to call the tower and request permission and all that?"

"Not if you want to get off the ground fast."

"But how do we know we're not going to crash into another plane?" I asked with mounting anxiety.

He gestured at the windshield, at the floodlighted airstrip, the big yellow lines and numbers vanishing beneath our wheels.

"You see any other airplanes?"

"No . . ."

"All right."

"But what about a plane coming from behind us?"

"He'll see us."

"In the dark?"

"We've got navigational lights."

"But what if he's coming in on top of us?"

"Listen man," Alex began, trying to keep his temper, "if you're changing your mind, tell me now because in a minute we're going to be *up there* and you're going to be stuck *in here*. Otherwise you've got to trust in the Kotsky aviatory skills and stop hocking me. There's one thing worse than a backseat driver, it's a backseat flyer, dig?"

"Dig," I said quietly.

"Good," he said and pulled back the throttles between our chairs. The engine noise swelled, the plane jumped forward, and the next moment we rose off the runway into the night sky, into a quiet, dark world where the lights of the valley sparkled like dewdrops on spiderwebs and matters like eviction seemed a million miles away.

"You know," I said after a minute, "this isn't bad."

"Are you kidding? It's great! Night-flying is the best."

He got the weather on the radio: clear all night with five-mile-an-hour winds. At least that's what he claimed they said; it sounded to me like the barnyard at feeding time.

From the upper corner of the window I could see a crescent moon and hundreds of stars that were usually overwhelmed by the city lights. I felt a profound peacefulness at being so high above the world, so far from the day-to-day scrounging that passed as my life.

When I looked back at Alex he was holding the U-shaped steering wheel with his fingertips, his eyes transfixed by the hundreds of instrument needles within their glass cases. The way he reached out to make minor adjustments reminded me of a piano tuner bringing an instrument to preconcert perfection. Presently he let go of the wheel, turned to me, grinning, held his palms up and said, "Look ma, no hands."

"Alex," I screamed, "this is no time to play games, hold the wheel, please . . ."

"It's okay, it's okay. Automatic pilot."

He showed me a square of instruments set into the center of the panel, which he claimed would keep the plane flying level and on course for as long as he liked; however, this did little to allay my anxieties. If anything, the sight of the steering wheel turning gently with no hands on it made me even more nervous. Now Alex spread out a map on his lap and started drawing in a course with pencil and ruler. I recognized the landmass as the Baja peninsula, the southernmost tip of the western coastline (if Italy is a boot, then Baja is a ballerina on toe).

"Here's San Ignacio," he said, pointing to an inland star just above the ballerina's arch. "It's about six hundred miles from LA. They've got half an hour headstart, maybe less if they went through the whole preflight and a wait for runway clearance. They didn't know anybody was going to be following them, so they didn't have any reason to hurry. We should catch up with them in . . ." Alex started to calculate.

"What if they have a faster plane?" I interrupted.

"Well, there aren't any landing strips around San Ignacio, so they probably use a cleared-off field, in which case they'll be flying a plane that doesn't need too much runway. And they don't want to attract too much attention when they run the border."

"Wait a minute! What do you mean 'run the border'?"

"Fly over the border into Mexico without stopping for customs and immigration. They can't stop if they've got Tony Valenti in the plane, can they? So instead they switch off the navigation lights and cruise across nice and low so the radar won't pick them up."

"Radar?"

"Hey man, will you stop worrying? I used to do it all the time when I was smuggling grass up from Acapulco. It's perfectly safe, except for the pursuit planes."

"What pursuit planes?"

"Oh, they've got souped-up P–Fifty-ones that come after you with machine guns and rockets—but that's only if they pick you up on radar. I'm telling you, I've run the border fifty times and they never caught me. The trick is to find a canyon and fly right down inside it." His right hand swooped like a bird.

"*Inside it?*"

"Look man, it's perfectly okay. That part's a piece of cake. The dangerous thing is going to be landing in that rough terrain."

"What rough terrain?"

"There are canyons and mesas all around San Ignacio, and three big volcanoes, Las Tres Virgenes. It's hard to judge just how high those mountains are. On a dark night like this a little mistake and . . ." He made a mountainside with his left palm and flew his right fist into it. "*KA-BOOM!* Hey, you know you're still a little pale."

"I'm fine," I said and took a few deep breaths. "You were explaining how we were going to catch them."

"Right. So I figure they're probably flying a light-weight twin-engine job, either a Beechcraft Baron, an Aztec or a Cessna Three ten. This is a Cessna Three twenty which is just an old version of the Three ten. The Baron's a little faster and the Aztec's a little slower. Chances are they're flying a Cessna just like this one—it's a very popular plane—with a comfortable cruising speed of two hundred. Now, we go up where the air's nice and thin, about twenty thousand feet, and we'll be able to squeeze out another fifty miles an hour—more if we luck into a tail wind. If they started a half hour before us then we should overtake them in, oh, I'd say two and a half hours."

"Alex, you amaze me. I never realized you were so knowledgeable about flying."

"I'm a many-faceted person, man."

"But there's still one thing I don't understand. Even if we catch up with them, how are we going to find them? The sky's such a big place . . ."

"Navigation lights. On a clear night like this we'll see lights from fifty miles, a hundred-mile radius. Maybe more since there aren't any surface lights to interfere."

"When we see the lights, how will we know it's them?"

"How many small planes do you think will be flying over a tiny town like San Ignacio at midnight?"

"Not many."

"Damn right. Now read me the letter."

"Oh my God, that's right!" In my excitement I had forgotten entirely about the letter from Mabel Edmonds. I took out the envelope and removed about twenty pages of pink onionskin written on with lavender ink in a flowing hand. I cleared my throat and began:

> *"Dear Mr. Pinkle,*
>
> *When I spoke to you yesterday it reopened wounds which I prayed had healed forever. All night long I lay awake struggling with my conscience. Dean Jamison and Rosalee Romain and all the rest came to my bedside. The voices of all those dear dead actors called to me. They told me I must make a clean breast of it. And so I have put down the whole story here on paper for you. This*

*is the truth and you must believe it, no matter
how amazing and astounding it may sound.*

*Soon after Mack Sennett brought us out to Los
Angeles to make movies, I met my first husband
Lance Carlyle. I told you that in my interview
but I thought I would repeat it to make the story
complete. I also told you that Lance was cruel and
ambitious. Well, he was. When he started acting
in movies he was earning three fifty a day and I
was earning five dollars! But back in those days
eight fifty a day was enough to live in comfort,
hard as that may be to believe now when a quart
of milk costs me fifty-two cents!*

*Lance was greedy and lazy and always thinking
up get-rich schemes. Around the time he came to
Keystone, there was a half-Mexican named Harry
Mateos also working there as a gaffer. Lance and
Harry used to play cards between takes and that
was how they became friends. Harry was not such
a prize either, cursing and drinking as he did.
Furthermore he had a glass eye that made it look
like he was always watching you out of the corner
of his eye, and gave him a particularly 'sneaky'
expression.*

*Harry told Lance that he had a map which his
great-grandfather had given to his grandfather
and his grandfather to his father, and so on until
it had come into Harry's hands. It was a map of
Baja California that purported to show the loca-
tion of the Misión San Juan Bautista, one of the
'lost' missions of the Jesuits. The King of Spain
had ordered all the Jesuits out of Mexico in*

seventeen sixty-seven, believing that they were planning to overthrow the government and put themselves in charge. A few years earlier the Jesuits, sensing something was in the air, made fifty Yaqui Indians gather gold and jewels from churches all over the gulf and bring them to the Misión San Juan Bautista, which was hidden in a mountainside somewhere near the three volcanoes known as Las Tres Virgenes. That was the explanation in a book I got from the library.

Such an opportunity for riches without lifting a finger was irresistible to Lance. He talked me into financing the adventure with all my savings plus what little my dear mother had left me, may she rest in peace. The three of us, Lance, Harry, and myself, set out on a steamship to Guerrero Negro, the nearest port where the captain would agree to put us ashore. We were so full of excitement at the beginning. Every night after dinner we planned how we would spend all the money on swell estates and motor cars and fancy gowns for myself. At Guerrero Negro one of the barges that brought the salt to the steamships took us ashore."

"Guerrero Negro's where the salt beds are," Alex interjected. "They used to have barges going back and forth from the salt beds to the big steamers."

"Interesting," I said and continued to read:

"We bought some burros and supplies and hired an Indian guide to help us search for the lost mission. In case you forget and think it foolish for

*two young actors, mere children in fact, to trek
into the Mexican wilderness, remember that Lance
was a cowboy. He had grown up on a cattle ranch
in Nevada and he was all steel and leather. He
could wrestle a calf to the ground and tie its legs
in less time than another man would spend tying
a necktie. And so I felt safe riding by his side,
despite the hostile desert terrain and the warnings
we had received regarding 'banditos.'*

*We rode four days by burro before we reached
the town of San Ignacio where we bought more
supplies, jerky and hardtack and coffee. Lance and
Harry got drunk and I visited the mission to pray.
The next day we set out for Las Tres Virgenes,
where the map said we would find the lost mission.*

*The flat desert with its scrub brush and cactus
gave way to a rugged terrain of mesas and canyons.
One of our burros twisted an ankle and it took us
a whole day and a half to reach the volcanoes. I
don't know how many times we aligned the compass points and paced off the distances on the map,
but we could not find one trace of the lost Misión
San Juan Bautista. Perhaps a rock slide covered
it or some other Act of God was responsible for
its disappearance. We did find something else,
however. What we found was a pyramid of stone
twenty feet high, with a flat top. Our ignorant
Indian guide was frightened and would not go
near, but Lance and Harry and I climbed to the
top. There we found many strange pictures
painted on the stone. We decided to sleep on the
top of the pyramid because frankly I am afraid of
snakes. I dropped right off to sleep but Lance and*

Harry stayed up talking, checking the map and trying to figure what had gone wrong. Sometime later I was awakened by a scuffling noise. Lance was asleep by my side, so I woke him too. Frankly, I was afraid it might be banditos. Lance jumped to his feet, aimed his rifle at the noises and told whoever it was to come out with his hands raised.

Then out of the shadows came the most frightening thing I had ever seen. It was a man with no head and a hole through his stomach. I could see the stars shining through the hole. Lance pointed the rifle at him and warned him to stop. Then he fired a shot. The next thing I knew, the headless man was gone and in his place was a man with a skull's head and claws instead of hands. He was moving quickly toward Lance, who held his ground. Once more Lance shouted a warning, once more he fired a shot. When the smoke cleared a giant black cat stood in its place. The cat screamed and leaped at Lance, and Lance wrestled the cat. They went rolling all across the top of the pyramid. Harry grabbed the rifle and tried to fire, but he couldn't get a clear shot. As for me, I nearly swooned with fright.

Then the frenzy ended and Lance was holding the giant cat as though it were a steer. Every muscle in his body seemed to be exploding from the tension. Harry aimed the rifle and was just about to fire when the cat disappeared and in its place was a beautiful young man, a Mexican I assumed from his shiny black hair and round face. Naturally we were all mystified. Harry put down the rifle and scratched his head. The young man *struggled to get free, but Lance kept a hold on him and demanded to know who he was and what he wanted. The young man spoke perfect English. He told us he was a magician and he was five hundred years old. He promised if Lance let him go he would grant him any wish.*

*Naturally Lance didn't believe him. He demanded to see some of this powerful magic. The young man asked Lance to let go of his arms. Then he held his hands up toward the sky and a thousand shooting stars traced their way across the firmament. I was speechless, but Lance certainly wasn't. Right away he said that he would let the young man go if he made Lance and me famous, more **famous** than anybody in the world. Lance figured anybody who had the fame could get the money, while the reverse might not necessarily be true, so by wishing for one he was actually wishing for both. The young Mexican said the wish would be granted if Lance would let him go. But I said, 'Lance, what about Fatty and Virginia and all our other friends?' So Lance amended the wish: fame for both of us and anybody else who belonged to the club we would form—the 'Inner Circle' of our friends.*

The Mexican said that granting the wish would exhaust him and he would need food to replenish his strength. When Lance let go of him, I noticed the Mexican was holding a stone chalice in his hand with an evil-smelling green liquid in it. In the other hand he had a length of rawhide with a little clay figure on it, a man with a skull's head and claws instead of hands.

'Who will feed me?' he said.

Lance grabbed Harry in a hammerlock. Before Harry could figure out what was happening, the Mexican had put the rawhide around his neck and forced open his mouth, so he had to drink the liquid and had no choice. Harry gagged and went into convulsions. It was so horrible I couldn't watch. I hid my eyes. I heard a screaming and a sound like a hungry dog makes. Then there was tearing flesh and bone being crunched. Well, I just ran. I ran and ran, and I fell down into a gully and I lay there until Lance came to find me.

He asked me why I'd run away like that and I told him it was because he had fed Harry to the Mexican who must have really been a wild animal. Lance laughed at me. He said that all the desert air and tequila were playing tricks on my mind although the truth was I'd hardly had a sip of tequila since departing Los Angeles. Lance told me that Harry and the young Mexican had become friends. They'd gone back to town to get drunk and find some women. We would meet Harry back in Los Angeles. I believed him. I was young and we were just married. People cling to their illusions.

By silent agreement we never mentioned the incident again. Of course that was the last we saw of Harry. When we got back to Los Angeles, Mack told us that he had decided to feature our names on our films, hoping that it would help to draw bigger audiences. Within three years Lance and I and the other people he had inducted into the Inner Circle—you can guess who they were—

were famous around the world. We were more famous than anybody ever had been throughout history, more famous than Hannibal or Alexander the Great, more famous than Newton or Socrates or Plato.

And do you know what? It didn't mean a thing! I thought the fame would change us but we were the same foolish people we had been before, and that was a very depressing fact. Oh, we had more money, we had motor cars and swimming pools and everything else you could imagine, but those things only made me feel better until I tired of them and then I had to buy something else.

And despite all my fame, the world still wouldn't accept me as a serious actress. That was what I really wanted to be, a serious actress like Sarah Bernhardt. But Mack kept me doing pie-in-the-face comedies, and when I quit working for him and formed my own production company, and produced The Tempest *with myself as Miranda, the critics sneered and the public threw brickbats, and the distributors said they'd stop handling my films unless I went back to comedy.*

I was depressed by fame, but Lance felt differently. Women were flocking to his bed; his life had become a roller-coaster ride of drugs and booze, sex and adoration.

Then came that awful night when Lance and Virginia disappeared from Mr. Hearst's yacht so near the port of Guerrero Negro. Suspicion stirred in my breast. And when he returned to Los Angeles with that ridiculous story about her being drowned, then I was certain. The veils of my self-delusion were torn away and I saw the truth which I had always known but had stubbornly refused to admit to myself.

I accused Lance right to his face of taking Virginia back to the pyramid in San Ignacio and giving her to the Mexican magician. He didn't deny it. He said that if I hated her so much, then what did I care? Which was just so typical of Lance. Then he told me that the Fame God— that was what he called him—the Fame God had come to him in a dream and told him he was hungry again. Lance planned to kidnap a bum from skid row, somebody who would never be missed. But the Fame God said that wouldn't do anymore. It had to be somebody who was already famous, a member of the Inner Circle. Fame had to feed on itself, like a snake consuming its tail. There were twenty members at that time and one of them had to die. Lance was to do the choosing, and the one he chose was Virginia Nightingale, his mistress, the woman who loved him. It was all too awful. I told him I could not bear to set eyes on him ever again.

He pleaded with me not to leave. He promised he would no longer be personally involved. He had hired a lawyer named Wallace Penny to induct promising young actors into the Inner Circle. He also mentioned a young medical student named Abraham Kellerman, a penniless German immigrant. Lance would support him through medical school and find him a position at a fancy Los Angeles hospital; in return Mr. Kellerman would administer the sacrificial drink, a concoction of

herbs, which was locally available, and sign the
death certificates, allaying any suspicion. Then
the body, in its deathlike sleep, could be shipped
discreetly to the stone pyramid in Baja to meet
its hideous destiny.

I told Lance that to hire another to murder for
him was even more despicable than to be a
murderer himself. I said I would no longer be part
of his Inner Circle. He could take away my fame,
he could take away my mansions and motor cars
—they gave me no pleasure. My swimming pool
was filled with the blood of my fellow actors, my
tennis court was chalked with the meal of their
bone.

But I could not leave! That was the terrible
truth. Once you had joined the Inner Circle you
were in it for the rest of your life. Try as I
might, I could not divest myself of the wealth, the
possessions, the fans and the lackeys. I could not
cleanse my soul. I felt like Lady Macbeth with
her spot that would not come out.

When I heard that Lance had died of drink at
forty-five, I prayed that might be the end of it.
But then in nineteen thirty-seven came the news of
lovely Jean Harrold—she had also been a friend of
mine—dead of mysterious causes while a patient at
Cedars of Lebanon. Her doctor had been a man
named Kellerman. It was then I realized that the
Inner Circle had a life of its own. Lance's passing
would not affect it. It was the God of Fame's con-
gregation and it would not be killed.

Its legions would grow year by year. It would
make its promises of Love and Happiness and

Fulfillment, its voice ringing with sincerity and then deliver the emptiness, the disappointment that was its true legacy, all the while cackling like Satan himself. For wasn't that the name of the young Mexican we found that terrible day? Who else would have such power? Who, I ask you?

Now I wonder why I am writing you this long, rambling letter. I want you to expose the Inner Circle and stop the killing, yet I know it is impossible. Nothing will stop the Inner Circle. So perhaps I am writing to warn you. I liked you very much, Mr. Pinkle. You are the kind of man I should have married instead of all those bastards I did marry. I say to you, please stop investigating the Inner Circle. Everyone who mixes with that unholy alliance meets one of two fates. Either they die or else they become a part of it. Please Mr. Pinkle, stop before it is too late.

Because I'm not sure which is worse.

Mabel Edmonds"

I folded the letter and looked at Alex. He must have disengaged the autopilot while I was reading; now he was steering manually again. I felt as though we were climbing and indeed when I looked down the earth was sliding away from us ever more rapidly. The lights of Long Beach were like talcum powder on black velvet.

"Well," I said, "what do you think?" Personally I was pretty disappointed. I had expected the solution to everything and instead all I had were bits and pieces of truth floating like meat in a heavy broth of occultism. Clearly Mabel Edmonds was farther along into senility than I had imagined.

"Far out," Alex said. He too seemed dubious.

"Surely you have more to say on the subject?"

He thought a minute. "I guess I've heard stranger things."

"Come on. What stranger things? I've never heard anything stranger than that."

"Well," he drawled, "in the winter of 'sixty-six me and my old lady—at that time it was a chick named Cynthia—"

"Oh, I remember her. The one with the pet boa constrictor."

"Yeah. So me and Cynthia went down to Oaxaca to buy some Mexican silver and get ourselves a little sun. We ran into a guy from Harvard, a dropout sociology professor who was living in the hills, getting high on mushrooms. He invited us up to his place to try some and dig it; for days afterward all the cats and dogs were talking to me in Spanish. The dogs all talked like Desi Arnaz. My mind became so powerful I could pick up Channel Four without a television set. It was weird."

"Yes, but that was when you were stoned. This woman was *straight*."

"How do you know? Maybe the Mexican guide was slipping a little locoweed in her stew."

"That would account for her vision of the headless man," I agreed reluctantly. "The skull's head might have been a mask and maybe the black cat was domesticated. I know a guy up in Soledad Canyon who has about ninety lions and tigers. He goes into the compound and plays with them; he rolls around on the ground with them and they lick his face. A lot of those big cats are really very friendly as long as they're well fed. You know, the ancient Egyptians kept cheetahs as house pets."

"No kidding."

"As a matter of fact, there's never been a recorded incident of a cheetah attacking a man—although they have been known to try to sexually molest women. Seriously."

For a time I was silent, thinking about the letter, reinterpreting the incidents in the cold light of rational thought. After all, I was a journalist of some repute. When I arrived at what I considered to be a suitable explanation, I tried it on Alex.

"Suppose the young Mexican is a Charlie Manson type, a psycho. He wanders around the desert with his pet jaguar, worshiping Tezcatlipoca, the god of his ancestors. When he meets a stranger, he decides it's providence and carves him up for a sacrifice. The jaguar eats the pieces.

"One night he stumbles on three Americans camping in the desert. He comes out of the bushes wearing the skull mask, leading the big black cat, intending to scare the hell out of them. But he hasn't counted on Lance Carlyle, who is too stupid to be frightened. Lance grabs him in a hammerlock and prepares to slam his teeth in. The Mexican says he's a great magician and to prove it makes a meteor shower. Of course, the meteor shower has been going on for days, but the Americans don't notice until he points it out to them. Thanks to the Mexican's personal magnetism—psychos can be very convincing—they think he's responsible for it.

"I know that part sounds unlikely, but remember: Lance and Harry are stoned on tequila and Mabel, the only one with any sense, is so frightened she doesn't know what's going on.

"Lance has blown all of Mabel's money on this expedition; he hasn't found the lost mission and he's desperate, he's grasping at straws. People's belief in the improbable is directly proportionate to their desperation. When the Mexican offers him a wish, he jumps at the chance to salvage *something* from the fiasco. He asks for fame and the Mexican says to himself, 'Sure, why not? By the time you get back to Los Angeles you'll be famous and if you're not, well, I won't be there to take the blame.'

"The Mexican has just about given up on getting a human sacrifice but now, witnessing Lance's gullibility, he thinks he sees a way. He tells Lance that in order to grant the wish he'll need fresh blood and a beating heart. Lance is so gung ho he actually volunteers to help. Maybe subconsciously Lance has been wanting to murder Harry ever since he got him into this wild-goose chase. They carve up Harry and feed him to the cat while Mabel runs screaming. The Mexican's overjoyed. He's made his first convert! He tells Lance to come back in a couple of years with another body to sacrifice.

"Back in Los Angeles, Lance's pictures are all hits. He gets more and more famous and as far as he's concerned, it must be the work of Tezcatlipoca. That's how superstitions get started, you know. A man wears a red tie the day he finds a hundred-dollar bill on the street; from then on that's his lucky tie. Lance has a run-in with a Mexican psycho and gets famous; he assumes one caused the other. You know, Alex, I feel funny—I'm getting kind of dizzy."

"It's the thin air. We're up to fourteen thousand feet." He took out two oxygen masks, plugged the hoses into the panel on his left and handed one to me. I pulled the strap behind my head and fitted the plastic triangle over my mouth and nose. After a few breaths my dizziness passed. The masks made talking difficult, so instead I stared at the silver moon and the occasional clouds, thin as lace. Presently Alex tapped me on the shoulder. He pointed to a meter labeled "Altitude," where one of the needles was creeping toward 20 ("✕ 1,000," it said at the bottom), then to another meter, "Airspeed," which registered 270.

"Tail wind," he said, grinning. "We'll overtake them in no time."

I noticed some blinking lights above us on the right and I pulled on Alex's sleeve.

"Look, there they are!"

"That's a Seven-forty-seven, idiot. When we spot them they'll be below us and traveling in the same direction. Obviously."

I guess I dozed off for a while. I'd hardly slept at all the last few nights and I'd been running like a madman during the days, expending the Manic Pinkle Energy, which, if ever tapped, could probably reduce our foreign oil imports to zero. The physicists say that energy has to come from somewhere and I guess the Manic Pinkle Energy is no exception. Carol says it's being manufactured at the expense of my heart and by the time I'm thirty-five I'll be dead, gone the way of my father and all those other Jewish businessmen of his generation, despite the fact that I'm an Artiste. But since the only alternative she can offer is Yoga and herb teas and health food, I think I'll pass, or pass on, as the case may be. I'm just not the kind who can relax for very long. If the Hindus are right about reincarnation, then I'll probably come back as a tree and spend two hundred years standing perfectly still, taking it easy while birds shit on me.

Sometime later I was awakened by the plane dropping very quickly.

"Alex!" I screamed, "what's happening?"

"Nothing. Relax, will you? Go back to sleep. I'll wake you when the stewardesses are serving breakfast."

"*What's happening?*" I insisted.

"Nothing! We're going into Mexico. I've got to lose some altitude so we can sneak across the border."

We were only a hundred feet above the ground and below us I could see nothing but desert and an empty riverbed with a broken cattle fence running along one side.

"The Mexican and the American governments both patrol the border with planes and jeeps and radar," Alex explained. "They think they've got it sewed up, but it's easy to get past them once you know the way. I discovered this particular arroyo back in nineteen sixty-three. I was flying a hundred and fifty kilos of Acapulco gold—*real* Acapulco gold—up from Ensenada. A prominent dealer in San Francisco was prepared to pay a hundred dollars a key, a good price in those days. It was the first time I'd ever made a run. I didn't know how I'd get over the border, so I came in real low and cruised back and forth a few miles south, looking for a way. And suddenly I saw this arroyo. It was wide enough to fly right down inside it and long enough to take me safely across to the States."

In the moonlight I could see the riverbed beneath us broadening into a narrow canyon lined with mesquite and sage, the walls striped with rainbows of sedimentary rock. Alex flew so low that I thought a fence post would rip open our belly; instinctively my right foot shot out for the brake.

"I called it Arroyo Kotsky," he continued, "and the next time I made a run, I was foolhardy with confidence. I picked up five hundred keys—the plane could hardly get off the ground—and I flew straight to Arroyo Kotsky. You know what happened? The fucking thing was filled with water. I forgot it was the rainy season."

"What did you do?"

"What could I do? I flew around for a while, looking for another way. Then I dumped the dope and flew back to Albuquerque empty-handed."

"Alex, that tiny canyon down there, that's not Arroyo Kotsky . . . ?"

In reply Alex nosed the plane toward the ground. The earth seemed to swallow us up, and then we were zooming along that narrow channel, like a log down a flume, at a hundred and fifty miles an hour. A vein on Alex's forehead throbbed from concentration; his eyes never blinked nor strayed from the canyon walls rushing by less than ten feet from either wing tip, and his fingertips urged the wheel with the finesse of a safe-cracker feeling a combination. Suddenly the arroyo, which had been relatively straight until then, began to curve in S shapes. Alex banked gently from side to side, neatly avoiding the outcroppings of rock never more than fifteen feet away. I was reminded of the penny-arcade driver-simulation games I had played as a child, where you steer a tiny automobile along a rolling strip of paper and every time you transgress the edge of the road a buzzer sounds; only now I knew the buzzer sound would be the scraping of a wing tip against a canyon wall, and the penalty points would be measured in lives.

Presently the arroyo grew shallower and Alex, to my infinite relief, brought the plane out of the canyon. For another ten minutes he followed the contours of the ground at only twenty or thirty feet, then he began to climb.

"Welcome to Mexico," he said, wiping the sweat off his face.

"Bravo," I said and applauded.

Tijuana was a dim nebula intersected by dark arteries: Mexico 1, the new Trans-Baja Highway, and Mexico 2, which runs east to Mexicali. Other than that there was nothing to see, nothing but desert pock-marked with sage and an occasional ranch. To our right the ocean was black and menacing, a promise of a slow, cold death while clinging to a scrap of wreck-age. The landscape was so barren that for a moment I imagined we were flying back in time, back to the days of the gold rush, back to the days of the Franciscans and the Jesuits, and earlier still, when Cortes first spied the Aztec's fabulous island city of Teoti-huacan. Alex nosed the plane skyward and climbed back to where the air was thin, and I replaced my oxygen mask.

About two hours later—at eleven thirty-five—we

spied, far ahead and below us, the faint triangle of navigational lights: red on the left wing, green on the right, white on the tail.

"Is that . . . ?" I asked.

"Maybe," Alex said, taking a big pair of binoculars from a side compartment and raising it to his eyes. He grunted with satisfaction and handed the binoculars to me. I saw an airplane very similar to our own, a small twin-engine craft. I strained to see through the windows, to distinguish the weak-chinned profile of Marty Rubin or Kellerman's stooped form, or even Tony Valenti with his proud Roman nose, but it was too dark and they were too distant.

"How long before we overtake them?" I asked.

"An hour . . . forty-five minutes."

Gradually Alex lost altitude and the other airplane loomed larger and larger. The landscape below had changed to the texture of crumpled carbon paper and in the distance I noticed three mountains, three black peaks rising from a sea of mist.

"Las Tres Virgenes," Alex said. "San Ignacio's just beyond them."

We were almost level with the other plane now, perhaps a half mile away from it. Still, the figures in the cabin were indistinct.

"How can we make sure it's them?" I asked.

"Hey man, who else could it be? Twelve o'clock at night, out in the middle of nowhere. It's the only plane we've seen in two hours."

"Fly a little closer."

Alex turned the wheel and we banked sharply; then we were almost next to the other plane, wing tip to wing tip. Looking through the binoculars I could see, quite clearly, Marty Rubin sitting at the controls and, in the seat next to him, Abe Kellerman clutching a revolver in two gnarled hands, aiming the muzzle at me.

"Alex," I said quickly, "is it possible to shoot a gun from a moving plane?"

The next instant I heard a metallic *ping*, and a hole appeared in the roof of the cabin. Air rushed through it with a shrill sound, like a policeman's whistle.

"Those fucking scumbag bastards," Alex muttered. He dove the plane out of range, grabbed the revolver from his belt and took off the safety. Then he opened the little triangular window on his left; the wind ripped it off the hinges and roared into the cockpit, spinning every map and Milky Way wrapper, every pencil and paperclip and anything else that wasn't bolted down, around and around in a tiny tornado. The roar was so loud I couldn't think, but it didn't bother Alex. He brought the plane up again, this time higher than Rubin's plane, and dove toward it at an angle so he could have a clear shot through the little window.

"Alex," I screamed, "don't—you might hit Tony!" but he couldn't hear me. He fired once and he fired again. Then, just as we were about to collide, he pulled up and away and circled back for another go.

I noticed that, while chasing the other airplane, we were getting lower; one of the volcanoes was not far below and if Alex wasn't careful the next dive might flatten us against the mountainside. I tried to warn him but his attention was riveted on the other plane. His beady eyes were slits and his mouth was working rapidly under the bunting of his mustache. He attacked in a steeper dive—my stomach felt wrenched from my body—and fired two more shots. As he pulled out, something pinged in front of us and a pin hole appeared in the windshield, a million jagged lines diverging from it, rushing to the edge of the glass—but the windshield held, it didn't shatter. The bullet must have missed my head by inches.

I glanced at Alex, who was grinning maniacally. As he circled away, I heard another ping, and seconds later the engine on my right became a fireball. Alex shook his head with disgust and put the plane into a nearly vertical dive. *Kamikaze*, I thought; Alex would sooner kill us both than try to land ignobly with one engine. Well, that was my reward for associating with mental deficients. We fell like a stone down a well of darkness, the air screaming through the holes in the cockpit, the shattered windshield beginning to buckle under the pressure, threatening at any instant to fly into a million pieces of shrapnel. The pitch of the screaming grew higher and sharper, and then I realized that my own voice was giving it the added edge. My eardrums were exploding from the pressure inside my head; my stomach was in convulsions. The black peaks came at us like daggers and when the end looked inevitable, when I was braced and prepared to die and waiting with more than a little curiosity to learn the truth about the immortality of the soul, we suddenly leveled off.

The right engine had stopped burning; the cowl and the wing were blackened with soot but there were no more flames. Alex had gone into the dive, I realized, so that the wind rushing past the engine would put out the fire. I swore never again to make snap judgments of my friends. I wanted to say something but the noise of the wind was still too loud; instead I slapped him on the back gently, so as not to interfere with his flying. He nodded with appreciation.

We had lost sight of the other plane. There was only one place it could have gone so quickly: behind one of the volcanoes. Alex began to circle those great dark shapes one by one. With only one engine, the plane listed slightly to the right, but it maneuvered well enough. The world looked like a kaleidoscope through the shattered windshield.

When we reached the inside of the first volcano, I saw on the mountainside opposite us a long rectangle outlined in flickering lights. I pointed it out to Alex, and he flew across to investigate. On closer observation it appeared to be a natural plateau that had been leveled off for a landing strip. Marty Rubin's plane was parked at one end but I saw no sign of the party, even with the help of the binoculars.

Alex flew away from the strip and came back from the opposite direction—to take advantage of the wind, I suppose. He came in lower and lower until I was sure he was too low and we were going to crash into the mountainside, but instead we hit ground at the very edge of the strip and rolled to a stop alongside Marty Rubin's plane. When he shut off the engine, the sudden quiet made my ears ring. I climbed out on the wing, stepped on the ground and fell on my face. The world was spinning like a roulette wheel, but I managed to rise to my hands and knees before the vomiting began. Then Alex was standing over me, holding my shoulders.

"You all right?"

He helped me to my feet but when he let go, I was in the dirt again. Finally the world settled down and the ground stood still long enough for me to get my balance. The night air was hot and dry and alive with the chirping of cicadas. The torches surrounding the airstrip were wooden staffs wrapped with cloth that had been soaked in kerosene. The airstrip was situated halfway up the mountain, about three thousand feet from the top. Across the way the other two volcanoes rose like massive walls protecting the bowl-shaped valley below us. In the center of the valley I could make out a pale shape, possibly Mabel Edmonds's pyramid.

By this time Alex was standing beside Marty Rubin's plane, admiring a series of bullet holes in the wing.

"Right through the gas tank," he boasted when I joined him. "Nice shooting, huh?"

"How come we caught fire and they didn't?"

"Luck." He shrugged. "They hit a fuel line in the engine. A little gas splashed on the manifold and exploded. Something like that."

At one corner of the airstrip we found a path that wound down the mountainside. Alex went first, holding the pistol ready at his waist. He almost shot the head off a lizard that leaped from a rock when we passed, he was that nervous. I followed at a few paces—the path was only wide enough for one—my heart hammering with anticipation. We didn't speak, not until I saw the two torches being lighted down in the valley. Then I whispered, "We better hurry."

We arrived at the valley floor, panting for breath. It was a dusty bowl filled with jagged rocks, dreamlike shapes all gray and black in the moonlight. Tiny blue flowers grew from between the cracks. The stone shape was indeed the pyramid Mabel Edmonds had described in her letter—although it was actually more of a ziggurat, big rough-cut blocks arranged in seven tiers, each about four feet high, each somewhat smaller than the one beneath, like the layers of a wedding cake. A stone stairway led up the center of each side to the stone altar on top, which was decorated with grotesque friezes and hideous gargoyles.

On either side of the altar stood a man—dark-complexioned and flat-faced like an Indian—dressed in Levi's and a checkered shirt and holding a flaming torch. Rubin and Kellerman, in shirt-sleeves, knelt in front of the altar. And lying on the altar, struggling against the ropes that held him trussed like a calf, was Tony Valenti.

Alive.

13
THE MEXICAN MAGICIAN

We scrambled across the valley, leaping the low stones, scaling the higher ones, until we reached the foot of the pyramid. Then I followed Alex up the steps, keeping low and to the shadows. The steps were very narrow, smooth, and close together, designed for men smaller than ourselves. There was no sound beyond the gentle whirring of the cicadas; yet despite the quiet those above us were so intent on their task that they neither heard nor noticed us. Only when we were almost at the top did one of the Indians see us and grunt with surprise. The other one turned, and Kellerman and Rubin both looked over their shoulders.

Alex leveled the revolver at them.

"Get up," I shouted, "and untie Tony." I didn't mean to shout, but I couldn't control my voice.

"No," Kellerman cried, turning awkwardly on his

knees, raising his hands to me. He had undergone a strange transformation since our last meeting: His shirt was soaked with sweat and clung to him so that every rib in his chest was defined and the vertebrae in his misshapen question mark of a spine stuck out like knobs. His skin was gray and porous, his eyes darted back and forth, refusing to focus on me or anything else for more than an instant; they shone with frightening religious fervor. "It's too late! He'll be here any second . . ."

"Who?"

"Him, the Fame God . . . He's hungry and if He's not fed . . ."

"Play ball with us," Rubin interrupted, "and you'll both be rich men." He climbed to his feet, crossed halfway to me, and stopped, glancing warily at Alex's gun. Somehow he'd kept cool through all this; his pants were hardly creased, his curly hair was all in place, his voice was calm and level, and he spoke with conviction: "Pinkle, I'll sell your screenplays; I'll get you top box office stars and a big bite of the gross!"

He stopped abruptly. We had all noticed it: The sound of the cicadas was gone and a deathly silence had descended over the valley. Although the night had been perfectly clear, now clouds drifted across the moon, muting its yellowness, darkening the landscape and chilling the air so that shivers raced across my flesh. One of the Indians crossed himself and began praying under his breath, while the other shut his eyes tight, his shaking torch making the shadows dance and tremble.

"Pinkle," Rubin went on, faster now, "you want to make it with a sexy babe? I can get you Yolanda

Roberts. She'll do stuff you never dreamed of. Think about it, Pinkle. Most men would give anything for some of that pussy."

"Untie him," I said. It was getting colder. I felt a few raindrops across my head.

"Don't make me do it," Rubin pleaded. "It'll be disaster for all of us."

"What's that?" I thought I heard a sound, a growling sound, like the grinding of a giant millstone.

"It's Him!" Kellerman said, his voice fanatical. "He has come for His supper."

"Pinkle," Rubin rushed on, "you love movies. Anybody in a thankless profession like screenwriting has got to love movies. Well, movies are movie stars, and if Tony Valenti isn't sacrificed tonight *there won't be any more movie stars.* No sex goddesses to star in your kids' jerk-off fantasies, no rough macho types for housewives to dream about while their husbands are banging them away like postage machines. No more glitter and glamor and Academy awards and screaming fans knocking down police barricades . . ."

A bolt of lightning leaped from heaven to the altar, a jagged white stripe, blindingly bright, exploding like a cannon shot and kicking up a cloud of dust and chips where it struck. The heavens opened and a torrential rain began almost at once. I thought I heard another clap of thunder but the noise was sustained, the way I had always imagined an earthquake would sound, on and on until my teeth were on edge and my ears were aching.

And then from behind the altar, creeping on padded feet, as silent as a winter's snow, came a great black cat. Its coat was so black that it was nearly invisible against the night sky; I could not really see the cat so much as its outline glowing like the corona of the sun during an eclipse. It opened its mouth and its teeth glowed white, as did its great sickle claws. It moved with an unearthly grace, and its shoulders were almost as high as my head.

"Don't move and He won't touch you," Kellerman whispered. "He only needs one man to satisfy His hunger."

We all stood like statues while it prowled across the top of the pyramid, sniffing us one after the other, then moving on as though we were rodents too small to be worth the trouble. When it came to Rubin, the lawyer lowered his head humbly; when it approached Kellerman, the old man smiled at it as if in the throes of ecstasy and whispered endearments as one might to a lover. The cat acknowledged neither of them. It passed by Alex with hardly a notice and then it started for me. Puddles were forming in the hollowed surfaces of the stone and I noticed with what little objectivity I retained, that the giant paws made no ripples in the water.

It approached me until its enormous head was only inches from my face, and I could feel its breath like an icy wet wind. I wanted to run screaming but I stood where I was. Its eyes were like luminous crystal balls, split vertically by jet-black pupils, thin as a knife's blade, totally without life or expression. It seemed to stand there forever, gazing at me.

Then finally it crossed to the altar and began to sniff at Tony Valenti's bound form. It bared its enormous fangs and a thick yellow saliva oozed from the corners of its mouth. Tony's hair was plastered over his face by the rain; his eyes were bulging and his jaws worked at the red bandanna tied across his mouth. The clay fetish hung from his neck, swinging back and forth like a pendulum ticking off the seconds of life. He tried to squirm away but the ropes held him captive.

Another flash of lightning and, faster than my eye could follow, one paw shot out, sickle-claws splayed, and drew back. Tony's body shuddered, a groan escaped from the bandanna across his mouth. Blood was pouring from four gashes in the side of his face, running down the rough stone of the altar, making swirls in the puddles of rainwater, beautiful swirling patterns like Indian endpapers. The cat trotted over and began to lick it away with loud slurping noises. It was playing with him. Like house cats I had seen dragging in near-dead birds from the garden, it would keep him alive as long as possible; first a finger would come off, then a hand pulled slowly out of joint. Finally a stomach torn open, a steaming pile of entrails on the cold, wet stone.

Rubin watched impassively; Kellerman, in ecstasy. How many times before had they stood here and watched a similar scene enacted? Rosalee Romain, her delicate white body tied across these same altar stones, ropes creasing her luscious thighs and breasts, her dress torn and her hair trailing in golden wet tendrils. Her beautiful little-girl face transfixed with horror as the very same claws rend open the ivory skin, the very same slathering teeth tug the viscera from beneath. She longs for death as she has never longed for anything; but consciousness lingers past all decorum and before the onset of oblivion she has seen her body mauled and disfigured beyond recognition.

Dean Jamison, only just out of his teens, only three movies to his credit, tied across the altar stones, screaming that it isn't fair for he has only just joined the legion of the great and he has barely had the opportunity to taste the fruits of his fame.

Dory Grayson, strong and brave and salty tongued, probably wisecracking up to the last.

Jean Harrold.

Francis Hertzel.

Virginia Nightingale.

The blood of every one of them had flowed between these rough stones.

I turned to Alex, but he was hypnotized by the strange vision before him; and I realized it was up to me. I waited, and the next time the cat retreated a few paces, I raced to the altar. I tore the rawhide necklace, the clay fetish, off Tony, and I ran over to Kellerman and tied the broken ends tightly around the old man's neck.

The cat seemed confused. It looked back and forth between Tony, Kellerman and myself. Then it started for me. I shook my head and held up my palms. I took one step back and another, until my heel went into a puddle and slipped out from under me and I fell flat on my back, hitting my head and my hip as I did so. The pain was awful but I forced myself not to groan. The cat kept coming, closer and closer, breathing heavy with hunger, saliva oozing from between its teeth. Then it stood over me, blocking out the sky, and I felt the drip of its saliva on my face. It was warm and oily and smelled like putrid meat. I was paralyzed with terror. Out of the corner of my eye I saw Kellerman struggling to untie the thong. "Yes," the old man cried with fervor. "Take him! Take him!"

Ever so slowly it turned and started after Kellerman.

"No!" he shrieked, "not me! I served you loyally all these years . . . I did as you told me in the dreams . . ."

The cat kept coming.

He tore at the leather thong, but the knot held. Then he backed away, and at the last moment he turned and ran to the steps down the side of the pyramid, vanishing into the darkness of the valley. The cat bounded after him. The few moments of silence that followed were like a reprieve. Then the walls of the valley echoed with Kellerman's screams and the growling, gnashing noise of the cat's savage jaws. Then again it was silent.

We all stood where we were for I don't know how long. The rain stopped and the sky cleared. Pretty soon the cicadas started up again. I had a feeling I had dreamed it all. I borrowed Alex's pocketknife and sawed the ropes that bound Tony hand and foot. When I took the gag out of his mouth, he was weeping. He put his arms around me and hugged me for dear life.

"Easy," I said, "easy does it. How's the face?"

The laceration reached from his cheek to his shoulder, but fortunately the claws had missed his eye. One of the Indians had a canteen, and I washed his face with the water. Then I tore strips from my shirt and wound them around his cheek and neck.

"I was right," he said while I was tying the makeshift bandage under his shoulder.

"About what?"

"You are my only real friend."

"I just thought it would make a good story," I replied.

When we were through bandaging Tony, we took him between us, Alex supporting one shoulder and I the other, and started down the narrow stone steps that led to the valley floor. The Indians went first, illuminating the way with torches. Marty Rubin followed at a few paces, very quiet and well behaved. He remained silent until we reached the valley floor; then, timidly, he asked Alex if his plane would fly.

"Can't make a single-engine takeoff from that little strip," Alex replied bitterly. "Anyway, my windshield looks like crushed ice."

Rubin nodded. "Me neither. All my tanks bled out through the bullet holes. I guess we're walking. It's not too bad. San Ignacio's only eight or ten miles."

"Think they'll have a doctor there?" I asked. "Somebody should look at Tony's face."

"I'm okay," Tony said.

"Sure you are," I said. "Think you can walk eight miles?"

"If we rest every couple of . . ."

The first Indian stopped suddenly. In his torchlight I could see what had surprised him: Ahead of us was a handsome young Mexican leaning on a rock, grinning as though we were dear friends. He wore thin white pants and a white shirt, and he was barefoot. He was chewing on a bone as casually as anybody would at a picnic. Except this bone was far too big to be a drumstick; it was nearly two feet long.

"Amigos," he said, "what a nice surprise. Share some of my food? I'm afraid the meat is old and dry." He made a comical frown and offered the bone to us, with its lump of flesh all red and soft and bloody. "Normally, I would not take it, but I know my amigos had trouble." He stared at Rubin, and there was no more humor in his eyes; they were cold and glassy like the eyes of the cat. The pupils, I noticed with a chill, were thin vertical lines. "Next time young meat, yes? Flesh that has been worshipped by a hundred million gringos."

"Yes sir," Rubin whispered.

The rest of us were too frightened to say or do anything.

"San Ignacio is that way," he continued, pointing the bone at a pass between the volcanoes. "Go to the right of the low mesas and follow the trail. You will see the mission tower to the south. *Vayan con Dios.*"

He nodded for us to go ahead, and we stumbled on like idiots. When we had gone about fifty feet, he called to us: "We will meet again, amigos? Ten years from today?"

I dared not turn around. We walked quickly ahead and despite the warmth of the night, I was trembling.

Tony was weak, but we didn't stop or even slow down until we were clear of the three volcanoes and well out in the open desert. Only then could I relax enough to admire the sky, a million stars undimmed by the desert air, and the landscape of low mesas and winding gullies and stovepipe cactuses ten feet tall. We all sat down on a big flat rock and the Indians let us sip water from their canteens. Alex came up with a few Milky Way bars, a whole one for Tony, another shared among the rest of us.

"I can't tell you how good it is to get these ropes off," Tony said, massaging his wrists. "The bastards had me tied up for weeks! Jesus, what they did to me."

I felt a surge of guilt. "If I'd let you stay at my apartment, none of this would have happened."

"Don't believe it, buddy. If they didn't get me that night they would have gotten me the next."

"How did you survive the car crash?" I asked.

Tony shook his head. "It was nothing. I've had worse crashes than that racing. I've *done the doughnut* and walked away from it. Porsche is built to take a beating. The trouble is, you walk away from a crash, you're not ready to punch it out with a couple of goons."

"You mean Billy Chou and Frank Pollacek," I said. "They're dead now."

"I'm not going to mourn them. They grabbed me and there was Kellerman loading a hypodermic with green stuff. He put the needle right in my stomach and a minute later I went into convulsions. I couldn't breathe or anything. It was horrible. Then my body went rigid and everything got sort of dreamlike. A crowd was standing over me—cops were everywhere —but I couldn't talk, I was paralyzed. I remember an ambulance. Thank God, I thought, they're taking me to a hospital. Instead they took me to some place in the valley, some kind of costume shop with dummies all around . . ."

"It was a wax museum," I said, "the Burbank Wax Museum."

"And they locked me up in a little room, tied to a goddamned chair for three weeks, with nothing to eat but Kentucky Fried Chicken and Pepsi-Cola, and the television running twenty-four hours a day. They wouldn't even untie me to take a crap! One day I heard your voice from the next room. I thought, Jesus Christ, Pinkle's trying to rescue me. At least somebody cares that I'm gone." He paused. "You know what I thought about all the time I was tied up?"

I shook my head.

"How I was gone and nobody cared. How I was alive but I could just as well have been dead."

This may sound self-pitying or simply crazy—the biggest star on television believing that his death went unnoticed. But if you know a couple of actors, then you know that their egos are like balloons: The bigger they get blown up, the thinner the walls are stretched. They live in constant dread of obscurity, of being suddenly forgotten. It's an ailment of the trade, the way dust inhalation afflicts coal miners, and cancer, X-ray technicians. And because it strikes the mind and not the body, that's no reason to take it lightly or label it indulgent. A Hollywood sound stage can hold just as much fear as a Kentucky mine shaft. So I spent a little time telling Tony about the grief that followed his death; and he listened with disbelief and finally with a little pleasure, one of the few who, like Tom and Huck, were privileged to know the result of their own demise.

"You may not believe this," Marty Rubin said when I had finished, "but I was pretty broken up too. This kid's like a brother to me, aren't you, Tony?"

Tony didn't reply. I could see from his expression that Rubin was treading on thin ice.

Rubin went on, oblivious: "I told Kellerman not to take you but he insisted. He does the choosing because he's been in the Circle longest. I was against it all the way. I said, 'Take Bobby DeNiro, take Travolta, what's the difference?' "

Tony snapped: "You cold bastard! We're not people to you, are we? No, we're numbers, we're box office. We're the gross of our latest film."

"Look who's the innocent!" Rubin said. "You blame me for the Inner Circle, but you're the one responsible. It's you actors who keep it alive. It's *your* greed, *your* insecurity, *your* hunger for success. Without you the Circle would have dried up years ago."

"Thank God it's finished now," I said. "No more murders, no more sacrifices. Kellerman's dead."

Rubin looked at me, puzzled; then he laughed. "Wallace Penny's dead too, but before he died he trained me to take his place."

"What are you getting at?"

"Kellerman did the same thing. He was an old man. He didn't have long to live so he picked out a successor."

"No . . ."

"Sure."

"Who? Tell me."

"Don't know. One of the kids in the postdoctoral program he teaches at the university."

"Tell me who, goddamn it!"

"*I don't know.*"

"You're lying," I said. I wouldn't accept it. The thought of that Hollywood-made monster called the Inner Circle going on despite all my efforts, consuming the youngest, brightest talents of every generation and leaving a trail of bloody footprints far into the future, enraged me beyond control.

Alex had just finished reloading the revolver and was wiping the grease away with the red bandanna when he noticed me looking at it. He handed me the weapon. "Go ahead," he said quietly, "I won't tell."

Rubin smiled nervously. "Hey, what is this? Some kind of joke?" The smile went away. "Tony, for God's sake, stop him."

Tony said to me, "We'll leave the body here. It'll be years before anybody finds it."

"No . . ." Rubin said. He turned desperately to the Indians. They turned their backs on him and stared steadfastly into the distance.

Then he began to back away from me, shaking his head, until he was standing against a boulder with no place left to go. "Louis," he mumbled, "Louis, you wouldn't . . ."

Closing one eye, I lowered the revolver and sighted along the notch in the barrel until it lined up with the third button on his custom-made shirt. I held it steady there for almost a minute. Then I handed the revolver back to Alex and told everybody that we had better get moving; soon it would be dawn and awfully hot for desert hiking.

Marty Rubin was weeping.

We reached San Ignacio a little before 5:00 A.M. A spring-fed pond ran through one end of town and date palms grew everywhere. We crossed the plaza to the general store, catty-corner to the big white mission, and banged on the door until the owner opened it a crack. He was a broad-chested, white-haired man, naked except for his shorts.

"*¿Qué quiere usted?*" he said sleepily. Then he saw

the blood seeping through Tony's bandages and he quickly ushered us inside. While he phoned for a doctor, we sipped instant coffee from tin mugs and ate a box of Ritz crackers. Ten minutes later the town doctor, a leather-skinned old man with quick, clear eyes, was cleaning the blood from Tony's face. Four red ribbons remained, crossing from cheekbone to clavicle.

"*¿Un lobo?*" the doctor inquired, puzzled.

The two Indians who had come with us weren't volunteering any information, so Alex took over:

"*Un gato grande.*"

The doctor raised his eyebrows and whistled.

"*¿Dónde?*"

"*Las Tres Virgenes.*"

Then the doctor said something to the store owner too fast for me to follow with my primitive New York public school Spanish. The store owner gave Tony a bottle of tequila and urged him to drink; meanwhile the doctor boiled water and sterilized forceps and scissors and a needle curved like a cat's claw. When he took the needle to Tony's skin, I looked away; I examined the shelves of canned goods, the ancient cash register, the ceiling fan and the single naked light bulb dangling from a cord. The store wasn't too dirty, but there were flies everywhere and a skinny old dog was scratching in the corner. Tony grunted with pain.

Finally the doctor gave him a tetanus shot and began to pack his bags. I had only three dollars in my pocket so I asked Marty Rubin to take care of it. Rubin gave the doctor a fifty—he had nothing smaller.

"*Es mucho,*" the doctor said, returning it.

Rubin rolled up the bill and stuck it in the doctor's pocket, and that was the end of it.

Seeing this exchange of money, the two Indians came forward and planted themselves in front of Marty with expressions that might have been expectant or hostile—it was hard to tell. He sighed, gave one of them a fifty and indicated in sign language that they were to share it. They grunted, turned and left together.

The store owner led us back across the plaza—dawn was turning all the stucco pink and the town was just beginning to stir—to a little house with a thatched roof. A tiny Mexican woman in harlequin glasses and a robe opened the door. The store owner explained the situation to her and she took charge, ushering us inside, showing us to our rooms, waking the girl who was sleeping in the kitchen and ordering her to make up the beds.

Despite our protestations she started to cook and soon the kitchen was fragrant with spicy smells. We sat down to a table heaped with plates of tortillas and frijoles, leftover chicken and pork back and icy cold Dos Equis. We talked very little as we ate. Hardly anyone touched the chicken or the pork.

I couldn't sleep; my blood was too stirred up, my mind was racing with images. When I lay on the thin mattress—I could feel each individual spring in my back—and closed my eyes, I heard Kellerman's screams echoing through the valley. There was a cheap crucifix hanging over the bed, a melodramatic Jesus with skin too red, eyes too plaintive. The bloody thorn holes in his forehead were turning my stomach. Furthermore, the partitions between the "rooms" did not reach to the ceiling, and I could hear Alex in the area adjacent to mine snoring furiously.

Then came a knock on the door and Marty Rubin entered.

"I thought you might be awake too," he said. "Mind if I come in?"

I shrugged.

He held up a checked shirt. "Hope this is your size. They didn't have too much variety at the general store." He tossed it to me. He must have bought it while the doctor was sewing Tony's face. Obviously it was to replace my own, which I had torn into strips to make bandages.

"Thanks," I said.

He sat down on the edge of the bed, took a few experimental bounces and made a face.

"I don't know what they make these mattresses out of. Boy, what I wouldn't give for one of those beds at the Beverly Hills Hotel, right?"

He grinned at me and waited for an answer.

"Right," I said.

"Listen, Lou, I can understand how you're angry at me. You've had a pretty rough time and I won't pretend that I wasn't responsible for some of it. Let's let bygones be bygones and start over with a fresh slate. When we get back to LA, I hope you're going to let me take you out for dinner at Ma Maison. And that date I offered you with Yolanda Roberts? Well, the offer still holds. She'll be your date for the evening *and* the rest of the night."

"She likes bald men?" I said dryly. My anger was gone and all I had left was contempt.

Marty Rubin laughed too loud and too long. "I love

that sense of humor. That's what I want you to get into your screenplays. We've got to set up some kind of deal for you next week. What do you say to your own production company, unlimited financing, total creative freedom? I can do it, I've got investment groups in Germany, I've got tax shelters in Montreal . . ."

"I'm sorry," I said, "but you're not going to stop me from exposing the Inner Circle."

The smile left his lips. "You *can't* write about the Inner Circle."

"And why the hell can't I?"

"Tezcatlipoca won't allow it."

"He doesn't have any control over me," I said.

"Yes he does. You made a sacrifice to him."

I felt a chill on my neck. "What are you talking about?"

"You sacrificed Kellerman. You placed the totem around his neck and gave him to Tezcatlipoca. There's no getting around it."

"I don't care, I'm writing the story anyway."

"Why waste your time? Nobody will print it. They'll say you're crazy. They'll put you in the same bag as those flying-saucer nuts who write for the *National Enquirer*."

"You're wrong. And even if I can't get it published right away, that's not going to stop me. I'll keep at it . . . I'll keep at it for years if I have to."

"Why kill yourself, Louis? You're going to have the success anyway, like it or not. It'll cling to you like dandruff on a black sweater. You can fight it for a while but sooner or later you'll have to give in. I can make it easier. I can tell you what you're doing wrong, like I did for the others. You see, Tezcatlipoca speaks to me in my dreams. I'm his servant, just like Abe Kellerman was. He told me that Rosalee Romain had to dye her hair blond. He told me that Tony Valenti had to play comedy."

I couldn't control my curiosity. "What about me?"

Rubin smiled. "Don't try to write fiction—you're a journalist. Turn your most recent experiences into screenplays."

"And it's as simple as that?"

"Simpler. What do you say?"

"Stick it up your ass. I've got friends in Sacramento. I'm going to get you for ten counts of murder. They'll lock you up and throw away the key."

"As you like. 'Night, Louis," he said and closed the door behind him.

14

EPILOGUE:
THE FAME GOD

We didn't have to wait long next morning before we met a rancher who was driving up the coast to Guerrero Negro for supplies. The four of us rode in the back of his pickup, bouncing against the metal sides, getting dust in our noses and eyes. Next we got a ride in a van belonging to a bunch of bleached-blond surfers from Redondo Beach, equipped with a fur-covered water bed, a mirrored ceiling and an elaborate stereo system. They turned off Mex 1 to try the surf at Bahía de los Angeles, and we hitched all the way to Ensenada in a Winnebago camper driven by an ex-army captain from San Diego and his pretty wife. That took most of the night. The dental student who drove us the rest of the way to San Diego was sure he had seen Tony's face before, despite beard and bandages, and kept asking if he'd ever been on television. We told him he must be mistaken.

We took Tony to the VA Hospital in La Jolla and had a specialist look at the lacerations. He said the doctor in Mexico had done a good job but plastic surgery might be necessary to cover the scars. At the airport Alex bought us all tickets while Marty called his chauffeur to meet us at LAX. I don't know what those Pacific Airlines stewardesses thought the four of us—baggageless and filthy, with three days' growth of beard—were doing flying first class.

Los Angeles made Mexico seem like one of those nightmares you half remember from childhood. We rode down Sunset in Marty's limousine, Alex snoring in the seat next to me; Tony across from me, gazing out the window, his brow furrowed in thought; Marty next to him, watching Tony with a calculating eye— or so it seemed to me.

Presently Marty said, "Well, Tony, it'll be great to get back to work, won't it?"

"I'm not going back to work," Tony said. His voice was cold, his gaze remained fixed on the gaudy mansions that lined the boulevard. After a long pause, he continued: "I'm getting away from this goddamned town. You know, Bini once said that if I ever went back to New York, she'd be my wife again. She's probably got somebody else by now, but I'd like to see her anyway. I'd like to see all my old New York friends."

"You're dreaming, Tony boy. You can't go back. What would you do?"

"What would I do? Sit on the front stoop with a

beer and watch the world go by. I used to love to do that. And once in a while, when I found something I really liked, I'd do a play. Off Broadway, Shakespeare in the park."

"You'll be climbing the walls in three days."

"Maybe, but I'm sure willing to try it."

"And we'll have to scrap the deal I've been working on."

"What deal?"

Marty pointed out the window. "Jesus, look what they did to that old white mansion! Painted it like a mosque. I hear some Arab oil sheikh bought it and spent five million on renovations. I tell you, in a couple of years Beverly Hills is going to look like Saudi Arabia."

"What deal?" Tony said.

"That Cyrano thing," Rubin said casually.

"Cyrano?"

"For years you've been talking about a film version of *Cyrano de Bergerac* . . ."

"Only if I can play Cyrano *and* direct."

"I know, I know. I've got it all set up with independent financing. Five-million budget. UA's distributing. Gordy Willis is your director of photography . . ."

"Fantastic!"

"But only if you start production in October."

"That's three months from now! We've got to cast it and build sets, work up a production schedule—and rehearse . . . I want lots of rehearsal, just like it was going on the stage."

"You'll get it," Marty Rubin said, grinning.

Tony grinned back at him; then his face fell.

"What's wrong?" Marty asked.

"Bini. I need her. This life's too scary to go it alone."

"She's been staying at your old house on Rexford, getting the place ready to sell. She might be there now."

"You think she'd want to see me? I mean, did she come to my funeral?"

"Cried like a baby," Marty said. He lowered the partition and told the chauffeur the address.

"Jesus," Tony said, "I'm so nervous." He felt his bearded cheek. "I must look terrible."

I shook my head. "Virile. Like somebody out of a Tarzan movie."

Tony laughed.

I sat back, regarding the young actor and his manager, and considered the strange ways of the film business. One day a man tries to murder you and the next day you're doing business with him. Agents and managers have this in common with the devil. They all know which offer will crumble the most adamant resolve.

The limousine turned off Sunset and glided south. It stopped in front of a quaint Tudor house framed in box hedge, shaded by elms. Alex and Marty waited in the car; I was going to wait too, but Tony asked me to come along.

"I'm terrified," he said as we walked down the flagstone path.

"Don't be."

He grinned at me nervously and pushed his hair into place.

The door was half open, but he rang the bell anyway.

"Come in!" Bini Valenti shouted. "If you're the cleaners, the carpets are in the hall."

Tony pushed open the door. I followed him into the hallway. The house was dark—all the blinds were drawn—and the furniture was covered with white sheets. Bini stood in the sunken living room examining a big Chinese vase. She was dressed in blue jeans and a white silk shirt, and the vastness of the room made her look particularly small and vulnerable.

"The long carpet is a very fine Bokhara," she continued without turning around, "so you'd better be careful. If there's any damage at all . . ."

She turned around and saw us.

"Oh," she said softly. "I thought it was the cleaners." She squinted. "Is that Louis Pinkle?"

"Hi, Bini," I said.

"And who's that with you? My God, for a moment I thought it was Tony."

She put down the vase and walked toward us. Tony descended the steps into the living room and they stopped a few feet from each other. Bini reached out and touched his face, traced his nose and forehead, ran her fingers over the bandages.

"Oh, Tony," she whispered.

She put her arms around him and broke down in a soft rhythmic sobbing. "I knew you weren't dead," she said, "I knew it."

"I was so scared you wouldn't want me," Tony said.

"Oh, darling, I always wanted you . . . always. I can't believe how good you feel! What happened?"

"They kidnapped me. A gang of Mexicans. They wanted half a million. Marty Rubin got the money together and flew down and rescued me."

"What about the body in the coffin? It looked just like you . . ."

"Somebody else," he said vaguely, and for the moment she accepted it. There would be more questions later, but by then he and Marty would have worked out the details. I was eager to see the final form of the fiction in tomorrow's papers.

"I guess we're pretty lucky we have Marty Rubin for a friend," she said.

"I guess," Tony agreed. He raised his eyes until they met mine (they were still embracing, Bini's back to me) and he seemed to be saying: *I know it stinks, but this is how it has to be. A movie actor is what I am, and Marty Rubin is the man whose help I need most.*

I shrugged and started silently for the door. On the way out I met the dry cleaners and showed them which rugs to take.

When the limousine stopped in front of Sunset Towers, I woke Alex and told him he was home. He yawned grandly.

"Hey man, did I dream it?"

I shook my head.

"Louis," he said, "this is one of the great adventures of all time. Someday we'll tell this story to our children and our grandchildren, and they'll listen real attentive, and when we're done they'll say, '*Bullshit!*'"

He laughed and I laughed with him because I knew he was right.

"It was far out," he said, shaking my hands. "It was just like the old days. Now you take care of yourself. I've got to get back to Santa Fe and check up on the business. You want to stay at my place while I'm gone? The fridge is full and there's an eighteen-year-old honey who's housekeeping for me."

"Thanks, but I think I'm going to Carol's for a couple of days. I need a good woman to nurse me back to health and make me believe there's still something worth scavenging for. To tell you the truth, after what I've been through I wouldn't mind making it a permanent arrangement."

"You couldn't find a better lady," Alex said. "I'll be back for the wedding."

Now Rubin and I were alone in the limousine, but we didn't exchange a word until we reached Toluca Lake and I opened the door to leave. Then Marty placed a restraining hand on my shoulder.

"If you're in any kind of financial trouble, you can come home with me right now and I'll give you a check—an advance against your first job. That's what kind of confidence I've got in you. Then I'll take you out to dinner to celebrate."

"You're unbelievable. I told you, I don't want anything to do with you or your lousy Inner Circle. You turn my stomach. Furthermore, despite my gracious manner I have in no way altered my intentions of blowing this whole thing wide open. See you in court, fuckface."

"Oh Lou, Lou, Lou. You're just delaying the inevitable. Once you're with us, you're with us."

"I am no longer with you," I said and slammed the door behind me.

It was Sunday as usual at Carol's apartment house. The brats were trying to drown each other in the pool, the divorced mothers were lying in deck chairs, reading Harold Robbins and turning brown. The sight of it all exactly as it should be, reassured me, certainly more than the sight of me, blue-stubbled and bedraggled, reassured them. They watched, suspicious behind sunglasses, while I trudged up the steps and rang Carol's door and waited. No answer. I rang again and again and waited. Presently one of the women lying by the pool called to me.

"If you're interested in renting that apartment, you should see the manager."

"I'm a friend of Carol Goodkind's."

"She moved last week."

"Impossible! She would have . . ."

She would have told me and she must have been trying to tell me just that. But my peculiar brand of tunnel vision had stopped me from seeing anything that did not figure in Tony Valenti's disappearance.

"Where did she go?"

"Chicago. Her grandmother was sick and she went back to take care of her."

"Do you have an address or a number?"

The woman stared at me suspiciously and shook her head. The way I looked, nobody was going to give me anything, except perhaps a handout.

I hitched a ride back to West Hollywood. My key didn't fit in the lock of my apartment. After a few minutes of fumbling with it, a young man wearing eye shadow opened the door. Behind him I could see two other young men hanging taffeta curtains over the Chinese-style windows. He told me he had moved in the day before yesterday; he had no idea what had happened to my furniture, my clothes, my books and my files, but he suggested I speak to Mr. Scheuermann. So I went next door to the white stucco building on the corner and rang the bell of Mr. Scheuermann's apartment. Mr. Scheuermann was watching the ball game. He told me that my furniture was in storage at the Bekins warehouse on Santa Monica.

"I've got to have my files and my typewriter," I shouted, rattling the screen door that separated us. "I'm writing what may well be the most important story in history!"

"Mr. Pinkle, be thankful that I am not pressing charges. If you want your furniture, you need only go to Bekins, pay the charges and it will be returned to you."

"But I don't have any money. And I can't make any money until I have my files and my typewriter. For God's sake Scheuermann, have a heart!"

He gave me the this-is-a-business-not-a-charity number and slammed the door in my face.

Well.

Quite simply, I was ruined. It was ninety degrees and I didn't have a hat to shield my poor naked dome from the sun. And yet I felt a certain freedom—probably what monks feel when they renounce all their material possessions and emotional ties with the world. Of course it must be even nicer when you do it voluntarily. When I reached the strip, I turned west and walked for a while, thinking about nothing in particular. I sat down on the curb outside The Cock and Bull, a popular lunch place for agents and producers and the like, and watched the traffic go by. It was the first time in years I could recall truly relaxing. I had no appointments, no stories to write, no obligations to anyone. Cars zipped across my field of vision; exhaust fumes made a pleasant burning in my nose. Two sun-ripened California beauties strolled past and smiled. I had three dollars in my pocket, enough for a cheese-burger at Schwab's and a big piece of chocolate cake. What happened to me after that, I didn't know and I didn't much care. Gradually I realized that someone was speaking to me.

"You're Bini's friend, the screenwriter, aren't you?"

I looked up and saw a big man on his way from the restaurant to the parking lot along with two other men, obviously coming from a business lunch. He was forty-five, with short brown hair—balding on top—a little mustache, a round face and skin around his eyes which crinkled when he smiled. His cigar must have cost five dollars and his suit, a hundred times that. It took me a minute to place him, then I remembered: David Pinkerton, the producer who had joined Bini and me in the Polo Lounge the day I had driven her home from the wake.

I stood up and we shook hands and exchanged pleasantries.

"How's the writing going?" he asked.

"So-so," I said, waving my hand.

"You know, I liked that idea you told me . . ."

"*The Climber?*"

"That's right—except it's too surreal. And I've never had success with movies set in the future. It's too hard for the audience to identify. But if you have any other stories . . ."

"*The Inner Circle*," I said on impulse.

"Oh?" He looked interested. "Tell me a little."

"All right. It begins on a summer's night in Los Angeles. A brilliant young actor—he's sort of a Tony Valenti type—appears at the apartment of a friend whom he hasn't seen for years, raving about how everybody's trying to murder him . . ."

So I stood there in front of The Cock and Bull talking nonstop for two whole hours while David Pinkerton and his two friends listened spellbound. When I finished, Pinkerton said, "I love it. I love it. You've got a deal. Who represents you?"

I hesitated. There was only one man I could think of. "Marty Rubin," I said before I could stop myself.

"I'll call him first thing in the morning."

He and his friends started for the parking lot, then he turned back to me.

"Louis, you've got a tremendous imagination. One of these day you're going to be very famous."

ACKNOWLEDGMENTS

I would like to express my thanks to Betty Kelly, who offered many excellent suggestions; Grace Griffin, who read the manuscript and encouraged me; Bardi McLennan, who typed it so beautifully (and so often); Kimo Kawa of the Hollywood Wax Museum, who gave me an afternoon out of his busy schedule; Charley Waugh, who flies better than Alex Kotsky; Shelly Pinchuk and Rick Ray, who provided more information about flying; those noble librarians at the Weston Public Library; and of course Erica, who nurtures my soul.